TRADE
$ECRET

TRADE $ECRET

EARLY VAN CLEVE

authorHOUSE®

AuthorHouse™
1663 Liberty Drive
Bloomington, IN 47403
www.authorhouse.com
Phone: 1-800-839-8640

First published by AuthorHouse   10/24/2011

ISBN: 978-1-4670-3687-0 (sc)

Printed in the United States of America

Any people depicted in stock imagery provided by Thinkstock are models, and such images are being used for illustrative purposes only.
Certain stock imagery © Thinkstock.

This book is printed on acid-free paper.

For Tear

Do not believe his vows; for they are brokers,

Not of that dye which their investments show,

But mere implorators of unholy suits,

Breathing like sanctified and pious bonds,

The better to beguile. This is for all:

—William Shakespeare

PROLOGUE

A blistering Midwest heat wave resulting in crippling drought can surely over time drive a strong man insane, especially when he trades the most valuable commodity on the planet for a living. The newspapers blamed global warming and the politicians blamed the newspapers, sending soybean prices through the roof causing international panic on global grain markets. Rioting in Moscow. Unrest in Beijing. Prices not seen in decades. Beans in the teens, they said. The Mississippi River was actually fifteen feet below its normal level. And then came the rains, a relentless biblical downpour that rolled across the Great Plains for weeks, drowning what foodstuffs hadn't already been committed to biofuel. Grand Rapids and Des Moines were underwater. The levees broke at Evansville. The Coast Guard had to ban barge traffic by closing a five mile stretch of the Mississippi to protect

Memphis. And downriver, New Orleans braced for the worst. But Louis J. Harper III was on the wrong side of the rally, which is what confused all the professional commodity traders and expert financial analysts at *The Wall Street Journal, Barron's,* and *The Chicago Tribune.* Something just didn't quite add up. Lou Harper was the last of a dying breed known for trading only one way—all or nothing, and he was not famous for losing money in Chicago's futures pits.

"Now's your chance, Lou! Let me take you out!"

Harper tried to ignore the words.

"Cut your losses." The words were wrong. They had to be. "This is as good as it gets, Lou!" The words belonged to his trading partner, Derrick Butler. "Jack tried to warn you a week ago," Butler jeered from the corner of his mouth.

"You know, I'm sick and bloody tired of hearing about the great Jack Diamond!"

"Take it easy, Lou. I'm your friend, remember? The rest of these whores would cut your throat in a heartbeat."

"Here to pile on, Mate?"

"Look, we've been standing here shoulder to shoulder on the same spot on the same step in this same trading pit for what? Five years? You and me. But you're definitely out of the zone this week."

"I've been upside down before, Mate. Dozens of times."

"You need Jack right now. He's just trying to help."

"I've cleared billions for his bucket shop. I know what I'm doing!" Harper shouted as his cell phone rattled against his chest. "Hello!"

"Are we confirmed for our meeting this afternoon?" she asked.

"Right."

"I'll need all of your trade confirmations for the past twelve months," she instructed.

"That's it?"

"Tickets, confirms, blotters, as well as account statements. Can you bring them?"

"I'll have the order filled by the closing bell. Cheers."

"Pissed off client?" Butler asked, leaning in.

Harper shook his head and wiped the sweat from his brow.

"Hardly. Impatient hedge fund with no vision, Mate."

Lou Harper was a gambler, and she knew it. And that's just exactly how she played him. She knew he was a position trader, not a scalper. He would hold his buys overnight, sometimes for days, and build towards one final monster score. Swing for the fence. Every cent of his own risk capital as well as his entire book of business—a play that would either haunt him, or define him. But that's how he worked, and all the other soybean traders knew it. Now beans were selling away from him and completely breaking down—the kind of breaking down that broke most professional commodity traders in half. All trading was halted, locked limit down for five days in a row. No one could get in. Worse still, no one could get out.

"Look, why don't you let me take you out," Butler offered. "We all get whipsawed every now and then."

"I said no."

"I heard we'll have enough volume by the close to dump your whole position."

"Bloody pit gossip."

"Monday's a new day, Lou."

"I prefer to let this market trade. That okay with you, Mate?"

"The smart money around here knows you're wounded."

"Which is why I refuse to pour more blood in the water."

Without warning the soybean pit began trading again, exploding into a jam-packed orgy of body parts—arms, hands, heads, and shoulders flailing seemingly without purpose as Butler started buying.

Disaster sneered from the exchange wall clocks as Butler back-pedaled to the pit's perimeter to catch his breath. "I'm on fire, Lou!" he bellowed, his face covered with sweat. "If we reverse by the close, we just might open higher on Monday with protection out to October!"

"You know something I don't, D?"

"I know you need a miracle right now just to break even, and that's the worst place to be," Butler gasped, scribbling orders by hand. "Plus, I've never seen you double-down like this."

"We're putting in a bottom today."

"I'll see what I can do for you, Pal."

Butler quickly covered his short position, momentarily running the price back up and reversing the week-long freefall. But Harper could do nothing. He was forced to watch in horror as the spot price for September delivery would rise slightly, only to remain well below his original buy in. He was frozen out. If he sold today, he'd suffer a five million dollar loss. But if he somehow held on, he just might climb back out and continue gambling on credit using his margin account. And that was his only chance.

"Mister Harper! Pick up line four! Mister Diamond, from California!"

"Jack's five for five this year, Lou," Butler shouted. "You might want to listen to him."

The runner stood up at the edge of the soybean pit with his hands on his hips. "Mister Diamond's still holding," he shouted. "He insists on talking to you immediately!"

"Do what you want, Lou," Butler said, shaking his head, "but I'd rather see you cut your losses now than cut your own throat on Monday. You're running out of time."

"You ever think about taking profits, Derrick? For good, I mean. You know, walk away from the insanity?"

"And give up the voices in my head, the sleepless nights, and the constant exhaustion?"

"I'm serious, Mate."

"Can't afford to."

"What if I told you I know a way out?"

"Why would we want out? We've got it made, Pal."

"We'll be replaced inside of two years, Mate. Maybe twelve months."

"No way."

"Electronic algorithmic trading on some ultimate virtual global exchange network? It's already here."

"There'll always be a place for a pit trader."

"We're too expensive, Mate."

"We're specialists. We're supposed to be expensive."

"Automatic markets are fabulously efficient and alternative trading systems bypass the exchanges now. Direct access to dark pools and crossing networks? No more spreads," Harper sighed.

"Who cares about spreads? Jack's never wrong."

"Electronic trading networks don't leak. Jack Diamond's edge will be gone."

"Never happen, Lou."

"Any system can be gamed, Mate. And more badge fees, trading fees, regulatory fees, transaction fees? I'm sorry but I'm getting too old for this crap."

"Never apologize, Lou. C'mon. Suck it up. Thirty minutes left."

Harper checked the scoreboard. Soybeans were dropping again, ahead of the weekend. Low of the day.

"Lou, we're almost limit down again. This is your only window to sell."

"Bloody hell!"

"C'mon, Lou. Work with me!"

"Let me think!"

The price per bushel continued to freefall. 12.20, 12.00, 11.70—"No time, Lou."

Harper chewed his nails and stared at the clocks.

"Make the call!"

11.50, 11.35, 11.30-

"Back off!"

"Let me get you out, Lou!"

"No!"

"You got no choice."

Harper's mind raced.

"Give it to me, Lou!"

11.25, 10.95, 10.90-

"Aaaauuggghhh," Harper shuttered, falling to his knees. His whole body broke down, he began shaking, and his skin turned ashen white. Then his shoulders collapsed.

"We're all on the same team on this one, Lou," Butler shouted as he raised his arms to identify himself as a seller.

"Don't give me that team player bullshit. Just dump it," Harper growled, watching in agony as the soybean pit's multi-colored hurricane of trading jackets swirled toward his partner. Through the deafening roar and rapid-fire hand signals, Butler engineered the sale of all five thousand contracts in less than five minutes time.

Lou Harper's black and gold-braided trading jacket was now soaking wet. He hadn't eaten all day but he began vomiting. His black trousers camouflaged the fresh urine stain over his crotch. As the gravity of his liability suddenly sank in, Harper lifted his eyes to see the Chairman of the exchange staring down at the soybean pit with folded arms from his prominent office overlooking the vast trading floor. By Monday morning, the CME Group would call for another two million dollar cash margin deposit that Harper did not have. Jack Diamond, the CEO and Managing Director of The Continental Trading Group, Ltd. now owned all of Lou Harper's soybean contracts, which meant only one thing. He also owned Lou Harper.

Harper fled the trading exchange, bypassing the crowded elevators as he navigated the concrete stairs that spilled into the Board of Trade's underground parking garage. He cranked his vintage Mustang, hurried through the downtown grid, and joined the asphalt river that rushed west, away from the city. As he drove, all he could think about was surviving the weekend and somehow formulating a strategy for recovery. But the more thought he gave the situation, the more he realized the fact that she was his only hope.

When she first approached him, her proposal sounded ludicrous. He'd refused to help, but now he could hardly wait to meet with her and spill his guts. Amazing how the mind changes under intense pressure. Sell the Frank Lloyd Wright in Oak Park? Liquidate his collection of classic muscle cars? Bankruptcy? And if he did help how could she possibly protect him? He'd have to testify, that much he knew for sure. Depositions? His name in the *Tribune*? A public trial? Witness protection?

The relentless rain mocked him, slowing the traffic to a glacier flow as he hurried to their meeting. But he'd resolved in his mind that he was doing the right thing. Hang in there, she told him. Your career as a trader will be over anyway. Everything will be fine as long as you cooperate.

The grey sky turned black by the time he finally reached the small suburban office complex near Aurora. He parked his scarlet Shelby Cobra against the end of the linear building and lit another Marlboro, desperately trying to calm his frayed nerves.

As he squinted at the darkness, a black Ford LTD slowly rolled around the corner without its lights, easing to a stop behind the vintage pony car. He checked the rear view, then his watch. She was early.

The misty drizzle stopped, leaving the surrounding asphalt sparkling like black ice. The driver of the Crown Vic stepped out hunched beneath an umbrella. Harper watched from the dry safety behind the wheel as the blurred figure walked slowly toward the Mustang's driver-side door.

A gloved hand rapped on the window as glass disappeared into the door, releasing the acrid cigarette smoke from the interior. "I can't do this anymore! I'll tell you everything!" Harper pleaded. "I just want out!"

"No problem," the driver uttered as the Beretta .380 automatic appeared and flashed once, burying a single, well-placed round into Lou Harper's left temple at a flat, horizontal entry angle. Harper slumped forward onto the wheel while the shooter wiped the gun clean, placed the pistol in Harper's lifeless left hand, then drove away.

1

The heart rate was at full throttle as he broke free from the dark tunnel, racing toward the blinding glare of daylight pouring through the domed stadium's skylight. He was used to the noise but tonight there was silence. He was aware of his hands because he could see them, churning with his legs, both a blur, but they were heavy, always too heavy, held down by the weight of his arms, straining and lurching upwards. His legs churned with great effort while his tall, rangy frame seemed to float as he galloped, certain he was running, but not quite positive, then peeling off in formation like mercury from a broken thermometer. He could feel the boom of thunder, and the pouring rain all around him, pelting his helmet, slowing his effort, making it difficult to see. But the harder he commanded his legs to run, the slower he moved through the two inches of water on the field.

There was little tactile feedback, only colors all around him, bright primary colors, reflecting off the flashes of lightning. Frozen glances in the crowd, on the faces of the other players, stolen peripheral looks. All motion halted by abrupt pauses, then fast forward. Thin tails of light streaming behind him but never quite reaching him, dying as he outran them.

He was quickly covered up by two defenders. He stole a step, then started toward separation. The spinning ball, chasing him down, arcing overhead, just in front of the shut-down corner, a shade long and just out of reach, but the rotation was flawless. He focused on the rifling ball, lit up by the glowing strobes of lightning. All motion slowed. More lightning. Then there was no crowd. No noise. No opponent.

The supple fingers at the ends of both hands contracted instinctively, tightening as the thin, elegant tendons desperately gripped like a vice. He landed hard as the scapula cartilage separated abruptly from the ball-and-socket joint that connected his left arm to his shoulder blade. Bone against bone. He tasted metal, cradling the football against his chest in a pitiful fetal position.

Everett Anderson was propped up in his bed at The University of California San Diego Medical Center, snoring softly. His bruised and swollen forehead was wrapped in gauze protecting fresh stitches, and a neck brace lifted his squared chin high into the air. A shoulder sling snaked around the brace that supported his spine and cradled his left arm. He used his right elbow as a fulcrum to support himself. Two day's beard and a shaved head revealed a white scalp against a sunburned face and neck.

The Wall Street Journal lay across his lap as Charlie Hayes stood in the quiet of the room. The heavy walnut door slowly closed behind him as the sharp click startled them both.

The eyes slowly opened. "Coach Hayes?"

"Hello, Everett."

"So they picked you for the exit interview?"

"I volunteered, actually. You good?"

He adjusted his body carefully and cleared his throat. "Well, let's see," Everett winced. "Aside from the constant chills from the anesthesia and the realization that I can't feel my left hand, I'm fine."

"I'm required to speak directly to you before day's end. They'll officially release you tomorrow morning."

The financial section fell to the floor. "So now my spot frees up before the trade deadline at week's end?"

"The game never gives anything to anybody. I don't need to tell you that."

"Look, I appreciate you coming down in person, and all."

"You know what I like about you, Everett? You have this way of setting your hands just before you make the catch. Never seen one of my receivers do that. That's all you."

"Coach, I know more about the art of physical therapy than your head trainer. We'll meet again."

"That's the problem. You're not afraid to go across the middle."

"But the rent gets paid across the middle."

"And careers are won or lost across the middle."

"Injury management. That the concept?"

"Both corners who tagged you were fined fifty grand each for helmet to helmet."

"But that's not how I was taught to play the game," Everett huffed. "Fines for contact? Then the game's no longer the game."

"I don't like it any more than you do, but new rules exist for a new kind of game."

"I'm not walking away."

"You showed up at camp hungry this summer. You were an undrafted free agent, you've been on the scout team, and you know what it's like to be inactive. You also impress me as the type of young man who has the good sense to get on with his life."

Nothing.

"Look. You had a concussion, Son. A bruised lung and a swollen brain, not to mention your shoulder separation."

"Right now, I just want to get through therapy and start working out again."

"It's not your first head trauma. I know your history."

"My agent will find interest for me. He always does."

"Quitting while you're ahead is not quitting. Don't tell me you'd settle for Europe, Canada or the UFL?"

"Thanks for the visit, Coach."

"Not too many players I know graduated college Phi Beta Kappa. Bet you didn't think I knew that about you."

"You can't protect all of us."

"That shoulder of yours will bother you for the rest of your life, along with your hamstring, and you'll fight through it. But you can't afford further brain damage once this game's done with you."

"Coach, without the game I'm just a wildcatter's son."

"You don't believe that," the veteran coach said as he shook his head. "Everybody's on the juice these days. Testosterol. THG. HGH. They're all virtually undetectable. But not you. I watched you in the weight room. You train angry and you take care of yourself."

"And I've gotten this far by ignoring the propaganda since grade school. I'm too light. I'm too white."

"I swear players are human projectiles these days. Bigger stronger faster. Can you honestly tell yourself you're as quick and as hungry as you were in college?"

"Great. Just about the time I figure out the game my body lets me down."

"Hell, there always has been a shortage of decent receivers in this league," the coach chuckled as he rubbed his thinning grey hair.

"And a real shortage of smart black coaches, too."

"Look. You're hurt and you're angry right now," Charlie said softly. "But it'll pass. It will. Believe it or not, I remember being in your spot, but the league's different now. All the cap money goes to the marquee players. There's a different front-runner loaded with talent in the playoffs every season. So don't give me that love of the game bullshit."

"Love of the game, huh? Let's see. Belitnikof recipient your senior year at Grambling. Two pro bowls. Offensive coordinator at Auburn. Never missed a bowl appearance yet passed over more than once in fifteen years for head coach."

"Coaching's all I've got, Son. Hell, we may not even have a season this year what with the owners threatening a lock-out and the league facing a concussion lawsuit filed in Los Angeles. Besides, I happen to know you come from a real fine family."

"I've been preparing for life after football since I was drafted in college."

"I've heard that about you," Charlie said as he reached into his wallet and removed a business card.

"You want me to call your broker?"

"Most players don't know who to trust when they first make a little money. Ham Walker and I go way back. He always had a knack for finances, just like you. So when the game got too fast, he figured out a way to make a lot of money for himself and his team mates in the financial markets. He's done a hell of a job for me."

Everett looked at the card again, his eye drawn to the middle of the thick, high quality parchment. Dead center was a black and gold embossed company crest. The circular design looked ancient, almost medieval—two black griffins, their talons locked in combat against a golden shield. "The Continental Trading Group? Never heard of 'em," he said.

"Word is you're on your iPhone trading between workouts, and making money in a volatile market. That's exactly what Walker does for me. Real exotic stuff, you know? Short selling, option spreads, derivatives," Charlie whispered. "They doubled my bonus last year."

"You're kidding. Two hundred percent in one year?"

"Everett I've been out of the stock market for years now. Walker calls it Fall Street. Margin Call Street. He put me in crude oil options, gold futures and I've been short the dollar for two years. We're making a killing in commodities while Wall Street goes bankrupt with scandal."

"Really?"

"All I'm saying is the move to California saved my life, Everett. It did. The timing was perfect. After the divorce, I almost gave up on life after coaching in that Alabama steam laundry for ten years. But hell, out here it's sixty-eight damn degrees every single day. Just thought you might want to stick around. You're facing weeks of rehab anyway, and the team hired a personal trainer and a physical therapist for you at La Costa."

"I don't suppose you had anything to do with my trade here in the first place?"

"I'd love you to think I had that much influence, but Dallas hired a Mississippi lawyer with razor blades for teeth when you were traded, and our new owner loves to run the ball. You were just trade bait."

"Any chance I'll see my bonus?"

"Sorry, but you never had a chance. Guess that's why I felt responsible for you."

Everett studied the business card one more time. "Can I sleep on it?"

"Fair enough. Rest up and clear your head, then pick up the phone and call Walker. Hell, you'll love California, Son. A young man could move out here and get in all kinds of trouble."

2

The Gulfstream G650 touched down at Lindbergh Field just before dawn. The gleaming ivory corporate turbo wound down from its high-pitched whine, hissing and rolling to a halt on the southwest edge of the concrete airport runway. Outside the airport perimeter fencing, a boot platoon of young leathernecks from the nearby Marine Corps Recruit Depot chanted loudly as they jogged in formation alongside the extended runway.

Jack Diamond watched as Derrick Butler rolled out the bulkhead steps and stretched in the doorway, then deplaned on to the tarmac gripping a large stainless steel suitcase with little effort in each hand. The heavy luggage was deposited into the idling limousine's trunk as the rear passenger door opened from the inside. Butler folded his well-muscled six foot six inch frame inside.

The voice drifted out from the blackness of the limousine's corner interior. "Your performance last week in the soybean pit was flawless," the voice said.

"Just another day at the office, Jack."

Piercing blue eyes shone through the dark, diffused light. "I took the liberty of arranging a suite for you at The La Valencia in La Jolla."

Butler squinted toward the voice. "Thanks, Boss."

"You've been in Chicago too long, Derrick. San Diego is a very spiritual place. Peaceful and productive. The energy here is incredibly powerful. Do you sense the sudden drop in air pressure?"

"I don't notice that shit, Jack. Have the cops called you about Harper?"

The voice took a moment to answer, which made Butler shift in his seat. "The Chicago police phoned me and informed me of his unfortunate suicide. Yes. In fact, they've been kind enough to invite me there for a deposition next week."

"I had to endure that crap for six hours straight."

"Compliance said you did fine."

"Jack, Harper was trading away from us with a handful of locals I didn't recognize," Butler snorted, "all wearing brand new badges and trading jackets, doing more looking around than trading for their own account. Plus he was nervous all week. I could tell he was up to something."

"Could you tell who he was trading for?"

"He must have found some private equity at the last minute to shore up his position. Could have been Camerone. Every trader in Chicago was after that hedge account he fronted. Hell, I watched him build his position for over a week. And when beans sold off, he panicked. I mean, what reversed that market? The news never got negative until after beans plummeted."

"Walker sure cleaned up for himself on that soybean rally."

"And Harper was on his cell all week to Walker," Butler said.

"Made a ton in his own account."

"Almost like he knew about it before it happened. And thanks to your skillful reaction, we covered with a nice profit," Jack smiled. "But your instincts were right about the buyers who tried to corner Harper's position."

"Harper talked about that very idea right before he melted down."

Jack narrowed his eyes. "What *exactly* did he say?"

"No more open outcry. Just high frequency electronic."

"Do you remember the merger of the Board of Trade and the Merc?"

"Of course. I got CME stock."

"Justice is forcing the separation of clearing and settlement. Fractured markets and more competition will give us unlimited offshore access while the CFTC is organizing a Technology Advisory Committee. They're ten years behind the curve on co-location, trade repositories, and swap execution."

"Speak English."

"If you saw a hurricane headline percolating in the Gulf just as it earns its name, what would you do?"

"Go long crude and OJ, just not all in."

"Exactly, and that slight bit of logical hesitation could mean the difference between boxcar profits or chasing a trend, which is what happened to Harper."

"I'm not following, Jack."

"Derrick, don't be a dinosaur. Speed defines markets now. No more pit push, just the pull of dark pools designed exclusively for high frequency trading, scalping a tenth of a point on Wall Street with millions of shares in a nano-second. That model is working its way to Chicago, putting you out of business."

"Like the flash crash last year? I'm already hearing about hyper-algorithms that can re-write their *own* algorithms, which then instantly replace themselves. C'mon Jack. I mean, what the fuck?"

"With the right software, our largest client was able to short bean futures days before the rains hit."

"How?"

"Camerone's sending millions of orders a second through all the international exchanges with no intent to actually trade. The bid and ask are so far from the market price there's no way they'd ever become part of the trade. But every now and then one trade gets through, at a huge profit. That was *your* trade."

"But it was a pit trade."

"Still, it's execution, regardless of the source, and that leaves patterns in the data that are invisible."

"You're crazy, Jack."

"Maybe so, but you scalped him rough and you manually saved me fifteen million US minus your ten percent, of course. I could never execute electronically without a loyal back-up engineer in the pits."

"You might make a programmer a trader, Jack, but you'll never make a trader a programmer."

"But *he* thinks you're connected somehow, and now Camerone wants to talk tonight to you specifically about an exclusive agreement."

"What kind of gross?" Butler asked.

"Twenty million a week."

"Jack, that's a billion dollars a year."

"Kind of makes Nick Leeson or that frog trader Kerviel at SoGen look like a piker."

"No shit, Boss. Makes me misty for the Nineties."

"Derrick, we're losing our window. This morning I bought another ECN, a fully registered secondary foreign exchange trading platform with branches in Bermuda, Monaco, Dubai, and Luxembourg. The Grand Duchy will match our investment one for one. And I know he's planning a labor strike in Rio and New Delhi. But tonight it's critical that El Toro understands that *we* own the information, not him."

"Information like that could cause a panic."

"I'm tired of his Tijuana donkey show. Begin building as large a position in sugar as soon as possible."

"Camerone has an army of traders," Butler warned.

"I've already made arrangements for your trading badge in New York. Tell him you'll easily cover his twenty-five percent inside the first week of each month."

The freeway traffic began to slow as they left the highway and took the La Jolla Parkway exit, which wound around Mount Soledad and led directly into the privileged international community. The limousine then turned south onto Prospect Street, the shopping Mecca of San Diego's super-rich. Gourmet restaurants, nightclubs, designer clothing stores and art galleries all lined the crescent-shaped curve overlooking the coves and cliffs of the Pacific in the heart of the world-famous enclave.

"No one knows he's here," Jack hissed. "Not even Washington. There's ten points in it for you."

"I'll do it for fifteen."

"Sweet talk the old bull for thirty points and your end is fifteen," Jack said as the limousine pulled up to the La Valencia's valet. "He's waiting for you in the Sky Room."

3

On the busy corner of Broadway and Front Street stood the most popular watering hole in the heart of San Diego's booming business district, The Aztec Athletic Club, a renovated barrel-vaulted brick basilica used in a previous life to house broken cars from the city's expanding trolley lines. Pure urban retro fashioned for yuppies specializing in micro-brewing its own beer. Massive copper tanks squatted behind glass walls enclosing the long curving bar. The high arched interior was light and airy with exposed brick walls supporting iron roof joists and exotic hanging plants. A dozen busy pool tables filled the rear corner of the large space. Tasteful and trendy, but relaxed and always crowded.

Following weeks of physical therapy and job interviews, Everett Anderson worked his way through the happy hour crowd—a confident collection of lawyers, stockbrokers, salesmen and accountants; young moneymakers with neat hair and well-fitting suits all starched and tanned, radiating prosperity and completely absorbed. He found an empty stool at the end of the long bar, ordered a glass of iced tea, and watched the front door.

The crowded club was now charging a cover as a jazz band echoed from the corner. The main floor was swollen with people when a loud, well-dressed group of expensive suits stormed through the front door. The crowd parted and Everett locked eyes with the tall, well-built black man leading the way. "So you must be Anderson," the man bellowed.

"How'd you know?"

He pointed to the crutches leaning against the end of the bar. "I'm Hamilton Walker," he said extending a hand. The big man had a powerful grip. "Charlie tells me you were traded during camp."

"That didn't quite work out."

"I watched the game on Monday night. Man, you got rolled up on."

"So let me buy you a beer," Everett offered.

"Your money's no good here." Walker barked at the bartender and a round of beers suddenly appeared.

Everett watched as Walker pulled a hundred dollar bill from the fat rick of bills held between the jaws of a platinum money clip embossed with gold. There was that company crest again.

"Coach Hayes told me you're having a hell of a year," Everett said. "He said you doubled his portfolio."

"Portfolio? The only stock I trade is livestock, my man. Hogs, live cattle, feeders and bellies."

"Commodities? That's risky business."

"Actually, we're more of a hybrid brokerage house. Futures, options, derivatives and private equity. The game changes daily and the public is scared shitless right now."

"Global recession is more like it."

"Exactly. Why play Wall Street roulette when you can handicap terrorism, energy, inflation, and interest rates? The futures market is the future, Baby. Buy the fear and sell the greed."

"A profession fraught with peril?"

Walker lifted his eyebrows. "Not where I work."

"C'mon. These are reckless times."

"We never lose."

"That's impossible."

"Look Everett, while you were running routes in Dallas, a derivatives revolution came along and permanently altered the world's capital markets. Wall Street had the system rigged so they heard the rumors first, and investors worshipped the bastards. But that was before Bernie Madoff and Sir Alan Stanford, and since then the politicians gamed the mortgage market and the bankers and the brokers fucked the public with worthless debt."

"I've noticed. I trade my own account."

"Then you know the smart money now trades in Chicago, Tokyo, London and Hong Kong, away from New York. The hedge fund managers and Goldman single-handedly destroyed the economy by selling shitty mortgages to their own clients, lied to Congress about how they structured them, then bet a billion against the poor schmucks. So while the Wall Street crooks cry in their single-malts at the Harvard Club, we've been in a decade long commodity bull market, and as brokers we're all just dealers at the table. I just happen to work for the top casino, and now we own the information."

"Do you know how insane that sounds?"

"Look, after three seasons in and out of four hospitals in Chicago I retired, just like you. I got my license, started trading for a few team mates out of our corporate headquarters, and it just snowballed. Now I'm making more than I ever made in the league, and I'm healthy enough to enjoy the ride, thanks to Charlie."

"I suppose Coach Hayes ought to be nominated the patron saint of broken athletes?"

"After he was promoted to offensive coordinator, I qualified for this west coast spot. Top rookie broker," Walker beamed as he handed over his business card.

"And you're still hiring?"

"We're always hiring. We just don't solicit and we never recruit. We refer from within, and that's the *only* reason we're talking tonight."

"So what's the bad news?"

Walker leaned in. "Higher suicide rate than dentists and rock stars."

"I'm well-adjusted, single, and motivated."

"Good. Wives just get in the way. Besides, rookie training is grueling enough, if you manage to get hired. Show up at five-thirty each morning, an hour lunch at one, then afternoon and overseas action in the evening. It's a major daily commitment, my man. Worse than two-a-days year round, but we never stop ringing the cash register."

"Damn."

"Survive the training, graduate to senior broker, and then everything changes. Seven figures a year. Your own hours. Luxury vacation every six months. Just produce and you become one of the chosen few inside the oldest brokerage house in Chicago. And the house always wins."

"So where do I sign?"

Walker finished his beer. "We're right across the street," he instructed. "Tell Big Tony in the lobby you're scheduled for an interview with William Peterson."

Everett straightened his tie in the mirror behind the bar as Walker pointed to the crutchesin the corner.

"You might want to leave those in the lobby."

The gleaming black marble and glass skyscraper rose through the socked-in marine layer of fog, frowning down toward the modern city beneath it. Built as a power statement during the peak of the golden state's recent real estate bubble, the landmark's place in San Diego's history was confirmed after the city council revised its restrictive building code to accommodate the height. Over-engineered with state-of-the-art earthquake specifications, it was designed by a German architect and considered a controversial architectural masterpiece.

Everett entered the sleek Minimalist lobby, signed in with the security desk, and was issued a temporary pass card. The etched glass button at the top of the elevator's panel bore the crest he'd seen earlier on Walker's business card and money clip. The button glowed as the card was inserted and the elevator lifted off. His ears popped as the lift finally slowed and the shiny doors parted, delivering Everett into the reception area on the building's fiftieth floor in ten seconds.

Although the front desk was now vacant, the lobby led to an open balcony that overlooked an enormous interior space. He heard the drone of the maintenance crew's vacuums in the distance, drawn to the cantilevered gallery railing overlooking the colossal trading floor beyond.

The floor was filled with Mahogany trading turrets. Custom-crafted detailing wrapped around the black high-tech quote screens, keyboards, and phone equipment, filling the electronic amphitheater beneath him, pulling his eyes across the large trading hangar which occupied the building's top two floors. The scale of the space was massive. The cleaning crew was dwarfed by the sheer size.

Appointed with ample walkways and plenty of seating, its roof soaring above the desks and consoles. The building's stark concrete skeleton, exposed wall buttresses, and rib-like roof rafters supported translucent ceiling panels overhead. Thick tinted plate glass windows surrounding the perimeter of the empty space offered unobstructed views of San Diego Harbor and the Pacific coastline stretching to the north. Downtown's lights twinkled across the crowded harbor below, jam-packed with anchored aircraft carriers, cruise ships, and an assortment of mega-yachts and luxury sailboats. Water traffic filled the bay while ferries and excursion tour ships passed in the twilight and the restaurants that lined the water's edge blinked with multi-colored outdoor lights.

"May I help you?" The voice sprang from Everett's right. A stout man in a precisely-tailored double-breasted suit stood next to him, meticulously dapper despite the late hour. His grey hair was raked straight back and his eyes shone with a soft green glow.

"I'm here to see William Peterson."

"You must be Everett," Peterson gushed with an easy smile. "Call me Bill."

"Thank you, Bill," Everett said as they shook hands.

The cleaning crew was escorted past them by a burly, pigeon-chested security guard. "Follow me please," Peterson motioned.

Everett carefully shuffled down the grand staircase that emptied on to the massive trading floor below, nursing his bruised hamstring.

"Are you okay?"

"Just a pulled muscle."

Peterson checked his diamond-encrusted watch. "I was on my way to dinner but we can chat briefly," he said as they snaked through a symmetrical grid of phone banks and trading desks. "It's a thing of beauty during market hours, but it's rather quiet tonight. Most of the office is still returning from Zermatt. Did Mr. Walker tell you about our last sales trip?"

"Not in detail."

"A week in the Alps. Nothing like it. So, tell me about yourself, Everett."

"I retired from professional football last month. One of my coaches arranged this interview."

"He must think highly of you."

"Charlie Hayes, he's pretty remarkable."

"Coach Hayes. I know him well. I've spoken to him on many occasions in Mr. Walker's absence. I assume he's been happy with his account?"

"Extremely."

"Mister Walker interviewed after he was injured and he turned out to be an outstanding trader, that is, when he's not bow hunting in Alaska or shooting elk in New Mexico."

"Hobbies make the man."

"You'll find that teamwork is our greatest asset. As you can see, we take very good care of our team."

"Absolutely."

"And loyalty is a prerequisite around here, Everett. Without it a team is nothing more than an undisciplined mob, wouldn't you agree?"

"No question."

"Step into my pro shop, Sport."

Everett took a seat in the plush leather club chair positioned in front of Peterson's desk.

"So, Mister Anderson. You want to be a commodity trader?"

"I've been involved in investing since college."

"First, please tell me why you're here tonight."

"I learned a long time ago to develop a skill for growing my own money that would serve me for the rest of my life."

"So you do have some experience in the markets?"

"I passed the series seven exam my freshmen year in college. I worked every summer as an assistant to a million dollar producer in Memphis until I graduated."

"Then you're aware that employment here requires a series three license?"

"Absolutely."

"This is commodity trading, Mister Anderson. We don't hire brokers. We develop traders. Hard core cannibals who are capable of split-second decisions. Most retail brokers today are half CPA and half insurance agent. He doesn't even call himself broker anymore. Now he's a financial advisor. The trader has been completely bred out of him. So tell me about your trading experience."

"I grew up on a producing soybean farm. My great grandfather was the first in the state to convert from cotton to soybeans after the Civil War. I negotiated at market and hedged our crop each season with a broker. And I learned to sell short during bad times to augment profits."

Bill leaned back in his chair and continued to read the resume. "Academic All-American from The University of Mississippi. MBA in Finance. Graduated summa cum laude. Honor society. When the hell did you have time to play football, Sport?"

"I was red-shirted my freshman year. I had a full ride, so I went to summer school and interned at Merrill Lynch in Memphis."

"What do you know about the futures markets?"

"Enough to know the retail side is risky as hell."

Peterson leaned back and steepled his fingers across his broad chest, exhaling. "We prefer to think of ourselves as a very misunderstood industry, simply because we can turn a faster profit than Wall Street with a smaller investment. Margin requirements are much more liberal than equities. Our foreign exchange clients like it that way. And we only deal with accredited investors because the average investor, quite frankly, is undisciplined."

"Which is why you exist?"

"Wall Street panics with a three percent intraday sell off while the average volatility in the crude pit alone is five times that. That's why most equity investors eventually lose, failing even to outperform the meager returns of the S&P 500 index."

"Why do you suppose that is?"

"Because unlike stock trading, commodities are a zero-sum game. Each dollar of profit originates from someone's losses, and for each one of my traders convinced prices will rally, there's another trader somewhere out there equally certain prices will fall. He's your competition, not the market. Capital simply gravitates toward the better trader. That's how we keep score in this game."

"So standard deviation. The reward outweighs the risk?"

"Only when research is accurate does time become a built-in component in futures speculation, creating what we believe is a unique sense of urgency. We deal with a perishable entity which demands immediate action. An investor can hold a stock forever if it drops in value, but a commodity inherently has a finite shelf-life. If its trading price doesn't rise or fall within a pre-determined window of time, its value as a vehicle for profit expires worthless. Ironically, Mister Anderson, just like football, anticipation is the key when you're working against a clock. And there's zero margin for error in this game. Have you interviewed with the local wire houses? They love MBAs."

"UBS, Wells, Morgan Stanley, and what's left of Mother Merrill. The usual suspects."

"You don't sound too impressed."

"Thirty percent rookie pay-out on agency trades working my way through some fee-based retail training program? Would that impress you?"

"If you were to solicit a million dollar securities transaction, what's their gross compensation to you?"

"Depends on the product, but standard ballpark maybe thirty thousand gross. After tax to me about ten."

"We'll pay you a hundred grand for the commodity equivalent."

"So why the big difference?"

"The big difference, Mister Anderson, is driving to work each day in an exotic import, dressed in a custom-tailored suit, raising risk capital and private equity in this sensational office. Versus the drudgery of slaving in indentured servitude for a giant national brokerage dinosaur while your publicly-owned employer confiscates the lion's share of your commission and grows fat on your hard work."

"Same game, different league?"

"You're a fast learner," Peterson said, "but I'm not quite convinced you'd fit in here."

"I know what it's like to work scared every day, to show up each morning just for a chance to play."

"Go on."

"I love the rush. Straight commission means I'm broke on the first but I'm rich on the last day of the month."

"That's right."

"Well that's the only way I've survived in college or professional football. Performance. I'm only as good as my last game, or my last catch. I know I look the part and I know I can think under pressure. It's what I do best. Frankly, I'm probably a better trader than I am a salesman, but I'd make up in profit what I lack in production."

"I like your passion, but I really don't have time for Wall Street wimps."

"I heard only one investor in ten ever makes money in commodities."

"So what's your point?"

"My point is I'm only looking for the same odds you give your clients."

Peterson's face lit up. "That's just about the best damn interview answer I've heard this year. All right, Mister Anderson. Understand that we invest a disproportionate amount of energy and capital in the training of our account executives. Consequently, our turnover is the lowest in the industry. The interview process alone typically takes weeks as each manager evaluates you up the food chain, not to mention exam prep and adequate study time. Background checks have to be made, references verified, that sort of thing. But you display a rather deliberate attitude. So, pass your licensing exam and you can join our last training class of the year Monday morning. You've got forty-eight hours, Sport."

4

Sunlight filtered through the tall, narrow windows as a passing train moaned at dawn. A blue jay's squawking echoed outside through the pecan grove that lined the gravel drive. The familiar smell of black coffee, bacon, and cigarette smoke made its way upstairs forcing his eyes open as Everett squinted at the alarm clock, and then sat up in bed rotating his sore shoulder. The painkillers had done their job—for the first time in months he'd slept uninterrupted for more than two hours straight. He stretched again, the cartilage popping and snapping, but the range was returning.

The large upstairs bedroom he'd grown up in was now a time capsule, filled with his awards—a punt-pass-and-kick first place medallion hung on the wall, a North South Senior Bowl MVP trophy rested on the shelving, along with black-and-white photos of team mates through the years in high school and college. Some had turned pro when he did. Some had made the sensible decision to marry and pursue a normal life. And some still elbowed their way through the league.

Haunted by the relentless ache, he quickly but carefully dressed, knowing she'd prepare more food than he could finish and he didn't want her standing over the stove very long. He covered his shaved scalp with a ball cap and hit the stairs.

His grandmother was stooped over the antique porcelain gas stove stirring scrambled eggs with one hand and removing bacon from a cast iron skillet with the other. He crept up behind her and gently hugged her frail, crooked frame.

"Well. Good morning," she said as she turned around slowly, touching his face. "Oh my. You're so tan. How did you sleep, dear?"

"Just fine," he said as he hugged her again.

"Can you ever forgive me for not greeting you last night?"

"You're forgiven," he said softly. "My flight was delayed and I didn't land in Memphis until after midnight, so I drove down sixty-one."

"With the window down, no doubt. You just love that old highway, don't you?"

"I love the smell of that dirt at night."

She wiped her hands on her apron. "You used to drive home from Oxford whenever you had a tough loss. I suppose you have a lot on your mind these days?"

"Blue let me in and Emma made me a sandwich."

"If I know you, you're still hungry this morning."

"Starving," he said as he carefully maneuvered into a chair at the end of the long kitchen table and eased into the antique chair.

"You move like an old woman," she jabbed.

"Is it that obvious?"

She stopped stirring the bacon. "You know, we have a brand new teaching hospital over in Greenville. Their physical therapy department is world class."

"Nice try," he said with a grin, sipping his coffee.

"I could drive you myself. Every morning."

"I have some news, Virginia. I've decided to stay in California for a little while. I interviewed with several brokerage houses downtown."

"Does that mean what I think it means?"

"I've been offered a position and I need a quiet weekend at home to study for the licensing exam. I only get one shot at it."

"Everett, that's wonderful! Just promise not to disappear on me. You'll always have this place to come home to."

"You have my word."

She carefully placed a crowded plate of eggs, bacon, sausage, and homemade bread in front of him, then she leaned over and kissed him again. "You'll never believe who I ran into last week."

"I give up."

"Shelby Ford was playing tennis at the country club and stopped by our bridge game to say hello to me. Wasn't that sweet of her?"

"How is she?"

"Well, I understand she's taken a modeling job in Atlanta."

"Good for her," he said.

"She asked about you."

"Virginia."

"She was only being polite. I told her Dallas traded you to San Diego. She didn't know you were injured so I didn't go into too much detail, but she wanted me to tell you hello. It wouldn't hurt to call her this weekend while you're home."

"My life is complicated enough right now."

"Very well. Blue is saddling the horses. He's expecting you this morning for a quail hunt. Can you raise a shotgun with that shoulder?"

He gulped his coffee. "I wouldn't miss it for the world."

"And the Rebels play at home this evening."

"I came to see you."

"You are certainly free to follow me around my rose garden, help me mulch my tomatoes, and drive me into town if you prefer."

"How about we plan on Bloody Marys before the game? Just you and me. I can study all day after the hunt and we can watch it on the back porch tonight."

"It's a date," she said as she sat down across from him with a cup of coffee and lit another cigarette. "Don't you dare look that way at me."

"What?"

"I know you hate these things, but I'm down to two in the morning and one after supper. An old woman is entitled to at least one vice."

He almost choked on his eggs. "You've outlived all your doctors. I say stay with what works."

"You've been through a lot, Everett. And it just breaks my heart because I know how hard you've worked."

"Positions have to be earned. You know that."

"But at what cost, Son? Why would they send you back in after you were hurt once at the beginning of the game? They just seem to use you and trade you like livestock. I just couldn't watch the last half of your last game."

"You never missed a game in college and now you won't watch me on network television?"

"I watched a video tape," she said. "Blue follows everything you do. He's taped every one of your games."

"I'm trying to focus on my future right now."

"And I applaud your decision. This is an important step for you. You remind me of Daddy."

"Really? How so?"

"He used to say risk is the father of danger and opportunity. I just wish I could convince you to interview back here, where you belong. Memphis has all the big name brokerages, or you could go back to work for Buddy at Merrill. I'm sure he'd love to help you get started in the business."

"I want to work for myself. Besides, California is this amazing place. The weather is picture perfect, the people are all beautiful and interesting and smart. Plus, this brokerage house I talked to is really something special."

"Well, I want you to be happy."

"You should see the office, Virginia! Top floor of the tallest building in downtown San Diego. Sweeping views north straight up the coastline. They pay the highest commission in the industry, and they're privately-held and family-owned. You'd love the place. Starched white shirts. All high tech, and very professional."

Her soft, blue eyes focused on his face. "I think it's a marvelous decision but I do still worry about you."

"You can stop worrying. I'll have a nice safe job now."

"I would scarcely refer to the financial markets as safe, Everett Anderson."

"But my great grandfather made a killing in the markets."

"Your great grandfather was a proud and disciplined war veteran who rose early, recorded with great detail the overwhelming complexity of this property in its heyday, and never speculated in the markets. He was a thirty-three degree Mason, and he also owned a bank. When the Depression hit, he was eighty years old, but he paid every depositor out of his own pocket. These days the government bails out every failed bank on Wall Street. I swear I don't recognize my country anymore."

"And he survived the Depression and kept this place in the family by hedging in the futures market."

"True, but your great grandfather was no gambler. That was your father's special talent. Daddy traded with a broker only out of necessity to hedge his risk and protect our crop."

"But farming is risky. Isn't that why my Dad drilled?"

"I suppose all Delta planters have to take risks to some degree, but your father was reckless, greedy, and extremely lucky at times. The family never talked about the lean years when he nearly lost this place, and the drinking that followed."

"Well, I'll be working as a broker. Handling other people's money."

"You're a grown man now and far be it from me to lecture you, but you've done a marvelous job with your trust. I only receive copies of your statements to satisfy Mister Pritchard, the trustee. Please don't make me regret voting in favor of control for you."

"Yes ma'am."

"And for heaven's sake, Everett, you're not even thirty yet. That trust is your retirement. Football could never give you that."

"It's in bonds right now."

"I'll say no more on the matter," she gushed, leaning over to kiss his forehead once again. "You had better finish up. Blue will be here shortly. His sons are dying to see you and you all should find plenty of birds over near the old well. I'm just delighted that you're here," she said, holding his face.

"It's good to be home."

"And by the way, I've got a very good feeling about this career change of yours."

*

Joseph F. Bailey, the Deputy Director of FinCEN, the U.S. Treasury Department's Financial Crimes Enforcement Network, entered the large corner conference room on the third floor of its headquarters building in Vienna, VA. The Chairman of the CME Group and two lawyers from the U.S. Attorney's office were already huddled around a circular meeting table which held an elaborate, high-tech encrypted speakerphone.

"Gentlemen," the Director said, "over three trillion dollars a year is laundered through the United States. It's a soar subject, but because of the fragmented nature of the present day regulatory trading environment we find ourselves in, my office has just concluded a preliminary investigation regarding legal but irregular transactions occurring on the newly-formed ICE and ELX exchanges which now compete directly with the Chicago Mercantile Exchange. As a result, our Commander-in-Chief and Treasury's newly appointed Secretary have initiated Operation Whirlpool, which we believe will ensnare billions in illegal offshore transactions. The Continental Trading Group just became our top priority. Jack Diamond's hedge business clears through several international sources. That much we do know. Working in a deep cover capacity, we now have an agent inside whose responsibility is to gather the physical evidence and provide the depositions and testimony, if necessary. We'll all need to work together. Is that clear to everyone?"

"Yes, Sir," came the response.

"For the moment, the identity of our confidential contact will have to remain protected, even within this room and inside our investigation. A rookie with the Secret Service, our contact graduated with honors from the United States Naval Academy with a Master's in accounting, and was recently promoted to the most elite unit of the Treasury Department. All future reports will come directly to my office. The Secretary wants transparency in our financial exchanges and we're shorthanded as it is, and I damn sure don't want any media leaks. Any questions?"

There was no response.

The console lit up as Bailey touched the power key on the conference phone. "Can you hear me?"

The speaker phone suddenly came alive. "Yes, Sir," said the distorted voice.

"Give us a briefing."

"The Chicago office is comprised of very aggressive sales talent, primarily in their twenties, fresh out of college. They're extremely careful about who they hire and the professional arrogance is remarkable. Their company research trades are micro-managed and never made public. Whatever their research analysts say is adhered to without question, with an almost militaristic obedience. By the way, I'll need to request an increase of capital for trading client accounts in order to advance my case."

"Now, wait a minute," the Deputy Director said. "We initially authorized two million dollars in front money."

"I'll need to appear well-connected."

"You're the salesperson; you'll just have to raise the rest."

"With all due respect, two million dollars won't even get me to the on-deck circle, much less out to San Diego."

"San Diego?"

"That's their flagship location where the top producers are awarded transfers to, once they've proven themselves at any of the other offices around the country. It's the only way I'll be able to get far enough inside to gather any hard evidence. And as far as my salesmanship is concerned, I've already raised millions on my own, using the leads they've provided for me, but I'll need additional capital to qualify for California."

"I'll see what I can do."

"The last thing you need is to come up empty-handed, Sir."

"As far as you are concerned!" he shouted at the phone on the table, "stop acting like you're having such a Goddamn good time! This operation could also make or break your career!"

"Yes, Sir."

"Your job is simple. Build a case from the inside and communicate through your SAT phone only, and no names on the airwaves. You've lost our Chicago contact in the pits. Now get me some one in the organization that will help us or your first assignment will be your last!"

5

On a brilliant, crisp, chilly morning Everett Anderson sipped his coffee and sat alone in front of the closet-size Coronado sidewalk cafe around the corner from his new address. A split-level Spanish-style two-bedroom close to the beach with the sound and smell of saltwater within walking distance, its balcony faced east toward the city's modern, serrated skyline. Charlie Hayes told him about the location after one of his players was traded to New England and Everett immediately fell in love with the tidy little military town, writing an offer on the new townhouse during his first visit with the realtor. Cloudless skies, bright sun, and soft Pacific breezes rushed past him and gave life to the picturesque seaside city surrounded by water on three sides just across the harbor from the business district. The high-priced peninsula serving as a natural breakwater to shelter San Diego Bay was also the perfect place for a young rookie commodity broker working downtown to live.

Confined in Eden, Everett walked the glowing beaches and swam in the Pacific, healing and learning the lay of the sparkling city and its postcard-perfect geography. The soft sun and Mediterranean climate accelerated his physical recovery and at times, usually while driving the modern race track-like freeway system with the convertible top rolled back, he wondered why the entire country hadn't moved to the southernmost city in southern California. She became a paradise full of mystery and movement—naturally lush, tropical landscaping with salmon-colored sunsets where seemingly perfect people were the rule and not the exception. The city made him feel as if he'd been an adopted citizen all his life, just as Charlie had promised. And in some deep, dark, silent part of his soul that no one would ever come close to knowing or learning about, he harbored a guilty sigh of relief, a well-deserved early retirement from the excruciating pace in the National Football League.

After riding the ferry across the bay, Everett walked the ten blocks to Continental's office. The soreness in the hamstring was almost gone and he welcomed the exercise as he strolled without crutches through the downtown area, which bustled with construction. The city was experiencing a renaissance in its historic Gas Lamp District—a dozen square blocks of converted warehouse lofts, art galleries, restaurants, and coffee bars catering to Baby-Boomers with retirement money.

Reaching the California Empire Bank building he entered the marbled lobby, confronted by a stocky, baby-faced man pacing in front of the main elevator. Dressed in a faded black suit and tie, the man rocked on his heels, rigid and erect, his stubby, calloused hands nervously pushed the up arrow while smoothing his tight-fitting trousers. The elevator lights repeatedly flashed red, refusing to open.

"Security's a real bitch around here. You got one of those special code cards?" the young man asked with a nervous grin. His appearance was pure southern California—blond buzz cut and a wide-shouldered frame. "I lost the one they mailed me. Can you believe that shit?"

Everett inserted the card he'd received.

"Thanks, Bro. Vinnie Cozzene," the young man announced, extending his hand as the doors opened.

"Everett Anderson."

"You one of the senior brokers?"

"I just moved to town and I start training Monday."

"Oh yeah? Welcome to the Hotel California, Bro."

The elevator doors opened on the forty-ninth floor to a gathering of suits and forced smiles on the company's trading floor. William Peterson greeted each broker as they all filed through the line straight to the open bar and the gourmet buffet.

At the end of the line was Hamilton Walker.

"Congratulations, Rookie. Guess the interview went well," the big man said.

Everett shook his hand. "I slipped under the radar."

"Bill told me you did fine. He likes you already," Walker said. "So what do you think about the place?"

"Incredible."

"You should have seen it when I interviewed!" Vinnie blurted out. "It was Friday morning, all hell was breaking loose, and the markets were on fire! I knew right then and there, I was going to work here if it killed me! This place just smells like money!"

Walker eyed Cozzene. "Actually, you could watch the fireworks later tonight, if you hang around. Asia opens in about four hours. Have fun and enjoy your last night of freedom, gentlemen," Walker gushed, shaking hands and disappearing into the crowd.

The rookies were easy to spot, pointing and marveling at the size and detail of the complex trading floor. Each wall of the great space held large, high-definition plasma monitors featuring Bloomberg, Reuters, BBC, and Al Jazeera, as well as CNBC and CNNfn reporting up-to-the-minute international news and updates on all global markets. There was even a section of screens with thermal maps of crucial agricultural regions, complete with international climate reports gathered from global TOPEX weather satellites. The walls seemed to pulsate as the color monitors flashed a dizzying barrage of data.

Like a dictator surveying the trading floor, Jack Diamond appeared overhead at the elevator lobby railing. A hush spread over the crowd as he flaunted his signature smile.

Vinnie leaned over. "Did you hear about one of our floor traders in Chicago?" Vinnie whispered.

Everett shook his head.

"Blew his brains out week before last."

Jack cleared his throat and took the microphone as Bill Peterson stood next to him with a graceful tilt. "Good afternoon, ladies and gentlemen. Permit me to officially welcome everyone to the west coast flagship office for the oldest and most exclusive retail commodity brokerage house in North America. According to Barron's, as of last Friday, Continental's equity just reached over fifty billion dollars. And the man responsible for this unprecedented growth is our one and only vice-president of trading, William Peterson!" Jack turned and began clapping, causing the floor to erupt in applause.

As the applause reached its climax, the elevator doors flew open below the railing where Jack stood. A sun-burned man with curly blond hair in a dark blazer strolled onto the floor. The blond man quickly found a spot to stand as Jack introduced the new brokers, one by one, including the company's top producers who'd been awarded a transfer from any one of Continental's dozen offices. Jack ended the ceremony with an announcement regarding bonus money for the second half of the year, followed by a photo montage from the recent sales trip to Switzerland. The type-A crowd headed for the buffet and the bar, grateful for an end to the formalities.

Everett and Vinnie inhaled lunch while Jack and the entourage that surrounded him worked the room like a political campaign. Jack was dressed in a dark navy blazer complete with Harvard crest on the jacket breast pocket, while the blond broker who arrived late followed closely, dressed in a similar blazer and crest.

"Mister Anderson, Mister Cozzene, nice to see you two gentlemen this afternoon," Jack said. "Have you two met the tardy Mister Valentine yet?"

Vinnie smiled and offered his hand to the blond broker in the blazer. "Vinnie Cozzene. How are you?"

"John Valentine."

"Say hello to Everett Anderson," Vinnie offered.

They shook hands. "Bill's told me a lot about you, Anderson," John said.

Apparently finished with introductions, Jack and Bill were immediately off to press more palms.

John instructed the bartender, "I'll have an ice pick, with a floater." The kid poured a full jigger of high octane clear liquor on top of the ice tea and vodka drink after it was mixed. He handed it to John who gulped the top half of the cocktail, almost straight booze.

"Thirsty?" Vinnie jabbed.

"That's quite a suit, Cozzene. Was there a death in the family?" John asked.

"Very funny."

"Well, I guess one slips through the cracks every now and then," John uttered.

"So what are you dressed for Slick, a yacht race?"

"Everyone wants to work here, Cozzene. How'd you talk your way into an interview?"

"Same way you did."

"An Ivy league education and a thoroughbred bloodline?"

"No," Vinnie said firmly, "bullshit and balls."

"Well, somehow you got in the door. We'll see if you stay."

"I can't spell, but I can sell."

"Our research is a well-guarded secret. Might even make you look like a genius, Cozzene, if you survive."

Vinnie glanced at the large office trading scoreboard and then looked at John. "Looks like we'll all be chasing the top of that board."

"I just had a great year last month," John bragged.

Vinnie focused on the office's production standings on the wall. "I see you in second place, Slick, below Vasquez."

As if on cue, the elevator doors opened and the crowd parted as she floated past the all-male group of rookies with a measured gait, her long blond hair pilled high in a conservative composition on top of her head. Slender wire-rimmed glasses rested on a petite nose and her tailored jacket and skirt failed to contain her ample figure. It was apparent that she'd struggled to button her blouse.

She walked past John. "You're late, Darling," he said.

The brokers at the bar studied the sky-high stiletto heels and the fitted designer suit as she passed. They watched as she handed a leather folder to Jack then ordered a glass of red wine from the make-shift bar and lit a cigarette. Several rookies approached her.

"Damn," Vinnie whispered, shaking his head. "Who is she?"

"Stop drooling. That's Jennifer Emerson. She's Jack's secretary," John volunteered. "She's also office manager. She processes all your paperwork and your paycheck, if you ever get one."

John melted into the crowd while Everett sipped his drink, but it was Jennifer he studied with interest as she walked towards the bar. "Another Merlot, please," she ordered, looking at him through her glasses. She slowly drew on her cigarette. "You don't look familiar."

"I don't know a soul here."

"Hmm. Honesty. That's original."

"But you, on the other hand, seem pretty popular."

"Anxious rookies. They make a little money and they think they can hit on every girl that works here. It just gets so old. So where did you transfer from?"

"I'm one of those anxious rookies."

The corners of her mouth turned up slowly. "Sorry. I'm Jennifer Emerson."

"Everett Anderson."

"Footballer from Dallas, right?"

"That's right."

"Small world. I grew up in Austin," she said. "but my mother moved us to Chicago when I started grade school." She sipped her drink slowly and watched him over the top of her glass. "This party's for you, you know."

"So is Jack as good as they say?"

She took a deep drag on her cigarette and exhaled away from him. "That depends on how you define good."

"Is he right all the time?"

"You'll see."

"So who's the top man around here?"

"What makes you think the top broker is a man?"

"Oops."

"The top *broker* is Victoria Vasquez. That's her over there talking to Jack and Bill." She nodded toward an attractive, young woman with short dark hair, combed back and dressed in a black designer outfit. "She just transferred from Chicago, and she's already over five million for the year."

"And her gross is ten percent?"

"She's all business. Uber-bitch."

"There's no shortage of free advice around here."

"Speaking of which, I'd avoid John Valentine, if I were you. He's always hanging around the junior brokers, usually for all the wrong reasons."

"Was he dropped as a child?"

"He's Jack's favorite pet and derivatives super trader from East Coast money. Born with a silver spoon up his nose."

"Is he up or down for the year?"

"He's up thirty percent."

"Nice, but it's almost Summer."

"Thirty percent this *month*."

"Shit."

"A real reptile, but harmless. John used to be the top broker in the office until Vasquez transferred here and stole his thunder."

"That explains a lot."

The drinks flowed and so did their conversation. They had enough in common to cause the party to fade away as they wandered outside and sat together on the leather furniture that covered the terrace.

As the brokers began to line up at the elevator banks, Vinnie re-appeared. "Looks like Valentine's throwing a shindig at his beach house in La Jolla," he announced.

Everett shook his head. "You actually get along with him now?"

"He grows on you," Vinnie said, "kind of like mold. Besides, the party's some kind of tradition. Need a ride?"

"I took the ferry from Coronado," Everett yawned.

Vinnie finished his drink. "Then I'm off like a prom dress."

"I don't usually do this but, I'm going that way," Jennifer offered. "If you need a ride."

"I haven't slept in three days," Everett volunteered.

"So that's why you scored ninety percent on your series three exam," she said. "That's a company record."

"I had a whole day to study for it. Would you be shocked if I took a rain check tonight?"

"I wouldn't be shocked. I'd be impressed. Just promise me one thing."

"Name it."

"Don't become one of them."

"You have my word."

"Then you better get some rest, Everett Anderson. Your whole world is about to change tomorrow morning."

6

In the cold pre-dawn darkness, the silver Mercedes S-class sedan glided into its reserved berthing in the climate-controlled garage. Jack Diamond stepped out with a leather briefcase under his arm and walked quickly to the small service elevator. Shortly after commissioning the construction of his Post-Modern masterpiece, the California Empire Bank had pressured him for years to sell but he hadn't budged. Instead, he agreed to allow the bank to pay him handsomely for the naming rights while his discreet brokerage house remained a large and anonymous tenant, occupying the building's top two floors.

The special service car ascended quickly to the mechanical floor strategically located halfway up the tall building in order to feed heating, air, and electrical to all the offices, effectively covering the least amount of distance in each direction.

Jack leaned forward and gazed in to the biometric retinal scanner next to the metal door at the end of the winding corridor. A red laser flashed into his right eye, confirmed his identity and the metal door unlocked, providing access to an elaborate, windowless command center bustling with personnel. Cutting edge state-of-the-art high-tech instrumentation wrapped around the rambling and spacious security bunker like a Las Vegas casino command center. Reinforced concrete insulated the entire services floor full of technicians as they monitored video screens, phone conversations, activity in the hallways, copy rooms, trading floor and restrooms while the relentless recording of client orders was fed to a bank of digital equipment which would embarrass even the most seasoned recording studio engineer. Dozens of OS-3 phone lines fed in to an array of computerized PBX and T-3 broadband high-speed fiber optic and Bluetooth phone equipment displaying every extension in the company, each coded to identify the name of the broker for which each line rang. Another bank of television screens displayed various surveillance camera angles throughout the top two floors. The cameras monitored everything. There was even a HVAC panel which controlled the introduction of pure chilled oxygen fed to the trading floor, creating a brisk environment at a frigid temperature of sixty degrees insuring the offices and trading floor remained at a fever pitch during market hours. And seated at a center control console panel filled with flashing red and green lights was Raymond Hood, Jr., Jack's well-paid bodyguard and Continental's chief of security. Standing behind Hood was Bill Peterson.

Jack tossed a detailed spreadsheet in front of Hood. "Have your people learn their voices, in case any of them make it. You finish all their background checks?"

Hood nodded, fussing over a new motherboard of computer wiring at the dashboard-like console directly in front of him.

"How was your deposition?" Peterson asked.

"Like a colonoscopy."

Hood spun around in his chair. "I've been in contact all morning with the head trader for Camerone Cane in Mexico City. We now have the ability to trade through international dark pools as well as the interbank FX forward swap market. Once an electronic communication network accounts for a large portion of total daily market volume, the regulators require prices to be quoted to the public. But for now, we're still under the regulatory radar."

"Brilliant," Jack added.

"Total anonymity," said Peterson. "With private buy- side *and* sell-side transactions, we can literally make our own market in any currency. Our new trading platform pulls in the various U.S. exchange feeds, including the AMEX, NYSE, NASDAQ, Philadelphia, and Bulletin Board, as well as Canada's TSX and Montreal Exchange, which then interfaces with your ECN overseas. No currency transaction reports *or* suspicious activity reports to deal with. But we are having a slight logistics problem with St. Martin and Tortola."

Hood handed Jack a spreadsheet.

"The British Virgin Islands are becoming a real bitch to work with, but the Dutch and French banks will still accept our transactions in pesos. Seems like everyone is running from the dollar these days."

"Wouldn't you, if you had millions on the line? Have it working yesterday, Ray. Take the Gulfstream down there if need be. How are our numbers looking to date for the month?" Jack asked.

"Vasquez did over a hundred in gross this month, and Valentine's nervous," Peterson offered.

"What about our rookie crop?"

"They're clean. Cozzene's family just sold their carwash franchise and left the kid with a little over a million. He's pissed half of it away already and carries a huge monthly nut. Loves to play the ponies and has a chronic weed habit."

"Sound's like our kind of man."

"And then there's Anderson," Bill said.

"The football player?"

"Cornbread and apple pie. Aced his exam and he's hungry as hell."

"How about family?"

"They own property in the South," Bill replied. "He traveled to Mississippi this weekend to visit the grandmother who raised him."

"So they're in real estate?"

"They grow soybeans," Hood grinned.

"Wait a minute. Let me get this straight," Jack snorted. "Our rookie cowboy escaped the farm to make it in professional football? Tall, handsome, and articulate. Make sure and put the NFL logo on all of his business cards. Our clients will love him."

"You can't make this shit up, Jack," Hood said. "His father was a drunk and an oil driller. Found the story in the local paper. Seems the family hit a pocket of crude near the Mississippi River, but never developed it."

"Why not?"

"Both parents died when the old man ran off the road."

"What's the estate worth?"

Hood began the furious input of numbers and digits he sensed would yield a profitable outcome. "Six hundred acres at four thousand per. Two point four."

"Who referred him?"

"Walker got Anderson his interview."

"So Anderson only met Walker that one time before we transferred him, right?"

"They met the night Anderson interviewed. One of our guys was following Walker and his crew into the bar."

"Keep an eye on Anderson, in case he survives."

At five A.M. sharp, Continental's main floor was already trading at full speed as Everett Anderson stepped off the elevator. Asia was shutting down, New York was waking up, and currencies opened in a half hour. The dollar was plummeting, again. The Fed was expected to raise interest rates. Oil was up. Bonds were down. The Russians were buying more gold and Japan missed their trade number.

Large plasma screens displayed an endless array of talking heads, throbbing and twitching and speculating in front of the latest combat footage or natural disaster coverage above crawling tickers dispensing pre-market fair value quotes and prices.

Senior traders were hard at work on their wireless Bluetooth headsets insisting upon more money and barking order confirmations at floor runners, rushing to time-stamp trade tickets on their way to the order desk, AKA "the cage." Continental's hand-picked top-producers were stationed at window seats around the perimeter of the great floor. It was an epicenter-like atmosphere, crackling with energy as news updates flashed like a strobe against the frenzy of movement, punctuated by the occasional shout "Tape!", while sales managers prowled the corridors of the mahogany consoles, monitoring orders.

"What in the hell are you doing here?"

Everett wheeled around, facing chin to chin with John Valentine.

"Research is about to start!" John bellowed. "Only senior personnel are authorized for the live report! You'll get the rookie version later along with the rest of the trainees."

"I couldn't sleep."

"You should be focused on learning our system right now! Period. Nothing more. Rookies do not rate access to the floor, Anderson. Right now you are a fucking clerk!"

"Well, Mr. Anderson, the trading floor looks a bit different during working hours, does it not?" Bill Petersen announced from the elevator doors. "That'll be all Mr. Valentine."

"Morning, Skipper. We're not through, Rookie."

"Walk with me, Everett," Bill continued, with an arm around the last rookie to be hired. "Jack's father, R.D. Diamond, established a reputation by hiring aggressive young athletes to work as his brokers on the exchange floor. We've built our operation around that business model. And we see that same potential in you."

"Thank you, Bill."

"We set the pace early on as the toughest and most discreet trading house in Chicago. Bare knuckles pit warfare at a time when your wits, your lungs, and your sharp elbows made you a rich man. Our reputation in the pits still bears testament to physical stamina and a passion for adrenaline—all traits our founder developed as a rugby forward in college. And although R.D. was also an avid sportsman, he sought out gentlemen, true gentlemen, men who understand history. You understand what I mean, don't you Everett?"

"Of course."

"And R.D. encouraged the hunting spirit in all his brokers and traders. Eat what you kill every day. He turned trading into a physical contest. The only replacement for the rush of competition. Of course, you won't be trading the pits in Chicago, but the company tradition has remained intact. Take a look around. With a direct link to daily operations back in Chicago decades before its time, we enjoy powerful control at the exchanges, yielding groundbreaking access to timely information. Order execution is our trademark, the brokerage houses' original charter."

"That explains all the security."

"Access to our trading floor is restricted during market hours to all but the senior elite who've earned the right. I hope you realize and appreciate the measures that we take to protect our clients as well as our brokers and traders. That's why you see all the limited measures being taken. Terrorists could affect the US economy if they knew what we know. Not to mention the occasional client who loses money and shows up at his broker's office with a pistol. You might notice surveillance monitoring equipment throughout the building to protect our traders, and our trade secrets."

"Makes sense."

"In case you haven't noticed, Everett, you're being fast-tracked. By the way, congratulations on your series three exam. Ordinarily, most junior brokers begin their training in Chicago, where they get the opportunity to meet and work with our exchange floor traders. But Jack saw your exam results and feels you have some very special talent. Our expectations for you are well above your classmates. Is that clear?"

"Absolutely, Bill."

"Our trading floor is where you'll hear the senior traders and their inside takes on every rumor, weather pattern, and price swing before and after execution. Not many broker-dealers allow their retail producers to speak directly with their floor traders at the exchange. That's what makes us different. Our participation often affects market movements. Consequently, floor privileges are what separates our ranked producers from the true players."

"Impressive."

"By the way," Petersen added. "You'll have to check out with John Valentine. He's been promoted to floor management following Walker's transfer to Chicago."

"Transfer?"

"John runs our private equity derivatives desk now."

"What happened to Walker?"

"Everett, I like you. I want to see you succeed. Walker was moved back to Chicago for more training."

"I hardly got to know him."

"You were lucky to get this shot. Just focus on your duties around here and you'll do fine. John was given control of Walker's team. You can learn a lot from him. He's proven himself to be a real team player as well as one of the top traders around."

They crossed the floor toward Valentine's new office. Peterson touched Everett on the back. "We'll talk later this morning. If you're hungry after your morning training, stop by my office and we'll go get some lunch."

Through the tall, wide perimeter glass windows which formed the skin of the high-tech tower, the entire city began to sparkle below in the early morning twilight. Stars flickered on and off over the ocean to the west as the downtown area began to glow at first light. Most of the commodity markets had opened with a vengeance as he made his way through the maze of trading consoles, dodging floor runners and sprinting sales assistants.

At the open doorway to John Valentine's office he stopped and knocked, staring at boxes filled with trophies, plaques, engraved crystal and sports memorabilia littering the oriental rugs which covered the stained concrete floors. What stood out around the empty office were bulls; some made of glass, metal, marble, even polished wood. In the middle of the clutter, John Valentine was on the phone biting his nails as he stood staring at the bay below. "What the hell, Pauly?" John snapped into his head set with his back to the door. "You want dinner first or you just want to fuck right away? The spread is way too rich." He waved Everett in. "The bid? The bid's an insult! You think I'm just some wire house whore with a couple million to waste. Call me back when you're ready to trade some size." John hesitated. "Yeah, you're right about that. Crude is a good buy right now. Good-bye house, good-bye car, good-bye yacht." John slammed the phone down as he reached inside the cherry humidor on his desk, extracting a sterling cutter. "Merrill Lynch. They put the bull in bullshit. Shmoke, Anderson?"

"Sure." Everett clipped the tip and lit the Montecristo with a long wood match as John turned on the hospital-grade air filter built into the ceiling.

"Relax, Sport. You're just the type of fraternity pledge we're looking for. And don't think we don't admire your initiative. Shit. Here at five sharp? You're just about the only intelligent jock Walker's referred all year. Last guy he brought us lost his own nest egg, burned through his parents' bread, then blew up his book in about the tenth month, which is pretty typical. But you've got nothing to worry about. Your background's solid. Receiver is still a skill position, isn't it?"

"So why are we talking?"

"I understand your family had a little money at one time."

At first the question startled him. A background check would be a necessary and logical procedure. Are they that thorough? "Why would my family be any of your business?"

"Your business is my business now, Sport. And my business is how much business you do from here on out. So, don't get defensive. Jack must've seen some thoroughbred in you and your background. He rarely hires anyone without a pedigree or a full week of interviewing, so this is our first date."

"Will there be a test?"

"Every fucking day, Ace. And on the floor, I'm in charge now. Remember that and we'll get along just fine. We run the hottest shop on the street, maybe the world, depending on which talking head you talk to. Research will tell you what to buy and when to sell. Just stick with the program and you'll get rich. This is trade by numbers, Zeke."

"So ten arbitrations makes you the most qualified to run the show?"

Valentine smiled. "You looked up my CRD number on the FINRA website. It's public information on the internet. I'm off special supervision this week," Valentine snorted.

"Congratulations."

"Anderson, if you can produce in this business, you can get away with murder. Your Series three is a license to steal, and it'll feel like charity. Hell, you'd have to stab someone on vide tape to lose your license."

Everett glanced around John's office, noticing the expensive and elaborate statues of bulls on every surface, shelf, table and credenza in every conceivable position cast in gold, wood or glass. Bulls fighting, rearing, horns lowered, charging, in repose, even black and white framed snapshots of matador and bull in the ring, all over the walls. "I'm curious. You ever been around a real bull?"

"So you need any more help with anything?"

"Just one question."

"Shoot."

"What happened to Ham Walker?"

"His team came up short. Won't happen on my watch."

"I thought he loved it here."

"He committed the unspeakable last week."

"What's that?"

Valentine leaned in, his smooth-shaven face shiny with sweat. "Went against research."

"That got him demoted back to Chicago?"

"If you don't learn anything else, remember that we're a special *kind* of team. That shouldn't be too hard for you, considering your Southern heritage," John said as he tossed the expensive investor package on to his desk in front of Everett. Hamilton Walker was pictured behind his desk, talking to a client. "Walker's hire was strictly affirmative action," John sneered. "He was even our cover boy."

Everett joined the other rookies later that morning as the group gathered against the gallery railing, gawking at the infinity of activity below. They sipped coffee and chattered nervously, watching the ferocious energy. But he couldn't shake the image of Walker's perpetual smile. *He seemed so upbeat, so positive,* Everett thought to himself.

Each trainee fixed their eyes on her as she marched across the lobby conference room. "Follow me please," she directed. Dressed in a grey linen pants suit, her short blond hair stacked and clipped in a bob, she made her way to the front of the large corporate boardroom as each rookie scurried from the railing to find a seat in one of the large leather chairs around the long oval table. She glanced at their hopeful faces, all hired on promises and dreams of making more money than they had ever imagined possible.

Everyone was quickly seated. "Good morning, everyone. My name is Katherine Fox," she announced. "I'll be your sales training manager for the next three months. First, let me congratulate you on your licensing exams. Unfortunately, I was in Chicago last weekend so this is my first time to meet most of you. I'm certain you've been introduced to many people and the names are blurred. Don't worry. Things will come together. Understand that you're all responsible for your own destiny around here. I've been with Continental for eight years now, starting as a junior broker and earning my way to the top. So forget everything you've ever been told about sales. You will learn to sell our way or you'll be out the door. Our way will make you very rich. If you listen carefully and apply what we teach you, you'll graduate to the trading floor, known around here as the Grinder. That's the good news. The bad news is eighty percent of you will never make it past our probation phase. So take a good look around. Roughly one in five will survive."

There was an uncomfortable pause as they glanced bravely at each other.

"Although your series three exam is required by federal law to educate you technically about the industry and license you as brokers, the pragmatics of selling will be taught here. The principles taught in here are not to leave this office. Clear?"

The room nodded in unison as she began passing out ringed binders to each of the neophytes "Read your compliance manual cover to cover tonight. You'll be tested on it tomorrow. Then sign the disclosure and return them to me. We will teach you how to carefully navigate through the minefield of calculated risk. Now turn to the first section and we'll review your pay scale."

The class obliged as she quickly covered the commission scale and production quotas. It was very early in the morning, but they were all wide awake now that the subject of money was being discussed. "Your monthly quota will remain at a hundred thousand dollars in gross new account production. Meet the minimum standards with this company, and with bonuses you'll earn well over two hundred thousand dollars your first year. If you fail to meet quota, it will then be up to your assigned sales manager on a monthly basis as to your future employment status. Any questions at this point?"

She scanned the room. "Good. Now, we have the next twenty business days together, before you start your phone training. We'll cover a different closing technique and trading tactic each day. If you remember nothing else, remember that we offer the riskiest, most aggressive and most profitable investment vehicle in the financial world. With that in mind, we have a treat for you. I'd like to introduce you to the top producer in the office, Victoria Vasquez."

In the doorway stood a striking young Hispanic woman, smartly dressed in a fitted charcoal jacket and skirt. Her dark hair framed her smooth tan face, punctuated with large brown eyes and full lips. Restless with excitement, the rookie brokers shifted in their leather chairs. "You've all had the opportunity to meet your managers," Vasquez said. "I suggest you get to know them intimately. They can make or break you. They will put constant pressure on you to stay on the phone. Their job is to patrol the trading floor and monitor your orders. They all have one thing in common. They were all exceptional producers. You will receive phone time reports twice a day to measure the number and duration of all your calls. Be mindful of what you say and stay on script."

Vasquez paused, her olive skin glowing in the early morning hours. "You've all passed a federal licensing exam. Your fingerprints are on record with the Commodity Futures Trading Commission and the FBI for a reason, to put the fear of God in each and every one of you so you do the right thing, all the time. Your license is a very precious opportunity. Protect it and your selves. You are dealing with other peoples' money, the most emotional component of their life. Be careful what you say, and always disclose the risk."

"Thank you, Victoria," Katherine said. "Now, why don't we take a break before we cover derivatives in detail. Then, I'll spend the rest of the day showing you how to make your clients fall in love with you."

7

The doorbell rang just before sunrise. Everett was already up watching the overseas, pre-open futures and cross market action on his Bloomberg. He looked through the peep sight and slowly opened the heavy wooden front door. "It's still dark," he yawned. "I thought you were picking me up at five."

"You can thank me later," Vinnie said with a grin as he quickly walked through the door. "Make us some java, Hombre. My caffeine level is dangerously low."

Everett looked through the open doorway and spotted Vinnie's Range Rover parked on the street. Two surfboards were strapped to the roof rack. One short. One shorter. He checked his watch. "You know we've got class in an hour," he said.

"Observation of the obvious, my brother."

They entered the kitchen and Everett reached for a bag of coffee beans in the top freezer, then began grinding. "You taking this training seriously?" Everett asked. "We can't be late, you know."

"You're in California now, Bro. You need to learn to relax."

Everett poured water into the coffee maker and the aroma immediately filled the kitchen. "Attitude, Vincent. Attitude."

"Hey, don't you worry about me."

They sat on the patio in the chilly morning air. "So how does it look out there?" Everett asked.

Scanning the waves in the distance, Vinnie sipped his coffee. "It's hurricane season south of Baja and there's a beautiful swell building out of the southwest. El Nino," Vinnie said. "Perfect waves for you. Low and smooth."

"As long as we're on time."

"Relax. You're gonna' love it." Vinnie said. "I'll teach you to give up a good wave every now and then to the rest of the tribe on the water. We all remember our first day. Just a little rule we live by."

"Guess this was bound to happen."

"Look. You're the jock. It's all about balance."

"I've hardly had time to do anything but study."

Vinnie frowned. "You're really buying into the program, aren't you?"

"Come again?"

"Don't you get sick of all that company-man, team-player, rah-rah crap?"

"Listen to you, giving up a wave for the tribe? I buy into results. You should have come to the mansion last night. Jack showed us how he charts the ag markets, especially beans and wheat, and natty gas is blowing up right now. Continental was way ahead of the crowd and all over the recent rally in grains and metals."

"Well, I know one thing, they'll brainwash you if you don't get out of the office every once and a while. You've been over at that mansion every night this week. You guys act like Jack's some kind of New Age guru. He doesn't employ brokers. The man has subjects."

"The man's a genius, and you can't argue with success. You'd do well to put in the extra time, too. You've flunked all the tech tests."

"I know, but I just don't get it. Buy long? Sell short?"

"Then how the hell did you pass the Series three exam?"

"Must be why they call it the Series three," Vinnie huffed. "It took me three tries to pass it."

"Look, you'll never close any business without the ability to explain to clients how we trade. Remember the Duke brothers?"

"Bo and Luke?"

"No. Mortimer and Randolph."

"Huh?"

"Okay. Let's try this again. You're a gambler. You only need to know one thing to trade. We love volatility and we make money for our clients on both ends, whether a market goes up or down. You're clear on that much, right?"

"Yeah."

"Then think in terms of direction," Everett said. "If you're selling short, you're gambling that a commodity's price will fall below its present price. Down is your direction. Your client shorts soybeans at seven dollars a bushel and buys the option to own the commodity at six, like placing a bet through a bookie without giving up any money. If the price does fall to six, you've sold it before you own it, and your client profits the dollar difference. Your risk is that the price doesn't drop. Short. Down. Make sense?"

Vinnie nodded. "Got it."

"And if you're long, you're gambling on a simple rise in price. Your client goes long beans at six then sells at seven. His direction is up. Again, the risk is that the price doesn't rise. It's that simple."

"What about limit moves?"

"Every commodity has to have a finite and limited range in which it can trade on a daily basis, otherwise currencies and interest rates would go haywire during political chaos, and crop prices would sky-rocket every time the weather changes. But we love uncertainty. It creates volatility and price movement."

Vinnie smiled and nodded. "I think I got it."

Most of the local surfing population was already in the water as dawn broke in the east beyond the mountains behind the city. Vinnie's truck slid into the corner of the parking lot under a Canary Island palm tree, slinging gravel and waking several sleeping surfers close by in the public parking lot.

"It's still dark!" rang out from the closest van.

"Go to hell, Rooster!"

Everett looked at Vinnie. "Friends of yours?"

"Yeah, I know those kooks."

"They call you Rooster?"

"I love daybreak. What can I say?"

They unloaded the boards and stepped into their wet suits just as the sleeping surfers began to stir.

"Do exactly what I do," Vinnie said, gesturing toward the chilly Pacific. He calmly squatted onto the sand and crossed his legs. His tone was suddenly stern and his face focused. "The ocean kills, my man."

Everett nodded and followed, stretching his stiff limbs and getting the blood moving through his athletic body.

Vinnie closed his eyes and began a rhythmic breathing routine. He inhaled and exhaled carefully, his posture rigid as the onshore wind rushed past him and the waves pounded violently into the sand. "Lie stomach down and paddle out hard. Once we pass the break, I'll walk you through the drill."

They paddled out together, pointing their boards perpendicular to the oncoming waves, allowing the water to break over their backs. They reached a point about one hundred yards offshore and then sat up on their boards, waiting for just the right wave to ripple under them.

"Your first impulse is to catch a wave that'll break too soon, but you'll learn in time to spot the swell," Vinnie instructed. "Squat with a low center of gravity, steady your feet and ride any way you can, and when you fall, try to fall shallow. We're over a reef."

Vinnie noticed a large swell in the distance. "See how the wave starts? You're looking for clean waves that roll in, then build. Stay here and watch how I drop in," he said.

As the swell grew, he paddled with the wave, his strokes matching its speed and his board slicing gently through the greenish blue water. He crouched on his short board and rode to the upside center, steering the nose into the fulcrum of the wave, slicing up and down on its smooth face. The wave lost momentum and rolled over, flattening out in the shallow water.

Everett quickly spotted his wave. There were very few riders on their boards yet. In the half-light of dawn, his wave began to build, its size pronounced against the smaller waves surrounding it. He was well positioned in front of the rising wave as the sudden exhilaration of the powerful water swept his large frame along with it, angling toward the shore line. As the swell pushed up through the surf, Everett forced his body up to a squat, parallel to the board. He wobbled, but managed to stay up and remain crouched. He couldn't believe the force of the ocean beneath him, lifting his body along on its back, carrying him swiftly through the wet stinging wind by the sheer force of its velocity. Adrenaline surged through his central nervous system for the first time in months. His eyes were wide open and the salty spray burned. With equally sudden force, a brawny blond surfer slashed through the water, cutting off Everett from the smooth water and slamming his body into the shallow surf. "Stay off my wave!" the man shouted, his piercing eyes red and angry. The slasher wore a short, black wet suit and he laughed as he passed. His wheat-colored crew cut was short and spiked, augmenting features chiseled and jagged. Then in a blurred moment, he was gone. But there was something vaguely familiar about the surfer's rage.

Vinnie paddled over. "You okay?"

Everett spit salt water and wiped his burning eyes. "Son of a bitch!"

The waves were now crowded and the blond surfer was gone. "It's just a territory thing," Vinnie said.

"That was more than marking territory. He was *definitely* on the juice," Everett noticed.

"You mean steroids?"

"He's been dosing hard. Did you see his face? His eyes were yellow."

"Let it go, Brother," Vinnie said. "Guys like that just need more room than most. We better get to work."

8

The Continental Trading Group's newest crop of would-be brokers were all well-versed in classroom closing by the end of the second week of training. Time to go live. And to further inspire them, Katherine Fox marched the rookies on to the balcony as Jack passed out commission checks, a company tradition every Friday morning. The floor was unusually quiet, and several of the female brokers and assistants were crying.

Katherine turned toward the doorway where Jack stood with his hands folded in front of him, dressed in a double-breasted, grey pin-striped suit. His sun-burned face glowed with authority against his crisply-starched white cotton shirt, accented by his red polka-dot silk necktie and pocket square. His laced shoes were buffed to a blistering shine.

They all applauded heartily as Jack made his way to the center of the trading floor. "Thank you Miss Fox, and good morning everyone. Let me get a bit of business out of the way. Effective immediately, all employees of the Continental Trading Group are prohibited from maintaining or opening securities or commodity accounts at other broker-dealers, online brokers, bank brokers, or any other financial services institutions. If you currently maintain an outside account you must make arrangements to immediately transfer or liquidate. Compliance will be reviewing new accounts, ACAT transfers, and other related transactions. Adherence to this policy is a condition of employment and those found in violation will be terminated."

Jack continued. "What I'd like to do now is personally welcome each of our rookies aboard and tell them we're very excited about the opportunity to offer up to you a king-size paycheck every Friday. In fact, we feel Friday is the most significant day of the week. As you've all no doubt noticed, we've intentionally provided you with an exceptional environment in which to work. We tolerate nothing but a relentless struggle for excellence. You'll be asked to push yourself beyond what you perceive as a mental and physical breaking point, then we'll ask for more. We'll show you how to dress, how to articulate your ideas on the phone, and how to ask for the order."

He paused, allowing his words to be absorbed as he paced the trading floor. "In time, you'll develop the mental radar required for detecting buyers versus people who will waste your valuable time on the phone. The senior brokers you observe on the trading floor once stood where you now stand, their heads filled with the same uncertainty and excitement which you now feel. We will remove that doubt and replace it with confidence. Our system works. They learned it, and they used it. We know that each of you right now has all the tools necessary to succeed. You need do nothing extraordinary to succeed. You need only perform the ordinary, consistently well."

He circled back to the front. "What I'm about to share with you is the single most important tenet in this organization. You work for yourself, and everything hinges on one concept, your attitude. Attitude is the single most important determiner of your success or failure here. The telling difference between one salesperson and another is not education, talent or genius. It's a winning attitude. A winner always sees himself as a winner even when he occasionally loses. We will insist that you promise yourself to be so strong that you will not allow anything but thoughts of excellence and success to penetrate your psyche. You alone stand guard at the door of your brain."

Each broker leaned forward on each word as the smiling face of their president slowly became serious, almost angry. "We are looking for those of you who strive for achievement in the face of uncertainty, and we expect you to project the public posture that you are unmistakably positioned at the top of the financial food chain. And learn to listen. Give every man thy ear, but few thy voice. It's that simple. You've each chosen to enter a world which is as dangerous as it is demanding. Working here is about learning a complicated game, building on mistakes, and finding that even when you do succeed, you realize how little you understand. If you survive our training, you will know what it means to be called a closer."

The trading floor responded with another round of vigorous applause as did the training class.

Jack composed himself. "I have some rather unfortunate news to pass along this morning. One of our best and brightest, Hamilton Walker, lost his life in a tragic hunting accident in Alabama over the weekend. He was an outstanding trader and we'll all certainly miss him."

The brokers looked at one another. A few shook their heads but no one seemed to be overly concerned as shrugs of apathy rippled through the floor. There was no time to mourn. Morale was sky high and the markets were running wild.

Jennifer was on the phone and Jack's office was empty when Everett approached her desk. Her hair was braided and a single strand of pearls hugged her neck just above her white silk blouse. "And just where have you been keeping yourself?"

"The training class from hell. What does Jack want?"

"Maybe Jack doesn't want to see you."

"Don't you find Walker's death a little disturbing?" he asked, oblivious to her flirting.

"I didn't really know him. Besides, brokers come and go around here all the time."

"It just seems a little strange, that's all."

"Why?"

"I heard one of the company's floor traders shot himself in Chicago?"

"You chose the world of high finance and unlimited risk."

"But does that sound like normal business to you?"

"No, it sounds like an unfortunate accident. Does full paralysis and the occasional death in professional football sound like just another normal day at the office to *you*?"

"I guess you have a point."

"Around here everything's on the line all the time, Everett. Most of the senior brokers never bother to get to know the rookies, until they break out and get promoted. It sounds like Walker was just in the wrong place at the wrong time."

He glanced into Jack's empty office. "So, you lured me down here on false pretenses. What am I going to do with you?"

"I have a few ideas," she said. "If you're interested."

"Infatuated with me yet?"

She rolled her eyes. "Obsessed to be exact."

"So how about lunch?"

"Impossible. It's payday."

"Then drinks after work?"

"Drinks would be perfect. I know a great little seafood restaurant in Pacific Beach and I refuse to work a minute after five on Friday."

"Katherine promised to let us go early. I guess that means right before dark."

"Scram," she said. "You're distracting me."

The satellite phone continued to ring in Jack's office after trading ended for the day. He ignored it as he watched Katherine Fox walk through the deserted trading floor toward his office.

"So. Are you too busy to play?" Katherine asked as she strutted through his office. "We had another record day."

"Never too busy for you."

"Haven't seen you in the office much lately," she said.

"Baby-sitting our biggest client is a full time job," Jack explained as he walked to his bar.

Katherine followed obediently as he handed her a drink. She took a seat on the leather furniture under the concrete overhang and watched as Jack removed a small bag of cocaine from his desk.

"Now, we can play," he said as he poured the sparkling white powder on to the stainless-steel counter. "You know what they say about all work and no play."

He chopped two long rails of coke with his black American Express card, and handed her a crisply rolled hundred dollar bill. "You are the devil," she said. "We have a lot of catching up to do." She leaned over, snorted both lines, then French-kissed him firmly. "God you taste good," she whispered.

He rewarded her with a smile. "I love it when you talk dirty."

Jennifer was waiting in the building's climate-controlled garage lobby. Everett followed her north up the interstate to

Pacific Beach, a funky, eclectic oceanside neighborhood with a mixture of sushi restaurants, rave clubs, tattoo parlors, and blues bars situated by the most popular tourist boardwalk in San Diego. After parking in front of the run-down but crowded Mexican restaurant they found seats on the patio overlooking the Pacific.

Sunny and sixty. Leather weather.

Once seated, she ordered a pitcher of the restaurant's specialty—frozen margaritas made with high-octane white tequila. While she watched the beach, he watched her as she closed her eyes and tilted her head back, absorbing the afternoon sun's glow on her face and neck.

She unbuttoned the top two buttons of her silk blouse, inviting the sun's warmth on her neck and ample chest. "Isn't this lovely?" she purred, admiring the beach and the setting sun.

"It's paradise."

"Do you miss Dallas?"

"Are you kidding? It's over a hundred degrees back there right now."

"So how's your training going?"

"Brutal. I'm ready to trade."

"Be glad you have the weekend off. You'll get your chance."

She studied his square angular face, focusing on his dark brown eyes as he scanned the beach where a make-shift game of football unfolded on the sand between two groups of surfers.

"You seem a million miles away," she noticed. "You miss it, don't you?"

"What's that?"

"The game."

"Now what would make you say that?"

"You never talk about it, you know, the fact that you played professionally. You still love it don't you?"

"Since I was five years old."

"I can tell it's still in your blood."

"What was your first clue?"

"You're very different than the rest of the brokers. You have this protective energy about you. It's where you find your confidence."

"Okay. So you're a psychic now?"

"No. Just alert to the fact that you're the exception to the rule."

"It's the price I paid for playing a game and calling it a living."

"Then why give it up if it means so much to you?"

"I was traded here initially to cash in my ninth life with a young team, but I lost my mojo."

"I'm sorry."

"Don't be. I've always been a late bloomer who's just ahead of his time."

"Wow. Rugged good looks and a sense of humor."

"We had a job to do."

"So what was your job, anyway? When you played, I mean."

"My job?" He smiled at the question. "I was a receiver. I caught passes."

She reached across the table. "May I see your hands?"

He guided them both toward her. She gently rolled each of his hands palm up, and for a moment she marveled at them. She'd never really noticed before but they were large and powerful, symmetrically perfect, the long fingers tapering into the trunk of muscle and tissue at the base of each thick forearm. "So did this move to California cause any broken hearts in Dallas?"

"So now you want to talk love life, huh? You don't waste any time."

"Life is short," she said, tracing her fingernails across his palm. "I see a southern belle back there in Dallas with you on her mind right now."

"Your fortune-telling skills are a little rusty. Do I look like a man with a past?"

"Every girl loves an athlete, and you impress me as the kind of guy who doesn't need his ego stroked."

"Look, I love it here," Everett admitted, "and I feel lucky again, for the first time in a long time. Okay? I plan to make senior by Christmas," he said.

"You do have an honest voice. That's half the battle."

"Jack makes it easy. He's amazing. I've entered every one of his trades in my own account and I'm up twenty percent in one month."

"Just remember what you promised me."

"I heard he studies migratory waterfowl patterns to predict weather anomalies."

"So what did you think of his currency trade this week? It was pretty risky."

"Get a hunch and bet a bunch."

"But you sold out two days before Jack did in your own account with a larger profit."

"How would you know that?"

"I'm an undercover agent for the FBI."

"Very funny."

"The girls in trading, silly. They're all talking about you. Remember, no secrets in the office."

"I plan to put clients into it, once we get on the phones next week. Why don't we talk about something else?"

She looked right at him. "Fair enough. I'm curious. Why didn't you make a pass at me that first night, after the reception?"

"You sure ask a lot of questions."

"I've been hit on by every fast-talking wannabe millionaire in that office, except for you."

"I was delirious. No sleep for three days? Remember?"

"I remember."

"I guess I'm just cautious by nature."

"Football player turned commodity broker? Cautious?"

"Regarding matters of the heart, that is."

"You're still playing a game, Everett."

"Yeah, and I've been waiting all my life for the game to come to me."

The sun had set by the time they finished their third pitcher. She'd matched him drink for drink. They were now both very drunk, and very loud. The manager asked them to quiet down more than once and they agreed it was time to go. She insisted on paying.

She then ran from the restaurant into the parking lot. He followed, and they stumbled to their cars, laughing. Then she threw her arms around him and kissed him deeply.

Her soft, warm wet mouth tasted like alcohol and salt and he inhaled her smell and pulled her ample body close. Her chest heaved into his as she shivered in the cold ocean air, feeling him aroused and hard against her.

"Let's call a cab," she whispered. "I don't live far."

They ran toward Mission Boulevard and flagged a taxi, making out in the back seat like teenagers who could hardly wait to get back to her empty townhouse and tear each other's clothes off. It was only a mile away but traffic was heavy that night.

They finally reached her Bird Rock townhouse and ran up the stairs, bursting through her front door. Once inside, they undressed each another violently in the blue darkness.

She pulled away from him and took his hand. "Follow me," she said as she led him to her bedroom.

9

At 04:30 AM Ray Hood pointed a large index finger at the jagged red line climbing across the flat panel monitor like an EKG reading on the technical chart in front of him. "Anderson sold right here," he said, "exactly one hundred basis points past the intra-day peak and much sooner than you, with a larger gain. And it's his second fucking week."

Jack watched in silence.

"Not to mention the fact that he came out way ahead of the rest of the office before the late day sell off," said Hood. "Biggest order of the day. They're all chattering about it on their phones. The new guy's lapping the boss."

Everett's face filled the computer screen as Hood focused the hidden remote lens, zooming in on the live feed from the conference room. "He's very creative," Jack beamed. "He not only followed my soybean straddle yesterday but he stayed in past my exit point. That took balls of titanium. The move came in the last thirty minutes and his patience was rewarded with a break-out rally which added another thirty percent to his position. Where the hell did we find him?"

"He found us."

"Imagine that."

"Look Jack, I know jocks make great brokers, but he could skew your curve. You've got a delicate balance of soldiers out there on your floor who don't question orders, but he's a loner. His hand-writing analysis profile screamed overachiever. You sure you want the friction?"

Jack stared at the screen, watching Everett as he sat alone at the end of the long oval table in the center of the sprawling conference room, devouring the company research. He was reading, scratching notes, diagramming the technical chart formations of each market, and pouring through the required chapters in the training textbook. "I haven't had a sparring partner in years."

"Well. It looks like Mister All-American's little family trust account just cracked a million bucks. Guess you got one now," Hood scoffed.

"Let's turn up the heat."

"It's what I do best, Jack."

All the rookies were assigned to temporary desks in the junior bullpen gallery overlooking the trading floor. Everett stared at the four-inch stack of index cards filled with sales leads on his desk as Katherine announced team assignments and the training class was equally divided among the many managers.

The firm's guidelines for cold calling were simple—at least five hundred dials per day. No exceptions. It was a pure numbers game garnered from past performance. Rejection was ignored and only focus was tolerated. Records were meticulously kept, they were told again. Phone time. A spread sheet including the number of dials and length of conversations for each extension would be delivered to every desk after breakfast, after lunch, and before they left for the evening. They were expected to immediately ramp up to this level of intensity, or resign voluntarily.

Each sales lead contained a full name, address, and phone number and the drill was to quickly make friends, or move on. The best leads, the virgin leads, consisted of interested investors who'd never been contacted by the brokerage house. The virgin leads were used as an incentive for the trainees. Rookie leads contained minimum information and most of these prospects had been called to death. The game was designed to test their resolve and it was agonizing work, but the motivation installed by Jack propped up the strong.

They experimented with different ways of turning the same phrase. One rookie quit after the first afternoon on the phone, he'd been in insurance and the rejection gave him a bad case of shredded nerves. The energy and volume generated by this rookie class impressed management and the one-liners flew like sparks from a welder's torch.

Everett dialed all day until after seven in the evening. The work wore him down. Mercifully, the end of the day finally arrived and as things began to wind down, his extension rang while he was returning from a coffee break. "Everett Anderson."

"Everett, Cyrus Bohaner."

"Hello Cyrus. How are you?"

"Old enough to know better," the investor from New Orleans said.

"What can I do for you, Sir?"

"Well," he said slowly, "I really enjoyed our conversation this morning. You don't push me like my other brokers, and you made a hell of a lot of sense. I like your firm's Euro dollar recommendation. You guys are the only group on Wall Street with the balls to sell short right now."

"I can fax you the paperwork and you'll be in before tomorrow's opening bell."

"You also said the Swiss franc should fall. I want to see how the dollar opens in the morning, then we'll talk."

"Tomorrow may be too late, Cyrus. It'll be Wednesday before we get your account open."

"Call me after the dollar opens in the morning. You've got my private line. I'll wire funds if I like your trade."

"What kind of dollars are we talking?"

"Five hundred, if your recommendation pays off."

"Then I'll contact you first thing. Have a good evening, Cyrus."

He was so engrossed in the conversation he didn't notice Katherine standing next to him, listening. Each phone console had a small squawk box speaker attached separately with a long cord. A manager could approach any time, pick up the speaker, adjust the volume, and listen to the conversation. Feeding lines to a new broker, without the client on the other end knowing, made a pro out of any rookie.

"That sounded a lot like your first order," she said.

"I hope Jack's right on the dollar."

"But that last conversation was not about Jack. It was about you. Normally I would urge you to push your prospect further, but I can tell he likes you. He's buying you, Everett, not the market."

"I'll need to call him early in the morning before currencies open in New York."

"I'll be opening the office this week. Incidentally, great job today. Most rookies don't open their first account until their first or second month, if then. You'll do fine here. Just be patient. Research will make you look like a pro until you get your trading legs underneath you."

"I appreciate your help, Katherine."

"Just keep up the hard work. By the way, Jack wants to see you before you leave for the night."

There was no open-door policy at the Continental Trading Group, not even for the most motivated employee. No one dared disturb Jack Diamond unless he wanted to be disturbed, even though the tall, see-through walls of windows that offered visual access directly onto the trading floor were typically open on the fiftieth floor. Exhausted, Everett stood in front of the nine-foot high, vault-like walnut engraved door and knocked three times.

The lights of the city sparkled beneath, from high above the streets.

"Enter!"

Everett reached for the sterling silver handle and turned it down, pushing the heavy wooden door open. It was his first invitation to the largest and most conspicuous corner office overlooking the trading floor. The angular redwood desk in the corner was all alone in the large room, situated in front of a wall of flat screens monitors, embedded in the unfinished concrete with exposed form lines. The room was cold and sparse, with stainless steel lighting giving life to scattered plants strategically positioned on the perimeter of the large corner office. No awards or family pictures or art hung on the stark, grey walls. Only black leather furniture surrounding the space with an accent of mahogany trim tying together the rust-colored Brazilian marble floor.

"Walk over here, Mister Anderson. I want you to see something," Jack commanded, with his back to the door.

Everett walked next to his boss as Jack pointed to the largest plasma monitor behind his desk. "December is a short month, for bonds given holiday activity and exchange closings around the world," Jack said.

"Why so far out?"

"Volume is down and we get super execution by going around Chicago straight to London or Tokyo. Most investors and traders relax and party, blind to the rich opportunity that sleeps during December. Very little activity and low volume. See how this price pattern rises, then levels, then rises, then falls, then levels, and then falls again?"

Everett nodded. "Classic head and shoulders formation."

"But you got in and out twice in your own account, with a handsome profit on both trades. What do you propose to do at this point?"

"You're monitoring my account?"

"I monitor every account, especially when I notice some real talent in your trading. You're aggressive when you need to be, but you're also patient and very disciplined."

"I set a target, like I was trained, and I'm content with the profits I've taken for the week. The down trend was confirmed by the second drop in price near today's close. I'm in cash now."

"So do you plan to re-enter this market?"

"Too risky to buy right now. If anything, I'd sell short right here. I think it's over-bought."

Jack walked over to his bar and poured two drinks. One single-malt scotch and one bourbon. "This market's about to plummet," Jack said. "You're right about that, but not for a while.

We'll rally once more prior to the next sell-off. Can you tell me why?"

"The Fed will probably continue quantitative easing this month. QE3?"

Jack pointed to the bottom of the screen. "That's just a fundamental head fake. What does your gut tell you about bonds from a technical standpoint?"

"Well, the open interest is decreasing while the option premium is rising."

Jack smiled. "You have great instincts, Mr. Anderson. It's time you learned the best-kept secret in the universe, the secret of balance," he whispered. "Balance determines motion, and motion becomes growth. Growth or lack there of in all things, including financial markets, is built by incremental increases, but the key to understanding that growth is balance. If you believe, as I do, that evolution is the explanation for our existence as human beings, then you can't ignore the fact that we began as primates and then learned to walk and then hunt."

Everett frowned. "I'm not following."

"The physical change in our human architecture that altered our sense of balance once we began walking upright occurred in the inner ear canal, and centered on the cochlea. The cochlea is shaped like a nautilus shell, which spirals outward in progressively larger rings. The proportions of those concentric rings increase and conform to a golden mean. A is to B as A is to A plus B. It's a system of measurement and proportion that dates back to the ancient Greeks and Romans, still evident in the timeless architecture of their temples. It's also in the bible. Therefore, when markets grow or contract, they typically do so according to the Fibonacci ratio rooted in nature. Balance and order. Two is to three as three is to five. Five is to eight as eight is to thirteen, and so forth. Demand increases and decreases in all markets at a specific and measurable rate and pace, and as a general rule, sudden weather events, crop reports or political upheaval are usually discounted in the trading of all commodities. Therefore, the trader who trades on the event and not the cause is nearly always wrong."

Everett nodded and sipped the bourbon.

"You've been working very hard, and your efforts have not gone unnoticed. I've been told by your managers that you have a natural talent for rapport with your clients, and that you're the first one in and the last to leave. You're an average salesman, Mr. Anderson, but you're an exceptional trader. The only element you lack to be the top broker in this company is experience. Wash that Wall Street crap out of your skull. Train your brain to go for the jugular with every client, now that your mind is no longer trapped in a football helmet. Learn to perfect our use of the golden mean and use it aggressively. You'll be unstoppable if you can combine the closing skills we teach you with your trading instincts."

"Thanks, Jack, for the words of encouragement."

"Miss Fox also tells me you're Mister Nice Guy on the phone. Surely there's a killer instinct inside leftover from the NFL?"

"I won't disappoint you."

"Oh, I'm counting on it, Ace. I only bet on a sure thing."

10

Everett checked his look in the mirrored elevator doors. The new suit he'd treated himself to hung elegantly on his muscular frame. The fabric and tailoring were just generous enough to disguise but not quite conceal the powerful width of his shoulders and arms. First phase evaluation time and he wanted to look his best first thing in the morning.

"Well, Mr. Anderson," Katherine said with a reserved smile, "congratulations on one of the biggest rookie paydays this year. Looks like you bumped Bohaner to over a million."

"Piece of cake, Katherine."

"It would seem we have little to discuss," she said, as she handed him his weekly paycheck, almost seventy-five thousand dollars, after taxes.

The tone of his voice changed. "I swear I've never seen anything like it before."

"Everett, you've been blessed with a real and genuine quality. Clients pick right up on that trait. That's your unique strength on the phone. Do you have any idea how hard it is to find and train what you possess naturally?"

"Is there a compliment in there somewhere?"

"I told Jack the first time we saw you, you'd go far with the company. Now, tell me about your trading."

"Endless hours reading the books that Jack gave me on Elliott Wave theory, technical analysis, and standard deviation. I reversed out of bonds and the Swiss franc three days before Jack and the rest of the office with a greater profit spread."

"Hard work always pays off around here."

"I re-entered this morning and plan to take another fifty percent out of the foreign exchange markets."

She studied his face and smiled. "Everett, being a successful trader means more than just knowing how to make money for your clients. It's about maneuvering in tight situations, knowing how to conserve equity by drafting behind a fast-moving trend, and knowing when to take a risk and when to hold back. Although the trader gets the glory, competing in today's markets is very much a group effort, from research to support staff to order execution on the exchange floor. Calculated and cool-headed trading based on experience will always triumph over aggressive gambling."

"But I thought that was why we were here. To make as much as we could."

She pushed a few keystrokes and checked the values in his open contracts. "You should have some very happy clients. You sort of went *around* research. Just be very careful about going *against* Jack's advice. Don't risk his wrath for a few extra ticks in price," she warned.

"I'm playing golf with Bohaner this afternoon at Torrey Pines and he's bringing two foursomes of oil and gas partners from Lafayette and Baton Rouge. I'm signing rollover paperwork for all of them, not to mention an unauthorized proposal I initiated to clear all their crude futures and drilling hedge business through The Continental Trading Group."

"What's their annual volume?"

"Thirty million, give or take."

"I like the initiative. Has Jack signed off?"

"Bill pretty much signature guaranteed that Jack would love it."

"You're not only covering your trades successfully, but you're also raising capital at a fever pitch. Why don't you go ahead and take off, it's almost one. Jack and Bill are gone for the day and you certainly deserve an early start on your weekend."

Katherine then removed a special security keycard and an account file from his desk. "I've decided to transfer one of Walker's accounts to you. I believe Mister Hayes was your coach at one time?"

"That's right."

She stood and led Everett to the door. "He has a rather substantial trading balance. Over three million. You'll also find an empty space in the executive garage on the third floor. No more parking on the street five blocks away. You've earned it. Have a great weekend."

"Coach Hayes?" the receptionist asked. "You have a guest. Everett Anderson. He has documents for your signature."

"Well then buzz him in, damn it."

The blackness of the canyon that surrounded the practice stadium swallowed the green rectangle in its center. The two men walked the perimeter of the practice field tucked into the eucalyptus grove. "So, how much money did you make me this week?" Charlie asked.

Everett was still in his golf spikes as the sun disappeared behind Mission Valley. "Well you really knocked the cover off the ball, Coach. A hundred thousand on the bond trade. More in currencies, maybe two hundred?"

"Three hundred grand in one week? That's what you're telling me?"

"Sounds like a lot, I know, but relative to your net worth that's only about ten percent."

"Only ten percent? In one week? That's a good year for most folks with retirement tied up in the stock market."

"We're not in the stock market."

"Listen to you. Never knew how broke I was until I made a little money."

"Well you're in cash now."

"Good. I'm glad you're on the account."

"You holding up all right?"

"So you're worried about me now?"

"I suppose the funeral was pretty rough?"

The seasoned coach took a breath. "Ham Walker came from a large family, Everett, plus there were lots of former team mates there. That was the toughest part, seeing all those guys he used to play with who I coached. He really was like a son to me. Hell, I recruited him."

"In college?"

"High school. I was driving home from a Friday afternoon scouting trip in Atlanta. Just as I outrun the city traffic in Montgomery, I throw a rod on the interstate, six months after rebuilding that '68 Camaro. The convertible finally rolled to a stop near the first access road and I pushed it into a dirt parking lot. They called it Harvard on the highway. Lincoln Memorial High School in Tuscaloosa, Alabama. After the tow truck left, I booked the cheapest motel room in walking distance, and flat-footed to the closest Stop-and-Rob to pick up a six-pack. Along the walk, I passed the local high school football stadium, if you could call a few bleachers off a gravel road in a hot, humid pasture a stadium, and the Friday night lights were on. So instead of a miserable evening alone drinking beer and trying to adjust the rabbit ears on the motel black-and-white, I bought a two dollar ticket to this 3-A Alabama high school football game. That night changed my life."

"Really?"

"I watched him run back a punt, kick a field goal, throw a flee-flicker for a touchdown and play safety. He went both ways for four quarters and barely broke a sweat. And the next morning he got up and fielded shortstop for the Lincoln baseball team, going three for four, and knocked in the winning run. Stole third twice."

"I missed playing against him by one season."

"Recruiting him got me hired at Auburn, and I was offered my first OC in Chicago because I engineered Ham's trade. Then San Diego called. He was old school, Everett, and my ticket out of south Alabama. Two-sport workhorse. Clearly ahead of time, and probably the closest relationship I've ever had the good fortune to create with one of my players."

"I'm real sorry, Coach."

"I never could quite put my finger on it," Charlie said, scratching his head, "but something started going wrong. I could sense it in his phone calls."

"Like what?"

"Almost like he was trapped, you know? At first he loved working there. He said the same things you say. 'We're three in a row so far, Coach!' 'Go with me on this one, Coach!' I keep telling myself just one more big trade and I'm out. Put it all in bonds and walk away. But your secret brokerage kept making me more damn money."

"You think he wanted out?"

"I know he was real disappointed when they moved him back to Chicago after promoting him to management here in California. See, he loved to hunt. That's the thing. You guys are cut from the same canvas. He's as country as you and me,

Everett. My plan was to assign you to him at Continental, just like the way I match the seniors with the rookies. My own personal mentor experiment. But he spent more and more time away from the office traveling to Utah, Colorado, Alaska, and Chile. I don't think his boss liked that. When he wasn't generating commissions, he was in the woods. I even got a phone call one time from his manager, Bill Peterson, asking *me* if I knew where he was."

"I heard around the office that he ran with one of our Chicago traders. They used to work together."

"Butler played for the Bears when Ham did. Bad seed."

"Coach, rumor also has it Walker used cocaine."

"No way. He was very disciplined about everything, especially his body, just like when he played. Weighed himself all the time. Tested his blood once a week. Obsessive about his nutrition. He was all about precision, that's the way he played. He'd run right at you, then slash or rip or spin right by. You know he was there, and then he was past you, fast and quiet."

"I guess that's how he was in the woods?"

"The best in the state. He was so poor as a kid he put meat on the table with that compound bow."

"Guess he had to grow up fast."

"Won archery awards since before he was a teenager. Folks called him the second coming of Bo Jackson. I just find it tough to believe he'd allow himself to get shot by accident."

"Why would you say that?"

"Bow hunters live by a code back there. They all know each other, and they all watch out for one other. Even the redneck crackers respected him. When Ham was in town they gave him room, especially when he was back home and headed for the hardwoods." The older man paused and bent forward, his hands on his thighs.

"Take it easy, Coach."

"He took me along one time in south Georgia. Hard core old school. He'd settle in hours before first light, listening, learning the smells, and he hated deer stands. He'd perch in a tree and you'd walk right under him. Never knew he was there, and he'd finally get one shot at dusk. That's what made him such a great broker. He was a pure hunter, and everyone loved his patience."

"Accidents happen. Even horrible ones. Right?"

"A compound bow is only effective inside what, fifty yards?" Charlie asked, pointing at midfield.

"You trying to say it wasn't an accident?"

"I don't know."

"But there was an investigation, right?"

"Yeah, a real thorough one. Conducted by the very capable and under-staffed county deputy sheriff's office in Dothan, Alabama."

Everett's cell phone came to life. "Excuse me, Coach. Hello?"

"Did you see how bonds closed this afternoon?"

"No."

"There was a huge sell-off in the final hour," Jennifer half-whispered. "And you had a rather large margin call."

"That's impossible."

"It gets worse. Jack just seized your family trust."

11

The football spiraled perfectly, traveling in slow motion across the trading floor, over computer kiosks, beneath the high tech halogen lighting, the ball continuing on its flight. At times it seemed to float, suspended over his head, just out of reach, and then it would speed up, slicing through the air away from him with its own natural momentum, obeying the laws of physics and gravity, yet extending beyond its target's fingertips with a mocking velocity. He charged through the walkways, dodging desks, spinning and cutting, ever mindful of the ball as it traced across the top of the high mahogany consoles. He was drawn to it.

The floor beneath him seemed to vibrate as he floated over the expensive oriental rugs that covered the exposed concrete through the bright sunshine that filled the trading stadium. The seats in the gallery overlooking and enclosing the massive arena were empty.

The large wide windows were open, exposing the trading floor to the outdoors, seven hundred feet above the downtown sidewalks. The wind whipped through the desks and chairs and credenzas, blowing papers and whistling in his face.

The sunlight was blinding, directly behind the ball, temporarily causing him to lose the flight, but a shadow quickly forced his eyes to once again focus and draw a bead on its flight. The arms simply would not rise—all he could do was watch with desperation as the ball sailed out the window, three feet in front of him, out of reach. He felt his body tumble forward, through the open window as he plummeted toward the fast-approaching street below.

The phone erupted on the nightstand next to Everett's bed. By the time he opened his eyes, he could hear his grandmother's voice on the message machine.

He lifted the cordless receiver. "Virginia?"

"Everett?"

"Yes ma'am. Good morning."

"We must speak at once."

He glanced at the alarm clock's glowing red numerals. "It's four AM here."

"I'm not very happy with you right now."

He'd considered calling her over the weekend, but he hardly expected that she'd receive notice so quickly. "They've sent out the trade confirmations then?"

She sighed one of those disappointing sighs he knew all too well. "I'll give you the benefit of the doubt by assuming you knew nothing of this margin call I received."

"No ma'am. I knew. I was told late Friday. I just didn't want to worry you over the weekend."

"Everett. How could you be so careless? They want a cash deposit wired Monday morning to release your trust."

"I can explain."

"You always do."

"I planned to capitalize the trust with my severance check from Dallas. The team is due to complete my final payment next week. It should be close to a hundred thousand, after taxes."

"But Everett, this margin notice is for over two hundred thousand dollars! That's almost one third of your trust."

"Virginia, please don't panic. There had to have been an error in my trade execution. I'll correct it when I get to my office later this morning."

"Continental Trading delivered notice to Mister Pritchard's office this morning, as the executor of your trust. They say that *they* now control the assets? Everett, what in the world did you sign?"

"There had to have been some kind of a glitch. I can assure you it's *not* what it looks like. It was a calculated risk with huge potential."

"That's still too much, Everett."

"But I'm up almost twenty percent in one month."

"The statement also lists soybean options? Currency option spreads? U.S. Treasury bond futures? I thought you owned bonds in your trust. The physical commodity. That's what you told me."

"I'll straighten it out when I get to work."

"I suggest you research these transactions and clear up this matter immediately."

"I plan to, first thing this morning."

"Your trust should never have been compromised with such recklessness. And I don't want to see any more speculation or reckless gambling. Is that clear?"

"Yes ma'am, of course."

She sighed again. "I understand your desire to grow this money, but please don't gamble with your future. You've only been working for three months now. Your trust is all you've got. And I am too old and too tired to relive your college problems."

*

Jack was seated at the head of the enormous conference table. Around him on the perimeter were Bill Peterson and John Valentine, as well as several of the top senior brokers. They sat perfectly still. All eyes in the room glared down at Everett as he stepped through the ten foot tall double doors.

John Valentine pitched a computer printout onto the table and leaned back. "So how was your weekend, Ace? Plenty of rest?"

"I'm more than a little concerned about my personal account, Jack. Can we speak in private?" Everett said.

"For an ex-football player with a few NFL contacts, you had one hell of an impressive training quarter," Peterson said, motioning to the only empty chair.

Everett took the seat. "I could have pushed it further."

The room remained quiet as Jack stood and walked to the wall of windows that defined his outer office. The trading floor beyond was teeming with excitement and energy. It was pure pandemonium outside as the price of crude oil just reached one hundred forty dollars a barrel. Jack pointed to the trading floor through the fishbowl windows and turned toward Everett, his eyes wide and candid. "What do you see out there?"

"I see a lot of hard work and dedication," Everett answered with conviction.

"Hard work and dedication, huh?"

"Sure," Everett said. "What do you see?"

"I see mostly followers."

"You say that as if it's a dirty word. Everyone around here follows your advice religiously."

"Not everyone," John Valentine blurted, narrowing his eyes. "Corn and copper last week, crude oil two weeks ago, and bonds on Friday. Any of these trades ring a bell?"

Everett cleared his throat and swallowed hard.

"We all trade together because we trust each other," John added. "But you saw fit to quietly and unilaterally challenge our research recommendations in those markets."

"Those trades were in my personal account. I never jeopardized any client accounts."

"And that's the only reason you're still employed. Those clients are not *your* clients," John scolded. "They belong to this brokerage house."

Jack eased down onto the edge of the conference table and stared directly into Everett's eyes. "And you were absolutely right on all of them, except one."

The room seemed to loosen a bit. Some of the seniors even grinned and snickered.

"I can only afford one rebel on my team, Mister Anderson. Mister Valentine has mastered that position."

Peterson stepped in again. "Everett, you cleared those trades in your own account with a larger profit than our research target. And you did it discreetly, without boast or swagger among your fellow rookies. We're the only ones in the office who know about this. That rarely happens around here. You're very poised under pressure."

"But there was that little hiccup in bonds," Jack said. "You sold short in the bond market when I placed a buy on it last Thursday. And as expected, the sub prime mortgage mess on Wall Street forced bond prices sky high in a flight to quality *away* from you. Your trust has been collateralized temporarily, in order to cover your margin losses."

"But Jack, my trust is a type one qualified account. I have margin privileges but I never trade type two margin. That bond trade was only a hundred thousand."

John handed Bill a copy of the trade confirmation. "Bonds are still limit up this morning," he said, "which compounds the cash margin call in his personal account. He'll need a huge sell off before expiration next month to recoup what's left."

Everett stared at Valentine. "You son-of-a-bitch! Those were cash trades!"

"They were coded type two, Sport. When you earn a sales assistant, perhaps you won't make such a rookie mistake," Valentine sniffed.

"I hand wrote those trade tickets and coded them type one and you know it because *you* signed them!"

"Not according to compliance. Maybe you should have read the risk disclosure you signed. All assets containing equity are subject to lien, and or forfeiture in the event of adverse market conditions."

"You can no longer straddle two worlds," Jack added calmly. "You know that, don't you?"

Everett frowned. "What in the hell are you talking about?"

"For the past few months," Jack continued, "we've observed you trying to have it both ways with your colleagues. You end up failing as a friend and as a leader. You do yourself and your fellow traders a grave disservice. You have some hard choices to make, and those choices determine your destiny."

Everett glanced at the production print-out stretched out across the long table. "What does all this have to do with my trust?" he asked.

Jack stood slowly. "It has nothing to do with your trust, or your production," Jack added. "But it has everything to do with your willingness to do what is necessary to get what I believe you want."

Everett didn't respond.

"You can no longer be a part of the people you were meant to manage," Jack said. "Especially in our present economic environment. We are in the midst of an unprecedented bull market in commodities while Wall Street implodes and feeds on itself. But you've displayed a focus and a diligence that I'm sorry to say I haven't seen in some of my senior traders in quite a while. What you see assembled here this morning are your future peers. I need empire builders on my trading floor who display focused clarity and conviction." He touched the control that closed his vertical blinds, sliding his hands in his pockets as Everett listened intently. "Almost ten million dollars in net new assets traded within your first three months? What's that, three hundred grand gross, without bonuses?"

Everett bowed his back. "Something like that."

"You're capable of producing that much monthly. Welcome to the senior ranks, Mister Anderson."

The room exploded with applause. Each senior broker stepped toward Everett and shook his hand. High-fives were exchanged and congratulations were given all around. William Peterson uncorked several bottles of champagne and set them on the conference table.

Everett turned to Jack, who was grinning ear to ear. "You're *promoting* me?" he asked.

"Miss Fox's rookie team set a record this month. Your production alone represented sixty percent of the entire team's total number. With the possible exception of Miss Vasquez," Jack added. "You're the only rookie to qualify for senior broker in his first quarter. Vasquez has slipped to third and right now, you and Mister Valentine are fencing for first place in the office. I'd say your learning curve has acquired a vertical direction."

Peterson began reading the offices' production report for the previous year, month by month, and then carefully removed his reading glasses. "Your trading clearly separates you from your class, Everett. We need a rookie prodigy and a real man at the top, not some bull dyke in a fitted Armani. Personally, I'd like to see you clobber Vasquez this month," Peterson said.

Jack stood in front of Everett. "Everything in life has a price, Mister Anderson. The question is, are you willing to pay that price?"

"What's my cost?"

Jack's piercing eyes were wild with latent energy. "Our international clients require a stable state with understanding leadership which can enforce the collection of their paper gains and the eventual conversion into hard assets from money center bankers. Consequently, our national allegiance is often called into question by The Commodity Futures Trading Commission, the FBI, and the Treasury Department. The men you see before you here in this room represent the best and the brightest from well-established families in the east, connected to other trusted individuals from similar heritage. More than once in our history, this brokerage house has been the target of regulators and we often find ourselves building a tightly-knit core of trustworthy brothers, as it were. An elite fraternity of traders."

"My blood is red, not blue."

"We all have secrets, Mister Anderson. As a family, we protect those secrets. And we have the power to pull that off in this day and age. You're part of this family now, and we expect you to help us protect each other. Kind of like your little run-in with the NCAA in college?"

"That was never proven."

"What if I could make that go away, forever?"

"You can do that?"

"Already done. No trace whatsoever of it ever occurring."

"Relax, Ace," John hissed. "You've proven yourself as a team player, which is why you're about to hear the whispers first."

"We want to see what you can do," Peterson said as he reached under the table. "We'd like you to shepherd some of the company's larger accounts which Mister Valentine can no longer adequately service."

John removed several file folders with account codes on their labels, then extended the folders across his desk. "All of Walker's NFL clients are in there. We need to know you're with us. What do you say we bury the hatchet, Sport," John said, extending his hand.

"I don't want to owe *you* anything."

"A man without debts can hardly be trusted," John said as Everett squeezed his hand until it lost circulation.

"Oh, and by the way, pick out a window seat, Mister Anderson," Jack smiled. "Your chair's on order."

Valentine pulled away, shaking his right hand. "Go ahead. Take a look, Sport. I know it's killing you."

Ten million in capital was spread out over forty different accounts, all with cash balances, just waiting to be traded. And easily another five million dollars sitting idle in the special reserve money market accounts of the remaining files.

Bill put his arm around Everett. "We're giving you this trade first because we believe in you. We want you to start buying as much sugar as you can. You're building a following out there on the trading floor. Whatever you buy, they buy. The formal announcement will follow research tomorrow morning. Come on, I'll walk you out."

As the door closed, Valentine stared at Jack. "He took that like a man."

Jack pointed his finger. "And *you* need to spend more time with him."

"Why do I always have to baby-sit the rookies?" John whined.

"Because I want him to play ball, Goddamn it!"

"You never give me any accounts anymore."

"Bury him with research. Give him even more responsibility and homework. He's a senior now. Maybe he'll make *you* look good. See how he handles it along with prospecting, trading, *and* raising more capital. You don't stand out anymore."

"Swell," John uttered under his breath, glancing at the production numbers on the computer printout for the month so far. "What the hell?" he whined. "So you're spooning accounts to Vasquez as well?"

"Vasquez works her ass off, just like Anderson. They were both in here every morning before five."

John flopped into the leather chair in the corner. "Jesus, I just had a stellar month."

"I leave for Mexico this afternoon. The pressure stays turned up until I return," Jack ordered, removing a small platinum mirror from beneath the corner console and pouring a pitcher's mound of cocaine onto it. After the assembled seniors had their turn, John hungrily snorted two lines, pinching his nostrils together.

"You're my eyes and my ears on the floor, Gentlemen. That will be all, except for you Mister Valentine."

Once the room was empty, Jack handed the mirror back to John. "Well done."

"We dumped all of Anderson's bonds at a profit, then parked his equity in the error account."

"Did he ask for a time-in-sales?"

"Oh yeah, but I showed him an identical trade in another account, and the time stamp matched perfectly."

"Your percentage will be wired this afternoon. Keep the rookies on their toes."

"Well, good afternoon, Mr. Cozzene. So nice to see you," John Valentine said, seated at Vinnie's desk when Cozzene finally arrived. "How was your weekend?"

"My wife's pregnant, John. We had a complication this morning."

John cut him off. "Why don't you meet me in my office and uh, bring your client book with you, Ace."

Vinnie poured a cup of coffee, grabbed his leather binder full of client account spreadsheets, and took the promenade stairs down to the trading floor.

John was on the phone when Vinnie entered his office. He turned his back as Vinnie sat down uncomfortably on the edge of the leather L-section.

"God, how I love the smell of volatility in the morning," John gushed as he finished his call. "Cozzene, I'm growing tired of your tardiness. Five hundred dollar fine."

"You can't fine me!"

"Then make it a thousand."

"Okay John, I'm sorry. It won't happen again."

"I thought I taught you never to apologize. It makes you look weak. Now give me your book."

"Look, I'll stay late tonight," Vinnie pleaded.

Valentine laughed and proceeded to rip out accounts at random. Calmly, John touched his speaker phone and stared at Cozzene. "Miss Emerson, would you ring Mister Anderson's new desk on the trading floor and ask him to join me?"

"Right away, John," she answered.

"You're on Anderson's team now, Cozzene," John snorted, pitching the remaining clients into Vinnie's lap. "Make the most of it."

12

Charlie Hayes quickly passed the word that Continental had tripled his signing bonus and the news spread like jock itch in the San Diego locker room. The company's recent success gave Everett and Continental a rock-solid reputation. The U.S. dollar was plummeting daily against all foreign currencies and the latest research recommendations were working beautifully.

Cyrus Bohaner referred Everett's name to every one of his oil and gas limited partners at the Petroleum Club in downtown New Orleans. Vinnie had the ear of every jockey, trainer, and owner at the Del Mar Racetrack. By the end of the last week of training, five gave up, five stopped showing up, and two were fired. Only two made it to the last day of the last week and based on production, only Cozzene had a chance to advance. The final week of training proved unpredictable and the race to survive was drawing to a close. It would take a miracle to meet quota on the last day. Rules were rules. No abundance of mercy.

As Everett sat down at his new trading console at five AM with a fresh cup of coffee, Jack's voice exploded from his speaker phone, like a shotgun blast.

"Well, good morning, Mister Anderson! Always nice to see an enterprising young closer in the office at this ungodly hour. How are you?"

"Outstanding, Jack."

"Pay close attention during research this morning. You'll have all the necessary ammunition you'll need to augment your production," the voice said. "I'm sure your new clients will be eager to add to their present positions once you've transferred your enthusiasm and related the necessary information. Did you celebrate last night?"

"I drank too much and I missed my job."

"I've brought in the cream of the rookie crop from the Miami and New York offices to give you some competition." The red light on the speaker phone faded, indicating that his highness was no longer interested in conveying compliments.

Everett used the time before research to call the east coast. With the three hour time difference, he was able to reach every new client that had been given to him. Now proficient with his new computer and trading software, he made copious notations regarding the details of each client's portfolio and asset allocation. Continental vigorously trained every broker to extract as much information as possible. Jack always said, get your clients talking about their money and themselves, and they'll open their financial kimono for you. All of the accounts were bloated with profits and all of them loved the sugar story. Katherine monitored two dozen of his orders before research began that morning.

"Ladies and gentlemen, may I please have your undivided attention?" Jack announced over the ceiling speakers. "Dr. Goldman has a very special message this morning. Go ahead, Max."

"Good morning, everyone. As we all know, the forces of supply and demand cause all commodity prices to fluctuate constantly. But does anyone remember the sugar shortages in the nineteen seventies when housewives were literally tackling one another at the grocery store for every available bag? World Sugar futures hit a high of sixty-six cents a pound in nineteen seventy-five! Back then, it was a magical time in the futures market. Sugar eventually rallied to forty-five cents per pound in nineteen eighty and guess what? History is shaping up right now as we speak to repeat itself. We feel that a fundamental situation is presenting itself in Brazil right now in raw World Sugar futures."

Early Van Cleve

Goldman began to cough. "Rumors abound that a small cadre of union dock workers are threatening a labor strike and we believe, according to international sources, that they intend to follow through. Their actions could potentially cause a force majeure condition, which will stop all shipments. It's a gamble, but we all know the mantra. Buy the rumor, sell the fact. Remember, it's your fiduciary responsibility to keep your clients apprised of crucial international developments such as this which may impact their portfolios. Sugar traditionally trades within a narrow range of six to eight cents per pound. We're presently trading at a slight discount to six cents. This is a dream come true, folks. We all know that stories sell. Contact your best clients and sell the sugar story. Paint as vivid a picture as possible of the potential for disaster."

He paused again to cough and then clear his throat. "The December six-cent call options are in-the-money for about fifteen hundred each, with commission. However, the seven cent calls are only a grand and although they're further out-of-the-money, we feel either option will pay off handsomely. We expect to see sugar reach at least twenty cents per pound or higher. That's a potential twenty thousand dollar profit for each option purchased. This creates a wonderful opportunity to roll all of your clients out of their currency and bond positions and place their profits into the sugar market at this extremely low level. And don't forget, people. Stress urgency! That is all."

"Well, I trust everyone gathered some valuable ammunition during this morning's research," Jack concluded. "On a lighter note, we are proud to welcome several of the more motivated junior brokers from New York and Miami. I'm confident everyone will make them feel right at home. We're also very proud of our newly-anointed senior account executive, Mister Everett Anderson. Join me in a round of applause, will you?" The floor responded with an enthusiastic hand as Everett nodded awkwardly.

"I'd also like to recognize Victoria Vasquez, ladies and gentlemen. Ms. Vasquez has just completed taping a magnificent new account for five hundred thousand dollars!" The entire office erupted again with applause as Vasquez emerged from Bill's office.

"Now that we're all assembled, I've saved the best news for last. As you all know, our annual Christmas Ball is scheduled this Friday at the U.S. Grant hotel downtown. "Unlike our Wall Street colleagues, we'll be continuing our company tradition!" he said as the group erupted. "I've taken the liberty of reserving all three dozen suites on a first come, first served basis. Please see Ms. Emerson regarding reservations. We don't recommend driving home after the festivities, of course. We'll also be announcing the details of the company's annual sales contest to Brazil. If there are no questions, let's all get back to work, shall we?"

The meeting concluded and everyone returned to their desks as the trading floor hummed with activity. Everett detoured through the senior executive lounge, which was now open to him. As he entered, Victoria Vasquez was pouring coffee.

"Congratulations, Vasquez. Nice order," he said.

She cocked her head to one side without looking at him. "Congratulations yourself, Anderson. Welcome to the show."

"Any advice?" he asked.

"Yeah. Stay the hell out of my way. You rookies come and go like the sales assistants around here."

"I plan on seeing my name above yours."

"Right," she sniffed, headed for the trading floor and passing Jennifer on the way out.

Everett shook his head. "What the hell's her problem?"

"I tried to tell you," Jennifer snorted. "Don't take it personally. So you want to meet for lunch?"

"Sure."

They found two empty chairs and were silent for a moment, watching the city's trolley roll past, its bell clanging sharply. She waved off the waiter, glancing quickly around the surrounding streets full of pedestrians as she nervously lit a cigarette.

"Everett, we need to talk," Jennifer said abruptly, adjusting her glasses.

"I know. I'm sorry. I've been busy as hell lately and I've been rude to you."

"Yes, you have, but that's not why I want to talk to you. Jack's been acting strange lately," she said, scanning the courtyard behind him. "Very strange."

"How do you mean?"

"Before he left for the week, he was wearing the same suit in the morning that he wore the day before. He's typically very dapper, not a hair out of place."

"Jack's a little eccentric, Jennifer."

"I should know, I've been working for him for five years, much longer than you. But he's been especially strange lately, even for him. I think he's spending his nights in the office, and he's gone during the day. I sit right next to his office but I never actually see him leave."

"He's a workaholic."

"As long as I've known him, he never has slept much. He's there when I leave and he's there when I get in." Her eyes darted quickly from side to side. "Lately he's been sending me on unusual errands in the jet that seem to have nothing to do with company business. I've been back and forth to

Cabo ten times, three times in the last two days. I mean, we do have a Federal Express account for Camerone Cane. Maybe it's nothing, but, you've spent lots of time with him lately. You don't notice it?"

"That's just Jack. I wouldn't concern myself about it if I were you," he said nonchalantly, glancing at his watch.

She drew heavily on her cigarette and stared at him. "You're probably right, but I thought you should know. You're the teacher's pet around the office now."

"Look, Jen, I said I was sorry, but I've got a lot of responsibility now, to my clients and to the company. I manage a large book and Jack's trusted me with some of the company's biggest clients. What do you want from me? Now I have to train and motivate a brand new crop of rookies."

She chewed on her fingernail and shook her head. "I knew this would happen," she said under her breath as she puffed. "I've witnessed the transformation too often."

He waved the smoke from his face. "What?"

"Congratulations, Everett. I hope you're happy. Now you're one of them."

*

Well after midnight in California, the sun was rising in Rio. Katherine and Jack had been up all night. The trading floor was silent and dark. The trading screens glowed green and the downtown lights around the perimeter windows twinkled across the sleeping city below. The Grinder often served as their after-hours playground.

Katherine held a crystal goblet filled with vintage champagne in her hand as she wandered around the trading floor, caressing the computers and dragging her nails across the desks as Jack pretended to chase her like a predator. They were playing a game that she often started when they partied late together. Jack was shirtless, in his trousers and suspenders and she hopped around the trading floor in nothing but her silk panties and high heels.

Camerone's account was so cumbersome that it had taken all day and part of the evening to carefully reposition his bond and currency trades without drawing undue attention to Continental's traders in New York. The sugar transaction had been excruciatingly complex, but well worth the work.

Jack was now celebrating and in a playful mood. "So. When did you last speak with our Mexican tycoon?" he asked.

"He phoned yesterday, but I haven't returned his call yet."

"Fine. We've completed the purchases and I think it's only fair to split your commission with your ex-husband. Wouldn't you agree? He did, after all, execute the orders for us."

"I have absolutely no problem with that, Jackson," she said, always calling him by his full name when she was horny, and Jack definitely made her horny.

"Why don't you ever take me back to the mansion?" she asked.

"Because I have all the necessities of home right here. I have enough rare scotch and exotic meats to survive a nuclear holocaust. I have access to international global financial market data twenty-four hours a day via state-of-the-art wireless communications equipment. I command a view of America's finest city that anyone would give up their first born child in order to enjoy, and I have a luxury turbo helicopter standing by at a moment's notice. Did I mention I also lay claim to the talents of one of the most beautiful women in the universe?"

"Sorry I asked," she said as she kissed him lustfully.

Jack picked up the desk phone, contacted his Hong Kong broker and closed out a dozen profitable warrant positions on the Hang Seng Index.

Katherine sat patiently in one of the leather chairs, watching him work. "You crave the risk, don't you?" she asked.

"A little risk never killed anyone, Darling."

She stood and walked toward him. "Let's give El Toro the good news, shall we?"

Jack began the lengthy dialing process. Two minutes passed as all the digits were entered and the super-high frequency signal was launched through the airwaves to deep space, deflected off of a satellite in geosynchronous orbit, and then zipped through the electronic real estate in the sky down to the southern tip of Baja California.

As it began to ring, Jack handed it to Katherine. "I want you to tell him," he said as he knelt in front of her and pushed her firmly against one of the trading consoles.

The phone continued to ring in her ear as Jack carefully slid his hands upward along the perimeter of her calves and over the outside of her knees and muscular thighs. Her long, tanned legs were smooth and clean-shaven and offered little resistance.

Fifth ring.

Sixth ring.

He kissed her warm, taut stomach and plunged his tongue into her navel as he gently peeled the waistband of her silk underwear down toward her high heels.

Tenth ring.

She stepped out of her panties and clutched a handful of his thick black hair as he firmly nuzzled his face between her legs.

Fifteenth ring.

She closed her eyes and her head fell backward against her shoulders. She almost dropped the phone.

The wireless signal connected. "*Hola.*"

Heavy breathing.

"*Hola?*"

"Don Carlos," she said slowly and softly. "I have some . . . very good . . . news for you."

"Ah, Katherine. What a pleasure it is to hear your lovely voice first thing in the morning."

She paused again, and exhaled into the receiver. "We have completed the purchase of . . . December sugar . . . for your . . . trading account."

"Jack tells me he believes sugar will reach over twenty cents."

"Oh, yes," she sighed.

"Do you really think it will rise that quickly?"

Her breathing became deeper. "Oh Don Carlos, I could . . . make love to sugar at . . . twenty cents," she gently moaned.

"This is exciting news, Katherine. You could give an old man a heart attack."

"Yes."

"Senor Diamond is very talented, no?"

"Oh God, yes! Yes . . . he is," she said, struggling for oxygen.

Her voice and her breathing became even deeper.

"Katherine?"

A very long pause.

She exhaled deeply and sighed, and then composed herself.

"Don Carlos, I can hardly wait to meet you."

"The pleasure will be all mine, Katherine. Adios."

13

The two-door convertible SL Mercedes came out of nowhere, but he immediately recognized her behind the wheel. His Corvette reached eighty miles per hour as it powered past the merge sign which warns all drivers that the two lanes of La Jolla Parkway converge to form one, leading south to the Interstate-5 merge pointing toward downtown San Diego. On the same morning at the same time, they both found themselves on the main road that wound its way out of La Jolla away from Mount Soledad. She was forced to downshift the pearl white two-door as he almost lurched against her, cutting her off at the ramp's entrance and edging in front. The two drivers then proceeded to test the structural integrity of the highway on-ramp at one hundred miles per hour.

The Mercedes roadster roared down the ramp and broke left, finding an opening behind the tight flow of twilight traffic. The 'vette was boxed. The morning merge was thick with cars and he couldn't move. She accelerated, changed lanes, and took the lead. Spotting a thin break in traffic, he shot the gap and launched past her through the S-curve which carved a banked path through San Clemente Canyon. She was pinned on the outside guard rail as they reached a straight section of freeway passing Pacific Beach.

Traveling south, the Corvette cleared the crest of the rise, privy to a glimpse of the downtown skyline on the horizon. It was still dark over the ocean to the right as the orange glow of sunrise behind the mountains to the east cast a silvery shimmer on the tall cluster of buildings in the distance. They were still seven miles from downtown. The Corvette was topless and the chilly morning air was unforgiving on his face. It helped improve his hangover.

The steering-wheel began ringing as a voice came through the speaker phone. "You know you're breaking the law, Anderson. This lane is reserved for car pools only." He looked in the rear view mirror. Victoria Vasquez was smiling from ear to ear behind a pair of designer sunglasses.

"You're as tardy as I am, Vasquez."

"I had to make love one more time this morning to the lifeguard on my beach," she said. "What's your excuse?"

"Jack Daniels buried a sledgehammer in my skull last night at Valentine's party."

"And I noticed you gave Ms. Emerson a ride home. I didn't know you lived in La Jolla."

"I don't."

"Dipping your Mont Blanc in company ink?"

"Very funny, Vasquez."

"So you're number one now. Tell me, what did you think about Jack's sugar trade?" she asked.

"A top producer like you asking my humble opinion?"

"Jack doesn't talk to me anymore. I want to know what *you* think."

"Technically it's long overdue for a breakout. Global expansion, low inventories in South America, huge demand for ethanol. I'm building a monster position."

"Care to wager your parking space? It used to be mine."

"You'll love parking on the street, Vasquez, if you can find a spot."

"Just try to keep up," she said as she changed lanes, merged back into the flow of traffic and edged past him as the two raced toward the Front Street exit to downtown, yo-yoing through traffic. Everett punched the accelerator, broke right, and zoomed through the exit ramp to downtown. He rolled in behind her at the intersection, revving his engine.

Anticipating the light, she turned left on Fifth in front of the oncoming traffic just north of Broadway as the signal changed to green. Everett had to wait and took the one-way alley on the side of the building. After the traffic cleared, he watched the white rear quarter panel of the Mercedes disappear into the garage entrance at street level. "Damn!" he said, slamming his steering wheel with his hand and shaking his head. His smile changed to a scowl when he glanced at the temperature and time clock on the exterior of the bank building. It read 59 degrees and 6:01.

He raced up the concrete ramp and quickly parked, his heart still pounding from the morning road rally. The sharp sound of his crocodile loafers ricocheted off the unforgiving concrete surface of the low ceilings and thick walls in the parking garage as he hustled for the elevator.

Out of the corner of his eye he noticed a profile waiting in the inky shadows outlined against the dimly lit garage. "Hello, Anderson."

"Hello, Vasquez."

"We need to talk," she said.

"Fine. You get it for a month, then I want it back."

"This is not about a parking spot."

"We're late, big time."

She stared at him without a word, until the silence became awkward. "Let's take a walk."

"A walk? We're very, very late."

She inched toward him. "Please," she said as she slowly reached up and held his face, then forcefully kissed him, full on the mouth.

He wasn't sure if he should pull away so he played along.

"Don't react, just trust me," she whispered in his ear, taking his hand. "Jack's watching."

As they rounded the corner at street level, Vasquez glanced around the crowded streets.

"So, why all the mystery?" Everett asked.

"I can't really talk about that. Not yet."

"Can you talk about the kiss in the garage?"

"I had to make it look like we were off on a morning romp. Jack has cameras everywhere, even in the garage."

"So? Security's no secret."

"What did Ham Walker say to you when you first met him."

"I don't know. Like what?"

"Like anything he might have fed you about guaranteed or rigged trades, or planted news stories that he knew would move the markets?"

"All he did was set up my interview."

"But he got his start in Chicago, the heart of the company, where all the information comes from. Walker never gave you a trade after you were hired?"

"He bragged about how great the company was and about what a trading wizard Jack was, but nothing like inside information. Then they moved him back to Chicago right after my hire."

"So all your recent success is your own independent doing?"

"I'm just following the same research as the rest of the office. Why?"

"But you're executing before and sometimes after everyone else, going around the company trades, and making even more profit. You're doing all that completely on your own?"

"You don't believe me?"

"Let's just say people around me lie for a living."

"That's pretty cynical, Vasquez."

"The whole office is buzzing about you. You're Jack's golden boy, and you're making a killing on inside info directly from the boss. Jack gave you sugar before the rest of the office, didn't he?"

"Why would you ask me that?"

"I watched you record and settle all those trades days before research announced the buy. That's front-running, you know."

"I've done nothing illegal."

"How do you think Bernie Madoff made all his money?"

"He lied to his clients."

"No. He started out on Wall Street in the Seventies as a market maker. Meaning he saw large blocks of shares coming through the system before he priced and cleared the trades, so he bought the same stock at a cheaper price for his own account before he priced it for the public."

"You saying that's what Continental does?"

"Man, have they got you sucked in," she said.

"You know something I don't?"

"That's all I can tell you, for now," she said as she stopped in front of the Empire Bank building. "Don't trust anyone and watch what you say all the time and everywhere you go in the building."

"Wait a damn minute . . . !"

14

The warm California sun beamed through the open French doors, forcing open his bloodshot eyes. He rubbed his throbbing temples as his patchy memory of the night before began to fill in the blanks. Happy hour with his new team turned into dinner, and then dinner turned into cigars and single malt and tequila shots and more champagne at La Gran Tapa, a traditional Spanish bar downtown.

A dog's constant barking in the alley outside echoed in the distance as he stared at the ceiling of Jennifer's bedroom. Everett sat up, arched his back, then stretched, planting his thick arms into the soft mattress and rising out of the cotton bed sheets. Through the open doors, he heard Jennifer moving about her townhouse against the roar of ocean waves as they crashed on the rocks at the end of the street. He could smell the turkey basting in the oven but he couldn't remember how he got into her bed, or where he parked the Corvette.

She appeared in the open doorway wearing shorts and a tiny bikini top, straining to support her chest. "This is becoming a habit with you."

"What time is it?" he groaned.

"After one. You've been asleep all morning."

"It didn't help. I feel horrible."

"I had to open the balcony doors. You smell like a brewery."

"I guess I really tied one on last night?"

"You earned it. Your team is top in the office for two months in a row."

"Sorry about the other day."

"I know. You must have said it ten times last night. Are you hungry?"

"Are you kidding?"

"Why don't you get up and go for a run. Windansea is two blocks away. The sun and the air will clear your head. I'm cooking for you."

"What did I do to deserve such treatment?"

"You obviously don't remember what you did last night after you snuck in and woke me up." She leaned over and kissed him.

"We can stuff ourselves and hide out together all afternoon before your flight," she purred.

"As long as I'm not late. Thanksgiving's always a big deal back home."

Everett rose slowly, and dressed. He stretched again, gulped down a bottle of spring water, and then polished off two bananas before leaving through the kitchen door.

The unmistakable smell of the Pacific Ocean and the chill on the morning air was exhilarating. Following the worn dirt path behind her complex to the beach, he ran bare-footed through the sand north until his second wind kicked in and relieved his headache. He broke a sweat, and as the ground began to pass effortlessly beneath him, his heart rate slowed. He watched the young surfers, already in the water, enjoying the five and six foot winter swells. He thought of Vasquez and how impossible her job must be. But there was something about her. *And what's up with the warning?* Her attitude, her toughness. He'd wrestled with the idea all night as he bought rounds of drinks for his new team. He'd been raised by the sturdy matriarch of his family and she'd taught him the value of a strong woman's perspective, helping him over time to forget the embarrassing bravado his own father had displayed, melting down often into a drunken tirade.

Last night started with happy hour at the Aztec for his new team of traders, but then turned into a walking tour of every new club downtown. *Am I drinking too much these days? Now what do I do? How much time do I have? Better make all I can, as quickly as I can. Another million and I win back my trust. One more quarter? Three more months?*

As he reached the rocks that surround the small patch of sand on Windansea beach, he felt a sudden rush of adrenalin. *What's he doing here?*

He wouldn't have noticed the man, except for the bright blond crew cut and the way the man ripped across the waves, cutting off the less-experienced surfers. But something made him stop. As he rubbed his bloodshot eyes he noticed the muscled slasher outweighed him by at least fifty pounds. He also noticed there were no lifeguards on duty on this crowded section of sand.

Everett reached the point of the beach where the surfer exited the water, now arguing with a young teenager. Angry words turned to shoving and Everett watched the big man beat down the young teenager, who was half his size. The slasher's face was bright red, the veins on his neck were bulging, and he was shaking with rage as he smashed the kid in the face, repeatedly. A crowd of the locals and most of the surfers started to gather behind him and when the slasher noticed he was outnumbered, he turned and sprinted toward the rocks, and then disappeared.

"You okay, Kid?" Everett asked.

The young surfer bled from his nose and mouth, and he shook his head. "Hell, no! That was my wave, and the bastard tried to kill me!" he shouted as an orange four-wheeler appeared, and the young surfer began recounting the story to the lieutenant.

The Anderson family had always been very generous when it came to the local Episcopal church. Miss Virginia, as she was called by the sisters of the vestry, had been blessed with a decent crop and coincidentally, Saint Stephens had been blessed with a refurbished pipe organ. She loved the old church and when Mother Earth touched her with a fine harvest, she opened up her family's main house to the whole congregation.

The pea gravel driveway was lined with tall, sparkling candles surrounded by glass decanters to break the breeze as guests began to arrive promptly at sunset. A slight chill was in the thick humid air and the dress was semi-formal. The ancient pecan trees which lined the main entry were trimmed with greenery and harvest color, and the front porch of the stately brick mansion glowed, decorated in earth tones.

The holiday celebration was in high gear as an airport van pulled up to the front door. The Bishop recognized him first. "Everett! Is that you?"

The crowded foyer erupted with whispers and smiles as he stepped through the front door and removed his overcoat. "Happy Thanksgiving, Father."

"So sorry to hear about your retirement, young man."

"I appreciate the kind words."

"We'll all certainly miss watching you play."

"Thank you."

Then she appeared in the entry foyer, dressed in a gray silk gown trimmed with modest diamonds at her neck. Virginia reached out with trembling arms. "There you are," she beamed. "I thought I saw headlights through the kitchen."

"Now, this is how I like to see the house look," Everett gushed as he gently hugged her. "Everything's perfect."

"Having you home for Thanksgiving for the first time in five years is perfect enough. You were always playing during the holidays. Come. Let's take a walk," she said, clinging to his forearm. "I have so much to ask you."

He wrapped her in his arms and they excused themselves onto the front porch.

"So. Tell me all about this job of yours," Virginia asked.

His mind raced, hardly able to pick a starting point. "Well, the last few months have flown by. Weeks felt like days and I've been fortunate enough to survive the training. I was just promoted to senior broker. And I manage a small group now."

"That's splendid, Everett. Any investment tips for your grandmother?"

"Sugar."

"You mean I can make money in sugar?"

"I've put millions of dollars in sugar futures, and I'm up almost three hundred percent."

"Not in your trust, I hope."

"No ma'am."

"Wonderful news, dear. I knew you could do it. And I suppose California still excites you?"

"Yes ma'am. I love it."

"Well that's good news indeed. And I must confess. I have been rather hard on you for a reason," she said, fanning herself.

"I understand."

"I'm not sure you do, Everett. You see, by design your trust was conceived as a very complex instrument by your great grandfather. He began buying bank stock during the Depression. He had such vision. There was no income or estate tax back then and he hated the government anyway, so he hid his wealth in many ways."

"How so?"

"Daddy always dreamed of heirs like you that saw the world as he did. Unfortunately I was forced to shepherd the assets because the men of this family were weak, until you were born. Your grandfather was a very sweet man but not cut out to be a Delta planter. The summer heat wore him down and he died early of exhaustion. And then your father turned out to be a reckless gambler who never had a chance to access the wealth available to him, causing us all a lifetime of frustration and disappointment."

"But Dad tried, didn't he?"

"There wasn't a person in the world your father couldn't charm. You got that from him. All the men in this family have been gamblers, but Daddy truly lives through you, Everett. I can tell you that. And although you're cursed with the family thirst for risk and adventure, you've managed to develop a strong sense of self discipline through your football training and the physical hardships you've endured because of it. So, I have a little secret to share with you, which I have nursed for over eighty-seven years."

Everett leaned against the porch railing, his eyes wide with anticipation.

"I want you to learn of our little family secret."

"What kind of secret?"

"A secret that was literally buried with Daddy."

"Did my father know about it?"

"No. He would have found a way to squander it. The smartest thing your father ever did was lease our mineral rights to Exxon Mobil corporation, back in the nineteen sixties. It was called Esso back then, I believe. And I made him place those stock shares in the trust. But had it not been for your great grandfather, your father never would have been able to retain the mineral rights."

"How did Dad know where to drill?"

"Because Daddy dug that water well on the northwest corner of the property, close to the river. He couldn't supply enough water to irrigate cotton, so he switched to soybeans, which are less delicate and more durable in the summer months. That aquifer irrigated our crop for years. But once the well was polluted by a small amount of raw crude, Daddy had to seal the well. So your father had the crazy idea that he'd hit oil by drilling next to that old water well. That's where the history begins."

"The suspense is killing me."

"Your great grandfather was a remarkable man, Everett. He was conscripted into the Confederate Army near the end of the Civil War, when he was only fifteen years old. That's how desperate the South became. He was an excellent hunter so he was assigned to a special scout detachment of sharpshooters that were ordered to protect the removal of the last of the gold bars from the Vicksburg Treasury just before the city went under siege. By then, the cause was lost and the governor had agreed to return the borrowed bars to the French magistrate who authorized the original loan in New Orleans."

"Real gold?" he laughed.

"Most of the men were killed that night, but Daddy managed to escape, wounded, with the wagon. The river was crawling with Union ironclads and he was bleeding badly so instead of loading the bars on a boat, he took the mule team north along the riverbank and made it here deep in the Delta just before sunrise. Vicksburg fell the next day after Gettysburg and the war ended shortly thereafter. The governor later deeded our property in exchange for Daddy's loyal service but was assassinated before the documents were signed or before the bars were returned. Once when I was just a little girl, some rather rough-looking men showed up, but Daddy shot two of them and the others took off and never returned. In the confusion of Reconstruction, Daddy brought this magnificent black dirt back to life. Eventually, he secured title to the plat we now own, but the bars were never found."

"But wasn't gold confiscated by the government in nineteen thirty-three?"

She stopped walking. "Is it getting warmer?" she asked fanning herself as she began to sway.

"Virginia. Are you alright?"

"Let me sit down, dear," she gasped, gripping his forearm as she lost her balance. He was able to catch her, but not before she completely collapsed in his arms.

"Help! Someone, please call 911. Hurry!"

15

Looking forward to nothing more than a bourbon and a few hours of catch-up on his computer, Everett stepped out of the cab in front of his condominium well after midnight. He loosened his tie as he strolled through the narrow walkway lined with cactus and tropical plants that led to his front door. His flight had been delayed and he was emotionally drained. Virginia had been rushed to the hospital in plenty of time and pronounced in stable condition over the weekend. He refused to leave her side. But once she regained consciousness and became her feisty self again, she insisted he return to work. It was considered a mild stroke and she was on her feet in twenty-four hours. Not too serious, but she was kept in the hospital for observation just to be on the safe side. As he slid his key into the lock, he smelled cigarette smoke drifting around the corner from the empty private courtyard next to his townhouse.

Through the wrought iron fence that surrounded the exterior of the complex he stole a quick glance and slowly opened the gate. Next to the sago palm squatting in the darkness under a large yucca was a young woman, slowly rocking back and forth with her legs tucked under her, chain-smoking and crying, staring down at the terra cotta patio tiles.

He squinted at the blackness that separated them. "Hello?"

There was no answer. Only quiet crying.

"Can I help you?"

"Oh, Everett."

"Jennifer? Are you okay?"

"No! No, I'm not," she screamed through a torrent of tears.

"What's wrong?"

The low glow of the moon revealed a purple bruise on the left side of her face. "I didn't want you to see me like this, but . . .Oh God, Everett, I've got nowhere else to go!" she cried reaching for his neck. "I'm sorry, I wanted to warn you earlier this week," she said, struggling to her feet as he supported her. "But you were going home for the holidays."

He propped her up, then slowly and gently examined her face. Her right cheekbone was swollen, her left eye was bruised and purple, and her lips were puffy. "Tell me what happened. Who did this to you?" He wiped the tears from her face and pushed her hair to one side.

"We have to go inside," she said, scanning the street behind her. "We can't stay out here. They might be watching."

"Who?"

She didn't answer.

"You're safe with me," he whispered as he carefully walked her through the front door.

She was still crying and trembling as he locked the door behind them. She collapsed into his leather love seat in the darkness as he turned on the dim lights over the stove, and returned with a dish cloth full of ice which he held to her cheek.

"I didn't want to drag you into this, but he made me."

"Who?"

She hesitated, then she spit out the words like poison. "It was Jack."

"You mean Jack hit you?"

"Of course not. He never handles his own dirty work. He's above that. He always has someone else do it. It's his way. He sent his bodyguard."

"He has a bodyguard?"

"It's such a long and ugly story," she said, shaking her head.

"I've got all night."

"Jack paid me a lot of money to cozy up to you," she said. "I've been spying on you, Everett. He wanted me to pick your brain, find out what you were trading and what you really knew. The coke makes him very paranoid."

"Jack uses cocaine?"

"He thinks the government is watching him all the time. But you were different."

"Different?"

"Jack picks one rookie every class and grooms him to be a franchise player, like in sports. Bill Peterson played baseball in college. John Valentine was almost good enough to tour the professional tennis circuit. All the senior traders have sports backgrounds. Jack collects athletes, just like his father. It's an unspoken tradition. But you did something none of them did. You actually out-traded the boss. And worst of all, you turned out to be this really honest, decent guy, which made it so easy to be with you. And when I got to know you, it wasn't an act anymore. I swear, Everett, I fell for you. I really did."

He walked to the window, looked out at the darkness on the street. All he could think about was Vasquez and her warning. "Why me?"

"You're the top broker in the company, and you're naturally good on the phone. People like you. Jack feels threatened because you don't blindly follow every one of his trades. He doesn't like to share the spotlight. He likes brokers with total obedience, and he likes to own people. I should know," she exhaled. "He owns me."

"But why would he hurt you?"

"Control. Just like you and your trust."

"How do you know about my trust?"

"Everett, I know everything that goes on in that office. I had to send the power-of-attorney documents to your trustee."

"Can't you just resign and leave?"

"Can you?"

"Not yet," he said.

"Join the club. Plus, my mother in Chicago has a very expensive form of bone cancer. She's all I have left in the world and Jack pays me very well, in cash. That's what he does. That's all he does. He finds a weakness and then exploits it. Who do you think pays the mortgage on my townhouse in La Jolla and the lease on my Porsche, and supports my expensive taste in clothes?"

"And now you're stuck."

"Just like you," she said, lighting another cigarette, defiantly tossing back her blond hair away from her face, and exhaling a stream of smoke. "When I first started at Continental, I was young and seduced by Jack and the money, just like all the brokers. One night when I was working late, the trading floor was empty. Jack showed up out of nowhere and raped me, Everett. Now he pretends like I like it rough. Then he gave me a lot of money to stay quiet. But when he drinks and snorts coke he gets mean. When you and I had lunch the other day at the deli, his bodyguard must have been watching us and thought I told you something. I told him you didn't know anything," she said tearfully, "but he wouldn't listen."

"We were being watched?"

She took another drag. "His bodyguard put his filthy hands on me and tried to have his way in the limo, but I wouldn't let him, so he slapped me around. You've got to pretend you don't know anything, or he'll come after you, too."

"Is there any way Jack could know you came over here tonight?"

She shook her head. "He flew down to Brazil this afternoon. That bastard who works for him put me on a plane for Chicago earlier tonight, but I snuck out of the terminal and took a cab here. I'm positive I wasn't followed, but I just had to tell you. I couldn't do it by phone."

"Then you're staying with me tonight."

"No," she said quickly. "No. I have to be in Chicago in the morning or they'll get suspicious. My mother needs me. I'm her marrow donor. She's being transferred this weekend. Then I'm taking a long, possibly permanent vacation. I've got a lot of cash in a safe deposit box in Chicago. Will you take me back to the airport?"

"You're in no condition to travel, Jennifer."

"I've got dark glasses and a scarf to wear on the plane. I'll be fine, really. It's a non-stop flight and I plan to sleep in first class with the lights out."

"You're sure?"

"I do care for you, Everett. Our love-making was no act."

"I know, Jen."

"We need to go," she said.

Everett snatched his keys and opened the garage door. After placing Jennifer in his Corvette, he pointed the nose north toward Lindbergh Field and rocketed over the Coronado Bridge for downtown. The cool night air filled the cockpit.

"There's one more thing you should know," she said as they approached Lindbergh Field. "I don't have access to every single one of Jack's personal trading files, but I stumbled on to something Friday afternoon. Something strange."

"Like what?"

"Everett, I think Jack's selling sugar in his own personal account."

The words gave him a sick feeling in the depths of his stomach. "What?"

"I overheard one of the routing clerks in the cage who was fired Friday."

"Fired for what?"

"For calling compliance about a huge sell imbalance through our head trader, Derrick Butler. He's Katherine Fox's ex-husband. The place is so incestuous."

"But Jack told me last week we could easily see twenty-five cents a pound or higher. Maybe thirty."

"He thinks I don't understand the markets," she said, "but I know Jack, and I wouldn't be surprised if he's selling all of Continental's sugar futures contracts to his own broker's clients, and none of them even know it."

"Which means he knows it's about to tank."

As they approached the terminal, Jennifer glanced around the empty airport's loading area. "It'd make a great story, wouldn't it? The brokers will jump at the chance to churn their books with the company's blessing."

"You're right about that."

"Corporate books billions in transactions while the great Jack Diamond not only takes profits, but makes hundreds of millions in commissions on top."

"Sugar is sky high right now, almost six times our buy in. I've watched it every day. My entire client book's in sugar," Everett said.

She gently touched his face with her hand and leaned over to kiss him. "Then consider this a gift. Jack would not be very happy if he knew I told you this."

"If I start liquidating my client accounts, he'll be the first to notice. He'll never approve of me going against research."

"Jack will be in Chicago next week."

"How do I know you're not setting me up, again?"

"Look at me, Everett! I'm black and blue. What do I gain by telling you all this? You've got to trust me!"

"I don't know who to trust anymore. If Jack sent you to spy on me once, what prevents him from planting a bogus story in your head right now?"

"You've got to believe me. I'm trying to help you!"

"I need proof."

"Alright, then," she said, finishing her cigarette. "A girl named Shelby has been leaving messages for you for months now, messages I never forwarded or gave to you. I'm so sorry."

"Why would you do that, Jennifer?"

"Because I want to be what she is to you."

"All right. Fair enough."

"Now do you trust me?"

He stared through the wind shield at the passengers who hurried through the futuristic concrete and steel terminal, then he looked her in the eye. "Yes, I do. But you've got to understand, she and I have history."

"I know. Be careful, Everett. Jack can make you very rich, *and* he can ruin your life forever."

16

Everett stepped in front of Victoria Vasquez's Mercedes convertible as she was leaving the parking garage at street level for lunch. He opened her driver side door. "Are you crazy?" she gasped. "I almost ran over you!"

"Move over."

She glanced around the street. "Don't talk to me like that," she said through clenched teeth.

"I want to know what you know," he demanded. "Now!"

She reluctantly climbed over the gear shift of the expensive Mercedes convertible. "Be careful, it's not mine."

"Then who the hell's is it?" Everett demanded, pulling into traffic and pointing the car towards the highway. "And why the warning two weeks ago?"

"Anderson. Listen to me."

"No, you listen to me! I'm tired of this crap! Everything! Right now!"

"You know, I've had to endure all the macho culture in that office contaminated by schoolboy locker room humor. Dirty jokes, porno on the computers, and sexual gibes directed at me. I'm the one asking questions, not you!"

"Cry me a freakin' river! You know, I had offers from every wire house in town, most with a long term contract and a six figure signing bonus!"

"Why do you think Jack seized your trust? To force your loyalty. He'll feed you accounts and make you filthy rich. Then after you've bought a beach house in La Jolla with a huge mortgage, leased a Lamborghini, and you're neck deep in sailboats and jet skis and monthly payments, he owns you."

"I don't work that way."

"Bullshit. All you guys are alike. Brokers, athletes, whatever, you're all jocks. Bunch of adrenaline junkies."

"How the hell did you get this far, Vasquez? What does he have on you?"

"Maybe it's time you knew."

"Knew what?"

She hesitated.

"I asked you a question, Vasquez!"

"I'm a Treasury agent, Anderson, working undercover."

"Bullshit! Then show me a Goddamned badge!"

"Are you insane? I'm risking my own life just revealing myself."

"And I'm just supposed to believe you?"

"You have to. You're the only person I can trust to help me."

"Help you? You're insane."

"Treasury underwrites all my accounts and my production keeps Jack off my back. I have nothing to protect. He owns everyone in that brokerage house. Peterson, Valentine, all the senior brokers. Why do you think they're so angry and bitter all the time? Now they have to play his game, or try to quit and wake up dead."

"Shit."

"He owns everyone and he talks to everyone. Ambassadors, Senators, kings, queens, dictators, European billionaires and players in Hollywood. He's the original mastermind. He's five moves ahead all the time. I'm not exaggerating. He's made money for a lot of powerful people over the years and I wouldn't be surprised if he really does get inside information that gives him an aura of being a guru. He's very intelligent and he's very hard to indict. We've been after him for decades."

"But what can I do? I don't know who he knows. I can't get inside his computer or his trading network."

"You just made senior. Now you're part of his little inner circle. That much Walker told me, before he was killed."

"Walker was murdered?"

"Just like Lou Harper, our pit trader. Once you reach that level, Jack tells you everything, like how he's Harvard Skull and Bones, connected to foreign nationals, currency traders, and heads of state. How he's privy to world events through international politicians, and how he manipulates his traders in Chicago based on inside information."

"I got the welcome chat last week."

"I knew it! That's why he promoted you so soon."

"How did I not see this coming?"

"Come on Anderson, you're a smart guy. This is the easiest money you've ever made. I know what you earned in the NFL. League minimum during your third year was what, four hundred seventy-five thousand, before taxes? And if you're cut for any reason, like an injury, the balance of the contract is voided. Only your signing bonus is guaranteed. Close?"

"So you checked up on me through the IRS?"

"At Continental you're on track to triple that. A millionaire before thirty, with a growing six figure trust fund. You're still young and hungry with an appetite for risk, and some might even say a tad greedy? NCAA accusations of gambling in college?"

"I never did what they said I did! I refused to throw a game and that bookie spread lies about me, which caused an investigation that was eventually dismissed! I pay my taxes and I've always played by the rules. And I've managed my family trust with discipline for over six years now."

"And Jack snatched it away from you in one afternoon, just to show you who's in charge. Now he's bribing you to play ball. You can't just walk away from the party now. He wouldn't like that, and he could always get to you or your family."

The convertible reached ninety, then climbed to over a hundred. He locked his elbows as he gripped the steering wheel, dodging and darting his way through the heavy traffic.

"What are you doing? Slow down!"

"I was on a roll," he snapped. "I had big plans!"

"Listen to yourself! You're as bad as they are!"

"I've paid my dues and I deserve over a million dollars in my pocket to pad my trust, all qualified dollars growing tax-deferred. Then I planned to retire back home and relax! Have my life back for the first time since I was a kid in grade school!"

"Anderson, Continental has never ever paid a penny in arbitration for settlement of a single client complaint. Any lawsuits or judgments for bad investment advice or adverse market moves fall squarely on the shoulders of the brokers. That's why Jack hires ex-jocks and kids with family money. And you're both. You can't just retire rich and walk away. That's what Harper and Walker tried to do."

"I didn't sign on for murder."

"Jack can get to you no matter what, but I can guarantee your safety."

"Like you did for Walker?"

"It's cold-blooded evil, very difficult to prosecute. Enron, Worldcom, Tyco, Lehman, Bear Stearns. The defense lawyers get rich, and the rich clients walk. Why do you think Jack plans these company trips to Zurich, Switzerland? Rio de Janeiro, Brazil? Nice, France? All non extradition countries. He's got equity buried all over the globe in numbered accounts and a plane ticket in his back pocket. The U.S. Attorney's office wants rock-solid, bulletproof evidence or else Jack Diamond keeps doing business, well connected to very powerful people around the planet, and he might actually get away with it."

"But for me, it's business as usual, huh?"

"We'll need some hard copy evidence. Client statements, articles of incorporation, trust resolutions, trade tickets, printed emails or memos, any kind of account documentation you can smuggle out of there."

"Good luck with that. You know how tight security is. Nothing client-related ever leaves the building."

"Then maybe we need some of your fourth quarter Hail Mary magic."

"What if I refuse?"

"Then we'll find you, and we'll eventually prosecute you. Trust me. I'm the only one who can save your life."

"I'll think about it."

"Well don't take too long. You're running out of time."

17

Early Thursday morning Everett hustled onto the trading floor as the last of the seniors prepared for the morning meeting. A few seconds of static and feedback silenced the great trading room and signaled the beginning of research.

Max Goldman's voice scratched its way out of the speakers. "Good morning, everyone," he growled. "Today's meeting will be short and sweet, no pun intended, and it will be perhaps the most important meeting of the fiscal year! In case this is your first bull market, I'd like to ask everyone with sugar contracts in their books to reflect on the powerful price moves of the past few months. We've all watched sugar rise from under five cents to over twenty cents. This move has put plump profits in our clients' accounts as well as our own pockets. We have much to be thankful for. But the most important move we can make is to parlay those profits into further gains."

A hush fell over the faithful.

"Corporate is therefore issuing only one recommendation this morning. We feel the upside is still very strong for sugar and we'd like to liquidate the profitable October and December options we presently own, and repurchase March options, which should give our clients more time for sugar to continue higher over twenty cents. Your individual offices will give you all the details. Have a productive day and great selling!"

Reactions ranged from stunned silence to restrained glee, but the buzz on the trading floor was immediate. High fives began around The Grinder. One by one they turned toward each another and it sunk in simultaneously as all the brokers, juniors and seniors alike, immediately grasped the concept. Churn and burn, baby.

"Settle down," Jack demanded. He stood in the center of the floor with his arms folded and his face beaming the triumphant look of a conquering hero. "Everything in life worth having, ladies and gentlemen, has fear attached to it. The fear of failure and often, the fear of success. Your client wants a strong broker, not some friendly voice who asks for the order, but a powerful broker who *tells* him what to do, without fear and with confidence and certainty. His money is at risk when you're uncertain, and as a licensed broker, you are a hired hunter. Man the hunter wakes each day alone and lives with no security. Man the hunter is respected and feared in the jungle. He lives to hunt and he hunts to live. He eats what he kills and sits proudly at the head of the fire."

Jack scanned the crowd of brokers, leaning forward in a trance-like state, hanging on every word. "Today's recommendation requires courage and conviction from everyone. Give every man thine ear, but few thy voice. We feel very strongly that sugar will continue to rise. Thirty cents is not only very attainable, it is certain. It will require even more courage to ride this market higher. You must reinvest those profits in March options. Your clients will resist. It's easy to win in this casino. They will want their profits returned, but you must be strong. Take profits now and be satisfied with a mediocre return in the face of surging bull market? Is that what we want?"

"No!" resounded from the entire room as the cheers began to build.

"I'm leaving for Chicago this morning. Roll everything into March!" Jack shouted as he marched through the Grinder to adoring applause.

*

Victoria Vasquez took the elevator to the street-level deli in the building's lobby. She slowly sat and watched Jennifer Emerson smoke a cigarette through the thick glass from a secluded corner behind a gigantic palm tree planted in the lobby, next to the sidewalk.

She quickly dialed Washington. "Good morning, Sir. I have some updated information for you, but I only have a minute."

"Go ahead."

"The company's number one trade recommendation was announced this morning."

"Which is?"

"They're basically ordering all the brokers to sell their profitable December sugar options, and then buy the March contracts into next year. They generate huge sell commissions, and then buy back the same commodity, generate even more buy commissions, but a later month into next year with an option expiration further out. They justify it by saying the market's going much higher and that they need more time, which apparently makes sense to all their gullible clients."

"Why didn't they purchase March sugar options in the first place and just hold on?"

"That question never came up. I'm just relaying to you the results of this morning's research meeting. They've got all their clients convinced they can do no wrong."

"How is the integrity of your cover holding up?"

"I'm confident no one suspects a thing. And no one has a clue what's really going on in Chicago. Jack has the whole organization brainwashed, clients as well as brokers, and between you and me, Sir, it's easy to get pulled in."

"Keep your head. We need you to stay sharp and focused."

"As usual, I'll need more big accounts to stay credible."

"How much do you need?"

"A lot."

"How much is a lot?"

"It's big, Sir."

"How much?"

There was a long pause.

"Another million dollars."

"Jesus Christ!"

"You want Diamond. That's what it'll cost."

"Why so much?"

"I need a hundred thousand dollars in production by month's end. I know this type of authorization takes time so I thought I'd tell you as soon as I knew. One more thing. The word around the office is that the firm's largest client is a wealthy sugar cane grower from Mexico. Don Carlos Camerone is a currency speculator who I suspect is laundering millions through Continental. He's well connected to the Mexican government, but my hunch is that he grows more than sugar in Brazil."

"We know all about Camerone, but he's the DEA's problem and he's out of reach. Jack Diamond is our problem. I'll suggest new client accounts spread out over the next few weeks. Don't get too close. Place your satellite cell calls to my cell only, understood?"

"Loud and clear."

"What do you think it'll take to get inside Diamond's office?"

Her eyes went straight to Jennifer Emerson, as she relit another cigarette. "Based on what I've observed of late, there's only one man who can get inside Jack Diamond's world, Sir."

"What's his name?"

"Everett Anderson. He's the top broker in the company."

He parked and quickly walked through the double doors marked Players Only. A voice rang out from the end of the long corridor that led to the dressing rooms. "Can I help you?"

Everett stopped and turned. "Charlie!"

"Security mentioned an intruder. I thought it was a scout from San Francisco. Can't be too careful after what happened with New England."

They shook hands. "Good to see you, Coach."

"So what brings you all the way down here?"

"Your office?"

Everett followed into the coach's quarters as Charlie poured two cups of coffee, loaded a fresh dip of Copenhagen in his lower lip, and they both sat down. "You look good, kid. Maybe a few pounds lighter."

"Too much sun and too much golf."

"Must be nice."

"Hey. You talked me into moving here. Remember?"

"And begged you to stay. Aren't you glad you did?"

"America's finest city."

"So how's the job?"

"Actually, I'm here on company business. I need to talk to some of my clients."

"So now you're too rich and busy to shoot the bull with your old coach?"

"As usual, I also need some advice."

"I heard sugar's over twenty-seven cents," Charlie said as he spit into a Styrofoam cup.

"Twenty-eighteen and a half to be exact."

"Damn."

"I want to take profits this week in sugar and sell short."

"You practically call me every day to tell me how much I'm making. I don't know what the hell you guys do downtown. All I know is, my statements tell me I keep making money and your company's research has made me very rich this year. If you think it's time to sell, do it."

"That's the catch. The office wants to sell alright, but they want to re-buy more contracts in order to give the market more time to go higher. They think it'll continue over thirty cents, but I'm content with the net gains in all my accounts."

"What did I always teach you?" the coach asked.

"Don't get arrested after curfew on the road?"

"No smartass. Trust your instincts. They're always right. If you're selling short, then I want a piece of the action. At least let me dip my toe in the water."

"How much?"

"I got another three hundred thousand in a CD."

"That's hardly a toe in the water," he said.

"I'd feel better if all of my money was with you."

"I'll trade your account on one condition."

"Name it."

"I'll take my commission and go with the company's buy recommendation in your account. If I'm wrong, you'll make back your bonus and break even. But if I'm right, you'll never miss the commission."

"I'll have a check for you this afternoon."

Charlie walked Everett through the locker room as most of the players trickled in from an afternoon workout. After securing a new risk disclosure and powers-of-attorney for each one of his clients, he shook hands and said goodbye.

18

The spot price of World raw sugar for October delivery opened on Friday morning at twenty-nine cents per pound, threatening and flirting with the thirty cent mark. Indonesia announced a 500,000 metric ton purchase and with supplies already tight from the previous year's short crop, the fundamentals were extremely bullish. Continental's research once again looked prophetically brilliant. Everett Anderson's client book had grown to over fifty million dollars. Sugar had been his salvation since his start date, and after nine hard months of raising aggressive risk capital and watching his clients' equity grow, he now controlled over two thousand October six-cent call options valued at close to twenty-five thousand dollars each, originally purchased for less than nine hundred dollars.

Research that morning was predictable—impressive to the ignorant but more of the same. The entire office was radioactive. In the middle of the morning research meeting sugar rallied and broke thirty cents, a contract high in the recent twenty-five-year history of the market. The spontaneous rally in the middle of the morning was a thing of beauty to watch. Seventy-five pairs of eyes tracking the same graphic on their trading screens, almost willing the market higher. The company's clients swallowed the research recommendation to buy more sugar. There was no resistance. To all the company's brokers, selling October and December and then reloading for more time with March options was a license to steal, and it didn't even feel like a crime.

Continental's managers were busy all morning, monitoring and signing sell tickets and tape recording buy orders for more options. As the morning wore on, Katherine camped out at Everett's console, ordered breakfast, drank her dark roast, and supervised the taping of all of his sell orders.

"You're lucky Jack's in Chicago. You know something I don't?" she asked sarcastically after monitoring Charlie Hayes' large sale.

Everett was focused. "The momentum's gone. I've worked too hard to build up all this equity. I'm not about to churn my book."

"Sweetheart, that's exactly what you're doing."

"No I'm not, and you know it."

"Excuse me, but I thought that was why we were here, to make as much as we could," she said.

"My clients get creamed if the market sells off without warning."

"Take a breath, Hon. You're a senior now. Don't worry, I'll sign your tickets, but why not just sell half? What if it goes higher?" she asked.

"Then I'll still look like a diligent account executive who pulled the trigger too early."

Katherine shook her head and continued signing his stack of trade tickets. "You're taking profits way too soon in my opinion, Everett, but it's your funeral."

"You never have a profit until you take it. I can always get back in."

"You're racking up quite a payday for yourself, and you're taking Cozzene down this road with you."

"I'm getting out today, Katherine. Vinnie's a big boy. He can make his own decisions."

"He looks up to you, and for what it's worth, I think you're making a big mistake, and a serious error in judgment. They all watch what you do, but suit yourself. All your clients have powers-of-attorney and that's all I need to know. It's your license."

She stayed at his trading desk for more than six hours and monitored every order. He'd scheduled calls every five minutes throughout the entire day. He had lunch delivered and never left his feet. By early afternoon, sugar was limit up at over thirty-one cents per pound. He'd sold into the teeth of the rally and reversed his entire sugar position.

Eleven minutes before sugar suspended trading in New York for the weekend, Everett taped his last order. His net commission was over five hundred thousand dollars. Exhausted, he walked into Bill Peterson's office and collapsed on the couch.

Bill was standing in front of his wet bar. "Nice effort this morning. Join me in a Bloody Mary?"

"Love one."

"See. My instincts were right about you the first time we met. I knew you were capable of this kind of production. Congratulations."

"You haven't publicly ruled yet on my insubordination. What do you think about my trade?"

"I think you just made a hell of a lot of money for yourself and this brokerage house this morning. Go buy yourself something nice."

"I'm surprised you didn't override me."

"I'm just the pit boss, Sport. You're my top senior trader now. You get to call your own shots."

Vinnie shoved his head into the office. "Que paso, Gentlemen?"

"Seems our star trader here is nervous about his little short trade today," Bill said.

"Oh, this is priceless," Vinnie said. "You just made a dump truck full of dough and now you're depressed?"

"Cozzene, get him out of here and go get him drunk or laid or something," Bill said.

Everett continued to stare out the window as Peterson's extension rang. He finally answered. "Yes?"

"Bill, there's an urgent call for Everett," the receptionist declared. "She's holding on fifteen."

"She?"

"Yes, Sir. Her name is Shelby."

Everett's heart flipped in his chest.

"Something tells me he'll take it," said Peterson, eyeing his top producer. "Make yourself at home, Mister Anderson. Cozzene, let's go pick up all your fills for the morning."

Everett jumped behind the big desk and looked at the blinking light on the phone console. He hadn't spoken to her in almost a year, which was a lifetime when you're single and twenty-seven. Even in college, he barely had time for her. Between twenty-one hours a semester of business classes, summer school, workouts, road games, meetings with agents and coaches, and his responsibilities back home, she found herself lost, becoming just another college girlfriend casualty that he had to schedule around. But she was more than that. After he was drafted by Dallas, she moved on and took a job in Atlanta. *It was probably for the best*, he thought to himself. They eventually lost touch, each on their own career tangent.

His hand slowly lifted the receiver. "Shelby?"

"Well hello, stranger. How in the world are you?" she asked, with a sugary drawl.

How do I even start to answer that, he thought. "I'm fine. How did you . . . ?"

"Know how to find you?" she said. "Your grandmother, of course. Actually, it took me this long to gather the courage to call you one last time. I thought you were ignoring me."

"It's along story, but I never got those messages. I don't know what to say."

"If I told you I was in California, what would you say?"

"Really? Where?"

"Santa Barbara. I landed my first job with an agency last month and we're shooting all week at the Biltmore."

"Wow. That's great. Good for you."

"I understand you're doing pretty well yourself. Virginia tells me you're this hotshot commodity broker making just a sinful amount of money."

"We've had good market activity, but that's a long story too."

"Then why don't you fly up here and tell me all about it."

"Well, aren't you full of surprises?"

"My schedule ends this afternoon," she said. "but I have my suite through the weekend. Can you break away?"

"Are you serious?"

"I'm very serious. I haven't stop thinking about you."

"I swear I've thought about you, too."

"Does that mean you'll come?"

"As soon as I can get there."

"Make it here by happy hour and we can have dinner."

"I'll be there tonight."

"Everett?"

"Yea?"

"I can't wait to see you," she said.

He felt a tingle in his chest. "I can't wait to see you either. I've got so much to tell you."

"And I can't wait to hear every word of it. I'll see you at the hotel."

*

The cell phone in his golf bag rang with a special tone that told Jack he had an important call that required his immediate attention. "Excuse me, Gentlemen," Jack said to the foursome of fellow Medinah Country Club members as he stepped away from his tee shot. "What is it, Ray?"

"You won't believe this shit. Anderson just took profits in sugar and then sold his whole book short."

"Who signed his tickets?"

"Who else? Your most trusted female manager."

"Anyone else in the office follow his lead?"

"Just Cozzene. You think it's just pure dumb luck?"

"How could he possibly know? The news won't be announced until Sunday night."

"You taught him too well, Jack."

"I'll be back tonight," Jack exhaled. "We can talk then. His whole book, huh?"

"All fifty million."

"Fine. I'll figure something out and deal with him next week. That sugar trade will cost him everything."

*

Katherine glanced around the deserted trading floor. Only the receptionists remained, still taking a tsunami wave of messages as she called the front desk and sent them home. She closed her door and mixed a strong drink of chilled vodka from her office bar. The sting of the clear liquor warmed her and steadied her hand as she held the highball glass against her forehead. She then spent the next two hours checking the sales figures on her computer.

She logged off the company trading system and began turning off the floor lights when the ringing sound of her phone captured her attention. "Good evening, Continental."

"*Hola*, Katherine. This is Juan Camerone."

"Yes, Juan," she said with a smile. "What can I do for our favorite client?"

"Do not tempt me with questions such as that."

"Did you see the one cent move in sugar today?"

"Of course. I am sorry I missed the move. What was the settlement price of my father's options?"

Katherine froze. "Settlement price?"

"Si. I phoned Jack on Thursday night and told him to liquidate the entire account. We believe the labor strike will end this weekend and sugar will plummet on Monday."

She hesitated, horrified by the implication.

"Katherine, tell me you settled the trust account," Camerone said.

"Senor Camerone, I was told nothing regarding your father's account. The account is too large to sell in one day, it effects the entire sugar market."

There was silence as the reality of what might have happened began to sink in. "Are you certain the sugar market will sell off on Monday morning?"

His words came very slowly. "Where the hell is Jack?"

Her hands began to tremble. She nervously lit a cigarette and walked onto the balcony with the remote. "You must understand . . . "

He stopped her. "I don't know what kind of game you are playing! You are my father's employee!"

"Jack told me nothing, I swear to you! I'm not playing a game! I was never told to sell!"

"If I discover you have misled me," he vented through the receiver, "I will have your head!" The line went dead.

She placed her shaking hand against her temple, massaging her forehead, somehow not believing her own senses. How could he do that? She felt trapped. She dialed Jack's cell phone. No answer. She dialed Jack's house. No answer. She dialed Bill Peterson. No answer.

She began to pace the floor like a caged animal.

She lit another cigarette, stomped through the trading floor and unlocked Jack's office. She rifled through his desk, drawer after drawer, tossing papers onto the floor. Then she found it, a little less than an ounce of pure cocaine in a zip lock bag in the bottom drawer.

She put the bag in her pocket with trembling hands and returned to her office where she snorted several long lines and tried to focus, but only fear and dread steered her thoughts. She tried to think, but only the darkest of outcomes filled her head.

Confused, she returned to Jack's office and logged on to his private network. He'd given her the passcode one night during their lovemaking and she had to know about Camerone Cane, SA. Once inside his trading records, she scrolled through the figures until she reached the hedge fund account. What she saw gave her a sick feeling. Under Camerone Cane, SA was a twenty-five million dollar cash balance. *Oh my God! Jack sold everything! I'll be ruined on Monday.*

She fled the office in a panic, and frantically wove her way through the Friday afternoon rush hour traffic, using the merging lanes and shoulders to pass. She drove north to Jack's mansion in Rancho Santa Fe, forty-five minutes from downtown. She was all over the road, finally finding the exit and swerving in time to make the turn.

The half-empty bottle of vodka sloshed around in the front seat of her Porsche. She reached for it and took a swig as the sun disappeared behind her over the Pacific.

After arguing with the gate guard at the exclusive address, she barreled up the long drive to Jack's house. Limousines and exotic sports cars were parked out front and the sound of people laughing told her there was a party inside. She came to a stop and staggered from her car, her dress wrinkled and her hair tangled.

She barged into the foyer, forcing herself through the amazed expressions of some of San Diego's wealthiest movers and shakers. She stumbled through the crowd, causing drinks to spill until she spotted him, surrounded by several men she didn't recognize. Jack was talking and laughing with one man she knew intimately, her ex-husband, Derrick Butler.

"Katherine, what happened to you?" Jack asked

"You son-of-a-bitch! You screwed everyone, including me!"

Jack quickly took her arm and looked around. "Why don't you calm down, Katherine."

"Why don't you tell your brokers and their clients what will happen Monday morning!"

"Katherine, what are you talking about?" Jack asked as he squeezed her arm. Several of Continental's wealthy clients were in attendance.

"Jack Diamond has a secret, everyone! He knows the future. That's right, he has a crystal ball!" She began to cry. "I just found out!"

"What are you talking about?"

"Now we'll all get hammered on Monday morning," she sobbed, her mascara bleeding black down her face.

"Why are you making such a scene?"

"Because I've got my life savings in sugar! I'll get wiped out personally and you could care less!"

The crowd began to mumble to themselves. All eyes were on Jack as he immediately tried to implement damage control. "Katherine, let's get you some coffee," he cooed and took her firmly by the arm.

"Let go of me!" she shouted as Derrick Butler watched silently.

"We've all been under a great deal of pressure and you've had too much to drink," Jack said between angry, clenched teeth, forcing her toward the foyer. "Let me call you a cab."

"You can go to hell!" she screamed, breaking free, violently shoving Jack out of her way. A confused and desperate look gripped her face as she scanned the room, hoping her ex-husband would believe her and come to her aid. Frightened and frustrated, she stormed out of Jack's house as Butler followed her.

"Good idea, Derrick," Jack said. "Please see that she gets home safely, will you?"

Butler sprinted through the front door and followed the red Porsche with his eyes as it pulled away, slicing diagonally through the front section of Jack Diamond's perfectly manicured lawn, leaving in her wake two deep tire groves through the mulched beds and bushes while chunks of expensive turf flew in all directions. The back tires of the Porsche 911 chirped loudly as they finally found traction on the soft black asphalt that led away from Rancho Santa Fe.

Everett rolled to a stop in front of the rambling, Spanish-style seaside hotel with white-washed stucco walls and a roof of red clay tiles. He parked and walked toward the restaurant under the crimson bougainvillea which crept up the corners and covered the trellises and overhangs. He could see her inside, watching and waiting for him. As soon as she spotted him, she ran into the small gravel parking lot and hugged his neck.

"I missed you so much," he said softly as he wrapped his arms around her. They held onto each other and he gently took her face in his hands and kissed her. She was just as lovely as he had remembered.

Without another word Shelby led him by the hand through the courtyard to their private bungalow. The whole world outside went away as he slowly undressed her and her tanned body was revealed, perfectly proportioned beneath her cotton sun dress. He lifted her body with his powerful arms as she held onto his wide shoulders and he carried her to the bed.

He gently traced the profile of her smooth skin with the tips of his fingers, carefully shifting his weight onto hers.

They made love for most of the afternoon, until they fell asleep in each other's arms.

As the evening sun reached through the windows of their room, he opened his eyes and sat up on his elbows. He studied her face as she slept. He watched her breathing, her chest rising and falling below the soft, wheat-colored blond hair that framed her face, lips slightly parted.

He showered and when he returned to the bedroom wrapped in a towel, her green eyes were open, following him as he walked to the bed. He leaned over and gently kissed her again. "Hey, sleepyhead. Did you dream about me?"

"Every night for the past year," she whispered, as he eased down onto the edge of the bed. "You broke my heart, Everett Anderson."

"I know," he said slowly.

She shook her head. "You just had to come all the way out here to California, didn't you?"

"At the time, I didn't have much choice."

"I know how much you miss playing, but I prayed and hoped you might finally retire and move back home. Back to me."

"Everything happens for a reason, and you were always the best thing that ever happened to me. You never gave up on me, did you?"

"I never gave up on us, Everett. Neither did you, even if you won't admit it," she said, touching his face.

"Up until now, I couldn't have given you a life. Not the kind of life you deserve."

"But any life with you was all I wanted."

"You're better than life on the road, in and out of hospitals and orthopedic clinics, and ridiculous media parties in hotel suites where party girls will do anything to get next to a starter.

You deserve a proper wedding and a big house where we can grow old with children and horses and dogs and a big green lawn in front where we can all run barefooted."

"I'd like that," she whispered, sensing the sudden excitement in his voice.

"I've always wanted to build more stables on the property, you know, with a guest house for your family, outbuildings, gardens, and more landscaping. Retire the fields and return the dirt back to the earth. Bring the place back to life, and make it a rambling southern villa."

"You used to talk like that in college. It's always been your dream, hasn't it?"

"And you were always a part of it."

She looked into his dark brown eyes, then reached up and kissed the fleshy, zipper-like scar that covered his left shoulder. "Does it still keep you up at night?"

"Not as much as being away from you," he said. "I never want you to disappear again, okay?"

"I never disappeared. Just promise you won't take off again."

"I promise. And I promise to make an effort to deserve you."

She sat up. "You've already made an insane amount of money this year. How much more do you need to just resign and start our life together?"

"Because I can't quit just yet, Shelby."

"Why not?"

He hesitated. "It's complicated."

"Admit it, you love the money."

"That's not it, not all of it."

"I just want to hear you say it."

He was quiet for what seemed like a long time, then he looked at her and smiled. "You hungry?"

She didn't answer. She searched his eyes instead for something, anything that might give her a clue that would unlock his thoughts. But there was that wall again.

"Well I'm starved," he finally said. "Why don't we dress up and go out for dinner. Lobster, caviar, champagne, the works. I'll order a limo and we'll do the town, spend some of my insane money. How does that sound?"

"I'd settle for pasta and wine on a blanket at the beach," she said softly. "As long as we're together again."

Inside her townhouse, Katherine continued to pace back and forth, unsteady, scared, alone. She looked out the window. After spotting her ex-husband at Jack's party, she remembered how he used to stalk her in Chicago after the divorce. She remembered how he would sit across the street.

"Oh, God, not again!" she cried out loud.

She phoned the police to report that her ex-husband was in town and possibly in violation of a restraining order. They said they'd send a car by later to check her place, but it was Friday night and they were busy. She was welcome to come in and file a report, they said. She slammed down the phone and poured herself another drink, pacing and continuing to chain smoke. She made one more phone call, then snorted the last of the coke.

Exhausted and drained, she finished the last of the vodka and passed out on the couch. The police drove by her place after midnight but the streets were empty and the olive green Defender parked on the street was gone.

19

The morning sun forced her eyes open as Katherine sat up, stretched, and smelled her own sweat. She'd been asleep for over twelve hours on her leather couch. With strained effort, she shook her head in a vain attempt to reconstruct last night's events in her mind. She realized she was physically intact. She looked around the familiar surroundings of her townhouse and then sank against the leather. Her back ached, her head throbbed, and her pulse pounded as she got to her feet and stumbled to the window to slowly push aside the linen drapes. The street curb beneath the oak branch was empty where the Defender had been parked.

But the headlights in her rear view mirror all the way home from Jack's came back. A Chicago judge had a restraining order against her ex-husband for his abusive behavior when they were married, and considering her panicked state, it made perfect sense. Nervous, neurotic and uncertain, she lit a cigarette and paced in her townhouse.

She poured herself a stiff screwdriver, gulping the drink. The acid in the juice burned her dry throat, but the alcohol calmed her and temporarily relieved her relentless migraine. She then searched frantically for her cocaine in all her favorite hiding places. Her bathroom, her kitchen, her living room, and her purse. She found nothing. She could barely function, much less concentrate. It hurt just to breathe. Her head throbbed when she tried to focus. Then she had a thought.

Still wearing her cotton skirt and wrinkled blouse, she hurried out to her Porsche. The dew on the morning grass felt wet and wonderful under her bare feet and she squinted her eyes, desperately trying to reach her vehicle. She was relieved to find it parked safely on the street in the shade. She unlocked the door and slid her aching body into the driver's seat and looked in the rear ashtray. She smiled and then removed the folded bindle full of white powder and stuck it into the front pocket of her blouse. She re-locked the car door and returned to her townhouse.

She changed into sweat pants and a white T-shirt and eased down onto the edge of her couch, unfolding the glossy paper that held an eighth of an ounce of cocaine. Her hands shook as she measured two long lines, rolled a bill, and hungrily snorted one of the thick lines. As she closed her eyes, the rush began to kick in within seconds. As she leaned over to finish the second rail, she immediately felt a sharp, painful burning sensation in her sinuses. The burning became worse, burrowing deeply into the soft tissue toward her brain. She dropped the bill, clutching her nose.

Blood began to pour from her right nostril through her hands and onto her white cotton t-shirt. With the speed and devastation of a lighting flash her body began to shake involuntarily. She grabbed her throat and her entire musculature cramped, stiffening in a grotesque, stroke-like convulsion. Her arms and legs locked in an uncontrollable spasm.

Her eyeballs rolled upward and she fell against the side of the couch and rolled onto the floor, desperately squirming and struggling to catch her breath. Her heart stuttered, beating in a strange, stalled rhythm. Her throat tightened. She couldn't breathe, and she couldn't scream. She clutched at her throat. Her body twitched and tensed, her jaw locked and her tongue blocked her trachea. Her sinuses swelled shut, her breathing ceased, and her eyes froze in a thousand-yard stare at the ceiling.

*

Parked outside Joe's Café in Santa Barbara was a masterpiece of Italian engineering. Even sitting still next to the sidewalk bar, the Ferrari looked like it was moving.

Joe's was loud and rowdy and packed full of UCSB college freshmen, but the attractive couple in the corner booth admiring the exotic red sports car could care less. Her long, straight, blond hair waved in the crowded, open bar as he stared into her crystal green eyes.

"I still can't believe you just walked in to a dealership and bought that car yesterday afternoon," Shelby said.

He stared off toward the bar, oblivious to the evening crowd.

"Everett .... Everett .... ?"

"I'm sorry, what?"

"I said I can't believe you just bought that car."

"The 'vette was five years old. Had to get here somehow."

"Yeah, right."

"Pretty cool, huh?"

"You want to tell me why?"

"I watched my teammates sign mega-contracts all around me for years. Mansions, super cars, even private jets. All I ever wanted was to be a part of that world."

"You know, I met other men after you dumped me," Shelby said, "but they all looked like you." She squeezed his hand three times, their little code for 'I—love—you'.

"I thought about you, too."

"So you're young and rich and you're living in beautiful southern California. You should be on top of the world, but I sense something. You're troubled."

"It's nothing, really."

"Nothing came up last night," she said

"We were a little busy last night."

She laughed. "You made love like a man just out of prison."

"And I went out on a limb this week with tens of millions of dollars. I could be wrong."

"But you made that decision based on your own good judgment, right?"

"Of course."

"If I know you, you did the right thing."

"That's just it. I thought I knew the difference between right and wrong."

"Now I'm confused," she confessed.

"The rush of trading replaced playing because my boss became my coach, and he taught me how to play a different kind of game, a game where the plays could be mathematically and logically charted. But now the one person who I thought was a genius is a person that I deeply distrust. It just feels like play money, you know, monopoly money." He reached across the table and plucked a sugar packet out of the stainless steel condiment tray. "See this little bag of sugar? It bought that Ferrari."

She stroked his hand. "Again, what's the problem?"

"I openly defied my boss and went against his professional advice in front of the whole office, which is against company rules."

"It sounds like it's a little late to worry about it now, but what's the worst thing that could happen," she said jokingly. "It's only a job, Everett."

He pictured Vasquez and Jennifer and their warnings in his mind. He didn't answer and he couldn't smile at her sarcasm.

"What are you saying?" she asked.

"What I'm saying is that this weekend, this moment, you've made me remember who I really am. I was a selfish bastard when I broke up with you. Can you ever forgive me?"

She lifted his hand to her face and kissed his jagged knuckles. "Do you have any idea what an effect you had on me back then when we first met? You were always the dreamer, and you never played it safe. And I never wanted to be the girl that tried to tie you down."

"You sat in the stands and waited for me since grade school."

"And I held my breath every time I watched you sprint across the field to catch a pass, right at the other team. And I know no girlfriend or coach or boss will ever change you. Now why don't you try to relax and order us another round of drinks. It's Saturday night, I'm ready to party, and I'm with the man I love."

20

Early Monday morning, Jack paced back and forth on his private terrace, perched high above the twinkling city. The building was located on the northwest corner of the downtown grid, facing the harbor just blocks from the airport as he stared at the planes taking off and landing in the dark.

CNN, Reuters, CNBC, Sky News, and Bloomberg were all abuzz about the international sugar market's force majeure condition in Rio de Janeiro announced that morning and the miraculous last minute weekend labor strike settlement. Concessions were finally given to the socialist rebels who had seized the loading docks with automatic weapons over the weekend. But when the light of day arrived after dozens of news crews flew in to cover the standoff, a last minute agreement was magically reached and management averted an international incident which would have crippled the ethanol, sweetner, and soft drink industry world wide.

Sugar's meteoric rise would be halted dead in its tracks now as trading would open later that morning to panic selling. Limit down. No one could sell. Continental's traders braced for the opening bell, comforting their stunned clients and dealing with a strategy of coping with what was left of their equity.

His external phone console lit up. "Mr. Diamond? You have two detectives from the San Diego police here to see you."

"Send them in."

The senior detective extended his hand as he stepped on to the terrace. "Good morning Mr. Diamond," he said. "Sorry to disturb you at your office. I'm Inspector Rogers. This is Johansen." They both flashed their badges.

"What can I do for you, gentlemen?"

"One of your employees, Katherine Fox, was found dead in her townhouse last night by her landlady. She had no next of kin and all we could find in her apartment was work related information."

"Well, she was my best manager, a real workaholic. First in and last out," Jack said, feigning remorse, folding his arms across his chest. "But this is very distressing. What happened?"

The two officers looked at one another. "We're not sure yet until the autopsy is completed," Rogers said as he removed his note pad. "When was the last time you saw her, Mr. Diamond?"

"Actually, I think the job was starting to get to her. She stormed into my home during a private party Friday night. Unfortunately, she was very drunk."

"We'll need the names of your guests, just for the record."

"Certainly."

"Was that the last time you saw her alive?"

"Of course."

"Were you aware of any drug use, Sir?"

"She used drugs?"

"Did you ever witness any drug use as her manager?"

Jack shook his head. "She did spend a lot of time in her office alone with the door closed. And she seemed a bit edgy lately, out of sorts."

"Edgy? How do you mean?"

"The timing on all this couldn't be worse, gentlemen. This morning we're in the middle of a bit of a crisis. Our company and our clients are taking a beating in the commodity markets."

"Back to Ms. Fox. Is there any reason she might want to take her life?"

Jack stopped. "We received news late last night, news which will cause Ms. Fox's clients to lose millions this morning when the markets open. It may have been too much for her to handle."

"She died Saturday night."

"She's been under a lot of stress lately. It's only a theory, of course, but it would explain a lot."

"How do you know that?"

"You see, we have indicators that tell us what the financials and futures are expecting before they open for trading. News is the biggest driver of performance and reaction in all world markets. Particularly bad news between trading sessions can positively or negatively effect how the markets trade, when they open."

"So you think she may have killed herself rather than take responsibility for some bad investment advice she may have known about in advance?"

"The stakes are very high in this business. Millions."

"Your company seems to have a high rate of suicide, Mr. Diamond. You lost an employee in Chicago last year, did you not?"

"Regrettably. Yes. Pressure does do strange things to people."

The detective handed his business card to Jack. "We'd appreciate it if you would make yourself available for questions, Mr. Diamond."

"Certainly, gentlemen. If there's anything further I can do to aid your investigation, just let me know."

Jack ushered the men out of his office as the entire trading floor was oblivious, staring at their screens waiting for sugar to open for trading.

Everett geared down from fourth to third through the shiny steel shifter gate between the tan leather bucket seats and cut his eyes to the dashboard clock for the tenth time in ten minutes. One hundred miles per hour.

He crested the freeway just north of San Diego. No turbulence in the cockpit. A remarkable absorption of vibration inside a civilized high-performance sports car that handled like a runaway bullet train.

He checked the passenger side mirror for law enforcement, shot cleanly across three lanes, feeding power to all twelve cylinders.

The decision to broom his book the previous Friday still haunted him but he managed to shove the doubt to the back of his brain all weekend, trying to savor every single second with her. He was certain he now knew what true love was supposed to be, defined as desolation when it came to saying goodbye to her. He tried to etch a lasting image of her into his mind as he sped south on I-5, passing through Oceanside to the west as the sun peeked over the mountains to the east. He checked the clock again.

The interstate was free of traffic and it took him very little time to rocket through the Los Angeles pre-rush hour traffic past Orange County so early in the morning. The car was a dream to drive. The sun was almost up and the cold morning breeze felt bracing in his face.

As he passed the Del Mar race track on his way south, his cell phone chirped in the console.

"What's up, Vinnie?"

"Dude, where are you?"

"Hey Rooster, do me a favor and call me on your cell."

"Why?"

"Just trust me."

Five seconds passed as the iPhone rang again.

"Look, I'm on my way in, Vinnie. Can you believe it! I just heard on Bloomberg radio that the Brazilian strike was settled last night. It's the biggest story of the morning! We'll clean up!"

"Everett, the cops just left the office this morning."

"Cops?"

"Yeah. San Diego police."

"What for?"

"Katherine was found dead in her townhouse this weekend."

"You're kidding."

"Wish I were, Bro. The rumor in the office is they think she overdosed on blow. Jack had a meeting about the whole thing this morning before research, right after they searched Katherine's office and found a couple of bindles with cocaine in them. Jack told us that they arrested her ex-husband, Derrick Butler, as a suspect. Apparently he's one of our floor traders in Chicago. Now they want to talk to you."

"Me? They mention why?"

"They checked her phone records and your townhouse was the last number Katherine dialed Friday night," Vinnie said. "They pegged her time of death around Saturday morning. The cops asked me about you and I told 'em you were in Santa Barbara last weekend with your college girlfriend. I know I don't need to ask you, but . . . "

"Relax. I didn't know anything about it."

He passed Claremont to the east, Pacific Beach to the west, and flew past the Mission Valley exit for Interstate 8, slowing for the downtown exit ramp.

"Everyone's talking about your sugar trade, man. Damn. How'd you know?"

"Vinnie, it was over-priced as hell. Just stupid luck."

"No shit. I'm glad I listened."

"Look, you're my back-up broker," Everett said. "Just watch my book, will you, in case someone wants to cover? And if any clients call for me, ring my cell."

"No problem. When will you be here?"

He quickly decided to continue south toward Coronado.

"I don't know. Give me another thirty minutes. Don't tell anyone you talked to me, okay?"

"Si, senor."

"How do sugar futures look this morning, pre-open?"

"Locked limit down, three cents," Vinnie said.

"I got to go."

"Hey. Take care of yourself, Bro."

Ray Hood switched off the speaker phone that had been monitoring Cozzene's wireless signal. Jack Diamond's usual poker face displayed a slight flinch, a minor twitching of the facial muscle beneath the left eye.

Bill Peterson was pouring gin over ice. "He's not stupid, Jack. He's now headed home and obviously he'll listen to the tape," Peterson said.

"Ray, send someone over to his place right away."

"Okay, but he must have it with him by now," Hood said.

Peterson glared at Hood. "You mean you didn't follow him this weekend?"

"He was in your office before he left on Friday. I've got my hands full here in town, watching the new class and the rest of the office. We can't watch every single broker, every single day, every single hour!"

Peterson gulped his drink and slammed the glass on the table. "Security's your fucking department!"

"Gentlemen," Jacks said calmly. "The only thing she could have told him on the message was that Camerone planned to end the strike on Monday," Jack said calmly. "Her little revelation died with her. We're fine."

"I still can't believe Camerone's office called and talked to *her*, of all fucking people," Peterson shouted as he downed his second drink.

"He was on a flight down to Rio for a meeting with his union people and she wasn't supposed to be in the office that late."

Hood shook his head. "Well, now Anderson's suspicious. He had Cozzene switch to his cell, and now Cozzene's confused. They could both be a problem."

"So what," Jack said, nonchalantly. "She's no longer credible. Now everyone knows she was a junkie and it changes their opinion of her. She was wasted at the party and on the tape, and she lied to protect herself. We have a house full of witnesses and we couldn't have scripted her appearance any better. That's what the cops think, and that's what I'll tell Anderson when he gets back."

Peterson poured a third gin and took a deep drink. "I don't like this, Jack. We can't keep murdering our brokers and managers. First Harper, then Walker, now Katherine?"

Jack spun around and turned a cold eye toward Peterson. "You are now ten million tax free cash dollars richer. If you don't have the stomach for hard ball, just let us know!"

"You look worried, Billy boy," Hood jabbed.

Bill leaned forward on his hands and stared at Hood. "You seem to forget who's responsible for her death."

"Don't even think about threatening me, Peterson," Hood said. "Without me, you're both lost!"

"Why didn't you check her phone, Goddamnit! You knew he shorted sugar on Friday. Why didn't your expert team of security spies follow him this weekend? Nobody's that lucky!"

"He could have checked his messages Saturday or Sunday or early this morning on the way in to work," said Hood.

A moment passed as the two stared one another down.

"Our first order of business right now is to find out exactly what Anderson knows," Jack said calmly as he watched the camera that scanned the trading floor near Vinnie's desk. "Cozzene's an idiot. I'll fire him. I'm more concerned about Valentine."

"What *about* Valentine?" Peterson asked.

"He'll roll over if he gets scared."

"We never should have told him anything, Jack. You gonna take him out, too?"

Jack slowly turned to Hood. "Don't let Anderson out of your sight, twenty-four seven from now on once he returns. He's our first priority. I'll worry about Valentine, and then Cozzene. Multiple problems are best handled one at a time."

Everett flew over the Coronado bridge, hit every green light, and parked on the curb in front of his complex.

After entering his condominium he threw his leather travel bag on the couch. It was almost sunrise as he hustled inside and re-played his messages:

Beep . . . "Everett, this is Katherine! One of Camerone Cane's sugar traders called this afternoon and told me that the labor strike in Rio will end over the weekend. But Jack didn't tell me! Now sugar will collapse on Monday and everyone will lose everything! Jack knew, Everett. He knew! God, I should have listened to you. Now someone's following me and I don't know what to do. Please call me!" . . . Beep

He drew a deep breath, looked at the time on the caller I.D., and yanked the micro-size cassette tape from the machine. He grabbed his leather travel bag, replaced another cassette, and headed to the office.

On the short drive over the bridge from Coronado to downtown San Diego Everett's thoughts turned to Katherine. His head was spinning. The whole thing had an weird, eerie feel to it. Nothing made sense. She seemed to be in top form to him. Beautiful, rich, externally full of life. Then again Jennifer appeared happy when he first met her.

He exited on to Broadway and wheeled into the executive garage at Front Street. He parked the Ferrari, entered the elevator, and checked his watch. He still had five minutes.

At first, no one noticed him as he stepped off the elevator. They were all too busy staring in disbelief as all eyes were fixed on CNN's lead story of the morning. The Brazilian labor strike standoff was on every network, cable and financial channel. The chaos and panic on the trading floor was deafening.

Everett froze in front of the large black plasma screen in the elevator lobby. As the digital clock in the lower right-hand corner of the screen ticked from 06:59 to 07:00, he stared in utter amazement as the futures price for October World raw sugar immediately plummeted three full cents on the open, locking limit down in the first second of trading from thirty-one to twenty-eight cents. No one could get in, and no one could get out. The limit move suspended trading for the rest of the day as the financial fire storm sliced through the whole office like the spiraling edge of an inbound tornado.

Everett's client book immediately grew from fifty million to over eighty million dollars in the first second of trading. He not only sold at the pinnacle of the six-month price advance on Friday, but he'd parlayed the profits into a massive short position. The premium values of the put options he and Vinnie had purchased at the end of last week for next to nothing had mushroomed to over thirty-five percent. He stood motionless in the center of the floor, staring blankly out the window. Over one-fifth of the entire company's eight hundred million dollars in sugar futures evaporated.

As the initial shock began to sink in, the chatter in the office slowly and reluctantly began again as Everett crossed the trading floor on the way to his desk.

Jennifer's desk was empty.

"I'll call you right back, Art," Vinnie said as Everett passed his trading console. He hung up when he saw his friend and rushed over to Everett's desk.

"You son of a bitch! How'd you know! Look at these pathetic chumps," Vinnie said, motioning toward the trading floor, his eyes wide and candid. "They didn't listen to you, but I did!"

Everett shook his head and tried to smile. "It hasn't sunk in yet," he said, almost listless, glancing around at the rest of the trading floor.

"Well, it has as far as your clients are concerned! Your extension's been ringing all morning. Jack wasn't very happy that you ditched research."

"He made it hard as hell for us to sell short on Friday," he whispered. "Why do you think that is?"

"Tell me about it. I had to spend half of Thursday and most of Friday getting signatures at the race track. At least I got half my clients to agree to go with me, and thank God Katherine signed my trade tickets."

Everett looked toward her office.

"You two were the only brokers missing this morning," Vinnie said. "Jack was pissed until the cops showed. You look terrible, by the way. You sleep in your clothes?"

"I need some java."

"Wait here, Pal, I'll get you some."

Everett's clients were backed up like eighteen-wheelers at an interstate weigh station as he reached his console and began returning calls, but he could feel Jack's eyes fastened onto his back as he addressed the barrage of stunned and elated clients. How could research be wrong? Worst shortage in twenty years they'd said. Twenty-five cents they'd said.

The receptionist broke through the phone system using a one-way feature that muted her voice from being heard by the client. She reminded him for the last time that Jack had a ten o'clock tee time and would like to speak right now. As he finished updating and congratulating his clients, Everett hung up the receiver and stretched.

He rubbed his eyes as his extension continued to ring. He'd postponed the inevitable long enough. "Everett Anderson."

"In my office. Now!"

He answered slowly. "Certainly, Jack."

Jack stood with his back to the door of the massive suite as Everett entered.

"Go ahead and get it over with," Everett said. "I'm too tired to fight you."

Jack wheeled around. "Were you under the impression you were fired?"

"You're not mad at my mutiny?"

"I wish I had listened to you, Champ. You were brilliant! I took a bath in my own account, you know. But you may have single-handedly rescued the entire offices' equity."

Everett tried not to laugh. "I just applied everything you taught me."

"You certainly did," Jack said as he walked around his desk and sat on the edge, danger close. "Which is why I want you to assume Ms. Fox's position."

"What?"

"You've displayed leadership and initiative. And now I need a fourth manager. You've also been assigned the Camerone Cane account."

Everett was unable to believe what his ears were telling him.

"I need an answer, Sport, if you plan to retain your trading privileges."

"Sorry Jack. I'm just tired."

"Well you better gather your strength. You've got some very happy clients holding for you who need guidance and direction right now. I suggest you calm their nerves and present a stoic image of confidence. After all, you called this sell-off like a master trader."

21

Continental's top broker returned home at sunset following a grueling but rewarding day of congratulations. As he rounded the corner and headed for his unit, he spied a dark four-door sedan parked under a tree across the street from his complex. Picking a parallel street, he slowly pulled around to the back through the alley. He parked behind the dumpster, several addresses beyond his unit and when he was certain he hadn't been seen, he eased out of the sports car and walked along the edge of the alley, entering through the rear door of his kitchen and into his den.

The place was ransacked. Furniture was upside down, leather cushions were ripped and shredded, plates were on the kitchen tile and scattered all over the floor. His compact disc collection was trashed, his computer and Bloomberg trading monitors were in pieces on the carpet, and all the papers from his desk were strewn about the living room.

"Stop right there."

Everett turned around as two men stepped from the shadows into the light cast through the open doorway. They wore surgical gloves.

"Everett Anderson?"

"Who the hell are you?"

"We're asking the questions, Son." The tallest of the two towered over him. The man extended his badge. "We're with the San Diego police department. Want to tell us where you've been all weekend?"

"Want to tell me why you're in *my* house?"

The short, stout one produced a neatly folded piece of official-looking paper. "This search warrant was our skeleton key. Now answer his question."

"Find what you're looking for?"

The tall one took over. "We suggest you cooperate with us, Mister Anderson. Your place looked like this when we walked in. Apparently someone else is looking for you as well, and I don't think they'll be as polite as us if they find you."

"Look, I've been in Santa Barbara all weekend."

"What about Friday night?"

"I stayed at the Four Seasons and drove home early this morning, before daybreak. I used my credit card all weekend and plenty of people saw me. Why are you questioning me?"

The short one held up a Ziploc bag full of cocaine. "You're coming with us, and we haven't even begun to question you."

Everett looked up from the bench in the holding cell as Victoria Vasquez marched through the precinct lobby and approached the station desk. She raised her badge and mumbled a few words under her breath to the detectives.

The duty officer pushed a button and unlocked the cell door. "Agent Vasquez? I feel safer already," Everett said as he walked out.

"Follow me," she said, reaching into her jacket and removing a long lens photograph of a tall man with a blond crew cut. "Have you ever seen this man?"

The image registered immediately. "Who is he?"

"You're positive? Look again."

"Sorry."

"His name is Raymond Hood, Jr.," she continued. "He's a real live soldier of fortune. Washed out of BUDS training in Coronado and hates the world. He's a psychopath and very violent. He's also Jack's personal bodyguard."

"I've never seen him around the office."

"You never will. He runs security for the entire company somewhere in the building, that much we know. Ray Hood is a mercenary, Anderson, and Jack's attack dog. He's been following me since I started. And he's had surveillance on you. Chances are he poisoned Katherine and rifled your place after her murder. And he probably planted the coke to set you up."

"So she didn't overdose?"

"No, she didn't. Her blood contained very slight trace amounts of succinyl-choline chloride, a neuromuscular blocking agent. It's very difficult to detect. She died a horrible, painful death. She suffocated slowly."

Everett shook his head.

"Come with me," she said as she motioned toward an open door in the precinct.

All the walls were covered with cheap wood paneling, except for the one with the large two-way mirror. Seated against the other wall was a short, overweight man dressed in a grey suit and an overcoat. What hair he had left was grey and thin and pushed to the side.

"I was sent to bail you out for a reason," Vasquez said. "I've been pulled off this case."

"What does that mean?"

"It means you're on your own right now, young man," the bald man said, extending his hand. "Everett, I'm Joseph Bailey, Deputy Director of the financial crimes enforcement network within the US Treasury Department. Please have a seat."

"Okay."

"So. You want to tell us about your top secret trading strategies?"

"What do you mean?"

"C'mon, Son. What did Jack Diamond tell you?"

"About what?"

"That the labor strike would settle and the sugar market would collapse over the weekend? Your trades on Friday were timed perfectly to profit from the Sunday night announcement."

"I analyze technical price charts and calculate their predictability. The whole market was technically overbought and extremely extended. It was pure dumb luck."

"Dumb luck or inside information?"

"Had I known in advance, I would have leveraged my family trust account, which is illiquid right now."

Vasquez handed the director a folder filled with statements. "He made over five hundred thousand in commissions for one day's work," she said. "Not bad. But it doesn't quite rise to the level of accessory."

"Maybe not, but it's got to be one of the most extraordinary coincidences in recent market history."

"And my clients made millions," Everett countered. "How come you're not questioning my employer?"

The bald man shifted his feet. "It would be a waste of time."

"So Jack's bulletproof now?"

"No. But it will take a grand jury, federal indictments, and the focused efforts of dozens of agents in my office, first of all. Diamond's wealthy enough to appeal for decades, and big enough to take on the US Attorney's office," the Deputy Director said.

"So why am I here?"

"We know Katherine Fox called you before she died. I want that micro-cassette."

"First of all, am I in any way implicated?" he asked.

"Everett, don't play games with us. You've already got Jack Diamond suspicious, and you're initiating international currency transactions for a Mexican drug lord as well. We're your only trade ticket out of this mess, and the only protection you have right now. I've had surveillance on you for weeks and Diamond's people are definitely watching you as well. In case you haven't figured it out, we're trying to save your life."

"Answer my question!" he shot back.

"Technically, yes, you're implicated. You've been set up. Diamond gave you the Camerone Cane account on purpose and since you're Camerone's broker, you're automatically dirty. But with your cooperation and testimony, we won't prosecute you. Of course, you'll have some explaining to do, but we're not interested in the brokers. You guys were just the pawns."

"And what about Camerone?"

"You return to work and go back to being a successful commodity broker. But we need information and documentation. Do all the trades you want for Camerone, in fact, churn the hell out of his accounts, and make yourself as much money as you possibly can. I personally don't care. I want Diamond, and we don't have much time."

"So Camerone's out of reach too?"

"Dealing with the Mexican government can be very difficult, politically, these days. Camerone's lined the pockets of the Federal Judicial Police *and* the Mexican Army. Plus, he's built a comfortable and legitimate reputation as an international banker and a business man. Former US politicians have been guests on his estate in Cabo San Lucas. But even with his connections to the national army, he's still an international narcotics dealer and head of the Baja cartel, and he's been laundering his drug profits through his currency trading accounts which you now manage. He prolonged the labor strike in Rio by using his union contacts in Brazil. Okay? Now then, let me ask you again. Did Katherine Fox leave you a message?"

"I've got your evidence." Mentally, he re-played the answer machine tape. He felt nauseous as he heard the sound of Katherine's desperate voice in his head. "But I think I'll hold off for now," he said.

"Anderson, don't do this," Vasquez pleaded.

"Nothing personal, Agent Vasquez."

"Everett," the deputy director said, "if you walk away today, then you're free to continue making money. But even with Vasquez on a leave of absence, we won't stop our investigation. There'll be another hotshot broker like you that will come along, and we'll go after him, or maybe one of the senior brokers will decide to do the right thing. And if that doesn't work, we'll continue until we find our man, or woman. And when that day comes, we'll come after you."

Everett rubbed his temples. "How did this happen?"

"Son, Lou Harper wanted out once he learned the truth. He was about to hand over detailed bank records, account statements, the whole shooting match. But Jack Diamond was one step ahead with powerful friends in Washington and around the world, and it's all in Continental's files, hidden in the sleepy little tourist town of San Diego, California."

"So every senior trader knows the truth?"

"Most of them, especially the big producers. They're the ones Diamond controls. They all started out just like you. Smart, aggressive, former athletes. Team players seduced by the fast money and the California lifestyle."

"Bill Peterson made it sound so easy."

"Jack Diamond's father started out in Chicago's trading pits. He started small, working for local gangsters and bookies. He grew up dirt poor on the south side and damn near killed himself building Continental from one seat on the exchange to the juggernaut it is today. Along the way he taught his only son how to shoot craps when he was only a kid. By the time Jack Diamond was seventeen, he was admitted to Harvard. Old man Diamond had finally bought his way into Ivy League respectability thanks to the political corruption machine in Chicago. And by the time the seventies rolled around, Jack Diamond scored his first big trade during the Russian wheat fiasco in seventy-two, and made his first million. Then he became unstoppable. We never could nail the old man, but I've made it my mission to arrest the son, and I'll do anything to get him. And Peterson plays along to save his own hide. But they're all pirates and murderers."

"And there's no client complaints or lawsuits?"

"Continental never screws the client, only the broker. You think you're the first broker to have his personal account seized and held hostage? Oldest trick in the book."

"How can the company continue to function? The CFTC and compliance are more strict than ever these days."

"Maybe with most retail equity firms on Wall Street, trading stocks and bonds. But commodities are a different story. The CFTC is under staffed and under budgeted."

"But the office is full of legitimate sales assistants, operations people, receptionists and floor runners, right?"

"We suspect tickets are rigged, orders are micro-managed by Diamond's insiders and input improperly using remote servers through offshore networks. With enough money, even honest, hard-working sales assistants and compliance officers can be bought. Think about it. Research is all verbal, delivered every morning under strict oversight by the senior management. Rookies are forbidden to hear the report until they graduate from training and earn a senior spot. No printed evidence of the company's recommendations ever circulates around the office. Management maintains obsessive control of all encrypted client transactions. Continental barely meets compliance with all regulations through their order routing system, which they contract out."

"How about a paper trail?"

"That's why we need you. Options and futures tickets are all hand-written, then routed to the exchanges through a complex, self-clearing international network. You've got to figure out how to get hard copies out of that building. There's no electronic order entry in place, and the brokers tape record every one of their trades after reading from a script. We think the back office doctors the live feed, time stamps the trade then shifts the burden to the broker on every single transaction. No internal compliance protection or company legal support whatsoever, and you guys don't even know it. If you get sued, you're on your own. The perfect financial storm, which is why you're brainwashed to follow research without question. Most of the staff employees are so well paid, they're too afraid to ever say anything. Diamond screws the brokers and rewards the clients, the exact opposite of every brokerage house on the planet."

Everett smoothed his hair back. "Unbelievable."

"You have a decision to make, Everett," the deputy director said. "We'll eventually shut Continental down, you can count on that, but you'll have to decide for yourself which side of the ball you want to play on, the offense or the defense."

"There's another crop of rookies starting in a month and a half. Why me?"

"Because you have less to lose than anyone there. Some of the brokers are married. You're not. Your only family is an ailing grandmother. Sorry to be so blunt, but you really are the perfect insider. You're intelligent, stubborn, and physically tough. And you're smart enough to actually pull this off. Harper got nervous, Walker got careless, and Katherine Fox just got caught up. You're not only our best shot, Son. You're our only shot."

22

When he arrived for work the next morning at 5 A.M. and approached his trading desk, Everett discovered that his computer and all his client files had been moved into one of the corner offices—Katherine Fox's former office. The view was spectacular as the stars sparkled to the east over the mountains before sunrise. But he couldn't help but notice the irony. Her office occupied the southwest corner of the building's floor plan, facing National City along Imperial Beach south, toward Mexico.

He walked in and slowly looked around. "Everett, the limousine's waiting downstairs," Jennifer announced through his speakerphone. "How do you like your new office?"

Before he could answer, John Valentine burst through the door behind him. "What the hell are you doing staring out the window? We've got work to do!"

Everett turned with a frown. "Come again?"

"Jesus," John whined. "Jack didn't tell you?"

"Tell me what."

"You're so busy taking time off after your miracle trade that you forgot about your first trip to Cabo?"

"Cabo?"

"You're killing me. Jack gave you the Camerone Cane account?"

"And?"

"And don't you think it might be nice to actually *meet* the company's biggest client in person and try to explain to him how we lost almost twenty million of his pesos in sugar?"

"Alright."

"Plus you get to bust your cherry, Sport. First trip on the Gulfstream. Besides, I'm looking to land some sweet blond tuna for myself while we're down there. Spring Break in Cabo San Lucas *and* Land's End? Hot and cold running California coeds."

"John, you two had better get going," Jennifer urged through the phone. "And Everett, I just hired two new sales assistants for you. Good luck on your trip."

Everett's assistants appeared immediately in the doorway behind Valentine. "Here is the paperwork for all of Camerone Cane's offshore corporate custodial accounts," said the tall blond as she handed John two briefcases and several bound folders.

"I've got the custodial paperwork!" John shouted. "I need the annuity and trust documents!"

"I have the trust papers," said the short red head.

"Great. Now go find the annuity transfer docs! Jesus! And where are the defined benefit account contracts?"

The tall one dug through the multiple stacks of account statements and other company papers on Everett's new desk, fishing out the proper documents as the short one rushed through the trading floor. "Anything else, Mister Anderson?"

"Yeah, bring me a Bloody Mary," Valentine barked. "And just make sure you find us the insurance paperwork. We make ten points on the annuity rollovers. Do the math!"

"Right away, Mister Valentine."

An hour and a half later, the G650 began its descent toward a narrow sliver of black asphalt carved deep in the desert canyon floor approximately ten miles north of San Jose del Cabo. Palm trees and cactus lined the private airstrip against the Sea of Cortez as the wheels touched down and the turbo engines on each wing were reversed, jolting John from his morning nap. They taxied into a small hangar with no tower and no runway personnel.

As the jet rolled to a stop, Everett heard Spanish and watched the cabin door swing open. The crew was escorted off the plane.

"Looks like the welcoming committee," John said. "Sit tight."

Everett watched as John disappeared through the doorway. Minutes later he was back. "At least our limo's here, Ace. Grab your shit and meet me on the runway."

Everett gathered the documents, loaded them into the leather briefcase and stepped onto the metal stairs. The hot, wet air hit him immediately. But the sprawling compound of white stucco buildings was incredible, reflecting the morning sun against the jagged geography beside the turquoise blue water. The air was humid and sticky and he loosened his tie, releasing the starched collar from his neck.

John was on his cell as Everett fell into the back seat of the waiting limousine, directing the air conditioning vent toward his face. "What do you mean he's not here yet? We made a special trip and we need signatures, Juan! Fine. Perfect. We brought multiple powers-of-attorney as well as the trust docs. *Mucho gracias.*" John snapped the phone shut. "He flew to Rio for God's sake, at the last minute, but his son Juan Carlos will meet with us. At least he's a signatory."

"Something about this trip seemed ill-fated from the beginning."

"At least it wasn't a wasted trip," John said. "We'll get plowed at the villa, have dinner in town, and fly back tonight."

As the sun began to set on the tip of Baja, one of the small hangar's doors opened slowly and four soldiers dressed in camouflage fatigues walked through. Their brown skin shone in the humidity as fifteen large metal suitcases were removed from the Gulfstream's cargo hold by four more dark-skinned locals with pistols on their belts.

One of the Brazilian mercenaries motioned to the Mexican Federal Police officer and all fifteen suitcases were off-loaded. "Rapido! Rapido!"

"One million each?" Hood barked.

"*Si.*"

"Did you count it!" the soldier demanded.

"*Si*. All in pesos."

"Get it loaded, then," Hood directed. "*Rapido!*"

23

Jack and another man were seated behind Everett's desk as research wound to a close. Everett noticed an extensive array of electronic equipment in his new office.

"How was your trip, Ace?"

"I guess I expected a little more than being stood up from my new client. Did you not know he was in Brazil?"

"Mister Anderson, I'd like you to ask your team to step into your new office, beginning with Miss Vasquez."

"Any particular reason?" Everett asked calmly.

"I have reason to believe we have a traitor in our midst."

"Meaning?"

"Meaning I'd like to test everyone's loyalty this morning. Turns out some one we both know is hiding a secret."

"Time out."

"Would you call Miss Vasquez in, please?"

"Dumb move, Jack."

"What did you just say to me?"

"It's politically incorrect."

"And?"

"And the first broker you want to polygraph is a woman?"

"I'm not choosing Vasquez because she's female, Mister Anderson. She's the hottest broker in this office right now, beside yourself, and I want to know why. You're next by the way."

"You can't test Vasquez or Cohen or Washington or any of my Jewish, black, Hispanic or female brokers. If you appear to make this little exercise in paranoia personal, you'll destroy the whole office's faith in you. And after the debacle in sugar, I don't think you want that."

Heads were indeed turning and eyes were carefully surveying the meeting through the offices' glass windows. The trading floor was watching.

Jack slowly walked to the desk and carefully closed the stainless-steel suitcase that held the testing equipment. He leaned over and whispered into the ear of the testing professional. They quickly shook hands and the man left.

The office returned to work and Everett breathed a sigh of relief, starting toward the door.

"Mister Anderson, we're not finished yet. Close the door," Jack instructed as he sat at an angle to Everett and spoke without looking up. "Mister Cozzene's production has fallen substantially since he followed your sugar trade. He's been coasting."

"I'll speak to him."

"While you're speaking to him, fire him."

"What?"

"You heard me. Fire him. He's on your team and he's late again today. You've been carrying him since the first quarter of this year."

Everett narrowed his eyes. "If you have something to say to me, Jack, spit it out. Don't pretend to try and manipulate another broker's fate to get to me."

"Either fire Cozzene or I'll fire you," Jack said. "Time to choose sides."

Everett pounded on the front door of Vinnie's Solana Beach cottage. Then he knocked again. The rundown cliff-side beach shack was being remodeled and construction debris littered the porch.

San Diego's recent real estate explosion had benefited many in the county, but none more so than those whose property was situated close to the ocean. Vinnie had purchased the beach relic years before and was the lucky recipient of a rising real estate tide that lifted all boats. But the recent mortgage meltdown and plummet in prices stopped the real estate market dead in its tracks.

Everett knocked a third time and heard some noise inside as the first glow of morning light warmed the surrounding canyon walls. Vinnie frowned in his boxers, squinting in the half-light. "I know. I'm late. Give me a minute to get dressed, will you?"

Everett walked past his friend through the den and entered the cluttered kitchen, staring at the ocean through the gapping roughed-out opening over the sink that would become a picture window at some time in the future. "You know how you always taught me that the best water is early in the morning?" Everett asked over his shoulder.

Vinnie shuffled into the kitchen. "Yeah?"

"So this morning I feel like surfing."

Vinnie's face perked up. "You? Mister team player, employee of the month? Cool."

They had their coffee on the porch as sea gulls honked overhead and Vinnie lit a joint as the coastline clouds rolled in. Everett pulled a bottle of tequila out of his backpack and took a deep drink.

"You okay?" Vinnie asked. "I've never seen you drop your guard like this before work."

"I don't feel much like working this morning," Everett said.

"No shit, Bro. The pressure's starting to show, even on you."

"What? I'm only twenty-seven."

"That's almost forty in broker years."

"Well, I wouldn't worry about going much further with the remodel if I were you, Rooster."

"What are you talking about?"

Everett looked at his friend. "Man, you're fired."

"You're kidding me, right?"

No response.

"You're not kidding, are you?" Vinnie asked.

"There's nothing I can do. Your numbers are down."

Vinnie hit the tequila bottle, hard. "Actually, I'm relieved. He wants to squeeze me out, fine. I'm out. I've been ready to quit anyway. I got a couple hundred thousand in the bank thanks to you, equity out the ass in the house, and a baby on the way. I'm ready for a break. I'll give you all my clients, Bro. You're the one I'm worried about."

"I'll kick you back my commissions," Everett said.

Vinnie nodded in agreement.

"You still in the mood to surf this morning?" Everett asked.

"With this weather and these swells? Hell yeah. How about Swami's?"

"I'm in the mood for Coronado."

"Why?"

"In the Spring hurricane season when south Pacific swells miss the rest of San Diego, Outlet is the place to be."

"Now you're learning."

They were quiet for most of the trip south. The city was just waking up and thick clouds hung over the business district, creating an orange canopy that reflected the sun rising to the east. Vinnie parked the convertible between two vehicles and turned off the engine.

"Hang on for just a second," Everett said as he scanned the incoming wave sets that melted into the sand as the morning light began to filter through the cloudy haze.

A few surfers paddled out as the light began to grow. The surfers bobbed between the kelp on the incoming waves as Everett raised a set of binoculars to his eyes. Slowly, he worked his way along the surf zone, squinting and struggling to focus on the individual features of each of the surfers. Everett shook his head to clear his vision, spotting something. Isolated at the south end of the beach, wearing a black wet suit, lying flat on his board, was a muscular figure with a bright yellow crew cut, glowing against a sun-burned face.

"There he is."

Vinnie reached for the field glasses as Everett pointed to the south. "I'll be damned," Vinnie confirmed, sliding down in his seat and then returning the binoculars. Vinnie shifted in the shotgun seat. "You didn't want to surf in the first place, did you?"

"I saw him at Windansea once, so he seems to like the morning waves with the least traffic."

Before the water got too crowded or the sun got too bright, the surfer had apparently gotten a full workout and waded back to the beach, hurrying up the sand to the back of the dunes. Everett and Vinnie watched him as he quickly dressed, climbed into an olive green Defender and pulled onto the Strand, merging into the morning traffic leaving Coronado.

"Let's go," Everett said as Vinnie kept his distance in the convertible. Following through Orange Avenue, past the toll gates and on to the Coronado Bay bridge, they kept the Defender in sight as it sped over the bridge.

Downtown San Diego sparkled on their left as they remained several cars back, well below the speed limit tucked into the morning merge. The Defender sped through the S-curve that wound past downtown, exiting at Broadway.

Their traffic light changed green, just as the Defender stopped and parked in the small adjacent lot, hidden in the alley behind the California Empire Bank building. They caught a quick glimpse of the blond crew cut hurrying through the mechanical door of the building's rear façade.

Vinnie looked at Everett. "What in the hell just happened?"

"I'll be damned. He does works in our building."

"Who is he?"

"Jack's body guard."

"How do you know?"

"You don't want to know."

"Man, this is creepy."

"Oh yeah. And he's a real nasty piece of work, too. Jack's head of security. Wonder what Jack would say if he knew the asshole blew his cover because he didn't want to share his wave with me my first morning out."

"Don't let me forget to thank you for firing me."

"You're welcome," Everett said as his cell phone rattled in his pocket. "Hello."

There was silence on the other end.

"Hello?" he said again.

"Everett, it's Shelby," she said slowly.

He smiled, relieved to hear the comfort of her sweet voice. "I bet you're mad at me for not calling. Look, I've been swamped, baby. I promise to.."

"It's Virginia, Everett. She suffered another stroke and they moved her back to the hospital. She's stable, but you better get home tonight."

He checked his watch. "I'll be on the next plane."

"I'm home for the weekend. I'll drive to Memphis and pick you up at the airport. Please hurry."

24

Shelby was waiting for him by baggage claim. She ran into his arms and he held her without letting go, oblivious to the crowded terminal surrounding them. Her hair was different now, shorter. And she was tan.

"She's been asking about you all night. She refuses to take her medicine until she sees you."

"It'll take us at least another hour to get to the Delta."

"Then we better get going," she said as she took his hand and led him to her car parked in the short-term lot.

They didn't talk much for most of the trip. She was afraid to ask too many questions and he was so deep in thought that the miles ticked away without notice. By the time they drove south and turned west on state highway 82 that led past Greenwood and took its drivers deep into the Mississippi Delta, it started to rain. The weather seemed to match the mood as they finally reached the Sunflower County Medical Center at two-thirty in the morning.

"Virginia Anderson," Everett asked at the nurse's station.

"Intensive care. Second ward."

The ICU was so bright and noisy Everett wondered how anyone could possibly rest or recover in such a cold, sterile, inhuman environment. He hated hospitals, spending his fair share in and out of them. Machines were beeping, pumps were wheezing and churning, and back in the corner, tucked away between a respirator and a kidney dialysis machine was his grandmother, propped up and dozing.

A heavy-set nurse stepped in front of him as he entered the small ward. "Can I help you?"

"I'm here to see my grandmother."

"Are you Everett?"

He nodded.

"I'm not supposed to do this, but follow me."

She pulled back the sheer curtain and motioned them into the corner where Virginia's bed was. "Maybe now she'll agree to rest," the nurse sighed.

Everett reached out and took Virginia's hand. It was cold and limp, with a large IV drip line inserted in her arm. He gently squeezed her hand and leaned over to kiss her on the forehead.

Her eyes opened slowly, as he straightened up and smiled. "I just knew you'd come," she whispered as the nurse handed her two pills and a cup of water.

"Are you giving your doctors a hard time?"

Tears streamed from her eyes. "I'm so very sorry, Everett."

"Sorry? For what?" he frowned.

"I've been so careless. Now I'm the one who has let you and our whole family down. Can you ever forgive me?"

Everett touched her face. "Virginia, it's not your fault. No one can help being sick. You're going to be fine. I'll stay with you as long as I need to."

She glanced at Shelby, who was now crying. "He doesn't know does he?"

Shelby shook her head slowly. "I didn't tell him yet," she sobbed.

"Tell me what?" Everett asked. "Why are you both crying?"

Virginia took his hand and held it to her face, then kissed his scarred knuckles. "The doctors found cancer, but that's not the worst part," she said with more tears. "Five men showed up at the house yesterday. They wanted to buy the property and turn it into a hunting camp. When I told them it wasn't for sale, the leader practically put the pen in my hand, and said he'd kill you if I didn't sign. That's the last I remember."

"Blue brought her in," Shelby said, "after she was pushed from the porch."

His heart pounded. "What did he look like?"

"He was a large man, with short blond hair cut square."

Everett shook his head. "Son of a bitch."

"Do you know him?"

"I know who he is. Listen, it's all right," he said with a clenched jaw. "We'll figure it out together."

"There's nothing left to figure out, Everett. It's all gone. Those men are probably still at the house now. They told me not to call the police, or they'd come back and kill you."

"You didn't sell, right?"

"I honestly don't remember," she cried. "The equipment we own is falling apart, and lease rates are sky high these days. We also had a bad case of rust on our plants this season and the chemical fungicide is so very expensive. I haven't bothered you with any of the details."

"Don't you think it's important for me to know?"

"You've been so busy trying to start a new career and have your life back again. Last year you were in Dallas and this year you were injured, so I guess I just wanted to shield you from the woes of our little farm. I have to borrow against the value every season and we're still behind. After everyone was paid this past year, we actually lost money."

"Listen to me," he said. "Everything will be fine. Don't worry. You just get some rest right now."

The medication began to kick in as her breathing was labored and abrupt. She reached for his neck, slowly closing her eyes. "The well, Everett," she whispered. "The well.."

He wiped his brow with the dirty sleeve protecting his right arm from the relentless sun. The August heat was almost unbearable. Flies and mosquitoes buzzed around his ears as waves of heat vapor rose from the rich black dirt. The sweat stung his eyes and dripped on to the ground as he stomped his foot. "Get up!" he grunted, urging the exhausted mule along by snapping the leather reigns across its' haunches which in turn connected directly across to his own sore shoulders.

The sturdy beast obeyed in fits and stalls, pawing at the dirt, then lurching the heavy iron plow forward through the soft black earth, then suddenly refusing to take another step.

He could easily understand the animal's impulse to resist, to rebel, to revolt inside. He could feel the familiar anger, smoldering so long he could no longer bear the memory, but the memory would not go away. It haunted him. It moved him to action in all things. In an effort to ignore the pain, it drove him daily to measure and calculate and record the daily operations of the sprawling, struggling farm in a vain effort to control the uncontrollable. He watched the quill pen dip into the inkwell, then scratch down number after number in the neatly recorded ledger resting on the old mahogany plantation desk. The inkwell began to gush with blue ink, which filled the room and washed over him. Then he was underwater, drowning. And sharks were chasing him. He paddled desperately, chasing the wave rolling across the surface above him. He willed his arms forward as he pulled himself through the active water and stood on his board, surfing the crest of an enormous ocean wave. He could see the sharks embedded in the water, following the wave. Surrounding him was a blue curving wall of water, inside the tube as the wave broke overhead, a perfectly round opening that began to narrow as the wave pushed him through the tube toward daylight. He tried to increase his speed, but the wave was in charge, decelerating his momentum toward the round opening at its own pace. He was just a few feet away, but the opening continued to close without him.

Gravity then pulled him backwards, forcing him back down the perfectly round tunnel. He could see the blue green walls around him. He tried to grasp the sides of the perfect tube, to stop his descent, but the concave walls were slick with algae and mold. He looked up and saw the hole growing smaller, closing in on itself, the light shrinking. He was falling down a hole, and no one knew he was there. He was all alone, certain he'd never be found.

"Mister Anderson," the nurse said softly, nudging his shoulder.

Everett opened his eyes and sat up in the aluminum armchair where he'd been snoozing.

"I'm sorry to wake you," she said, gently. "She's being moved to a private room."

Shelby knelt next to him. "She'll be fine. I'll keep an eye on her for you. Don't worry."

"I should have taken better care of her, and handled her affairs. I should have been here for her."

"Everett," Shelby said as she hugged him. "It's not your fault either."

"She begged me to move back home, and work in Memphis," he said, his voice cracking. "None of this would have ever happened if I hadn't been so selfish."

"That's not true."

"I bought that ridiculous car and I've been chasing my own greedy dreams clear across the country, while everything I've ever wanted or needed has been right here all long, just waiting for me." He gently touched the side of Virginia's wrinkled face, then bent down and kissed her on the cheek. "Now maybe she can rest," he said.

Shelby stood next to him with her arm around his waist. "Please let me help you," she offered, wiping the tears from his cheeks. "We'll need to run by the house and pick up some things for her. Her nurse said she'll need to stay here for at least the week."

"You're incredible. How did I ever manage to live this long without you?"

"Now you don't have to anymore."

25

The sun was rising behind them as she drove him toward home. Shelby said nothing, just as she'd given him room on the trip from Memphis. As they passed the outskirts of the modest little town he'd grown up in, he scanned the historic brick buildings, renovated warehouses, updated rail station, and the ante-bellum homes, recently painted bright white with green shingle roofs against the fresh black asphalt. Casino money had launched the state into an historic revival unprecedented in decades. And now his generation was moving into the hundred year old homes and investing in their future. Suddenly the Delta was the place to be in the state.

"Do me a favor and stop at the top of the hill just before you reach the main gate," he asked.

She nodded and smiled sweetly. As they crested the hill, she pulled to the gravel shoulder and parked under the long low branch reaching out like a great arm attached to the mature oak that guarded the road. He got out and pushed past the thick brush, looking through the tall grasses surrounding the entrance that had grown along the perimeter fence. There was a large padlock on the front gate, and five high-performance, off-road, four-wheel-drive vehicles were parked at the end of the driveway, covered with mud and circled in front of the grand old house he grew up in.

"What would you do, I mean, if it is too late?" she asked.

"I guess the answer is I really don't know," he said, shaking his head and staring across the green, rolling five acre vista that separated the main house from the county road. "I'd always dreamed of settling down back here, after I got tired of playing, accepting the knowledge she wouldn't live for ever. I just thought I'd have more time with her."

"She knew you had to travel most of the year, and she would plan all year long for your homecoming every Spring in the off season. And, oh how she talked about you when you played. Bragging about you around town, and especially at church. If you'll let me help you get through this, I will."

He squeezed her hand. "You don't want any part of my life right now."

"I wish you'd stop trying to protect me. I was raised an Air Force brat, you know that. I adapted just fine to every new school in every new town until my Dad was transferred to Mississippi when I was a teenager. I can take of myself."

"That's what I've always loved about you," he said softly.

"Then why don't you tell me what's really going on?

"Why are those men at your house?"

He looked right at her. "You really want to know?"

She nodded and squeezed his hand again.

"Well for starters, The United States Treasury Department is investigating my employer."

"What exactly do they want?"

"They want me to help them shut the place down."

"Everett! Are you doing something illegal?"

"No. No. Not at all! I'm not. I would never break the law. I'd resign first. I'm a federally licensed commodity broker and I've never taken advantage of a single client, even the ones that gave me full discretionary trading power."

"So what's the problem?"

She hung on every word as he explained how his coach set up his interview after rehab, referred by Ham Walker, followed by Walker's hunting accident. He talked about the margin call on his trust account, then Katherine's suspicious overdose. He told her about Lou Harper's alleged suicide and everything Vasquez had told him along with his meeting with the deputy director, and the trades he'd already placed for Camerone.

"So that's why you were acting so strange in Santa Barbara?"

He nodded.

"And now you can't walk away, can you?" she asked.

"If I do, I'll lose the trust and my future, that's for sure. But if I rat out the company, I'd be sentenced to life in Montana or Iowa or Rhode Island under some witness protection personal prison. And if I do nothing and keep working, they threatened to arrest me at some time in the future."

She paused. "Well, whatever you decide, I want to stand with you."

"I could never ask you to give up your life and trade it for an uncertain future with me. No way."

"My father was shot down in Iraq and I'm an only child. It's just me and Momma now."

"Shelby, you're too young and this has been a very confusing year. Somehow along the way I made some real bad decisions, and I lost my way. I'm not about to pull you into this mess with me."

"You still don't get it, Everett. You're not like any man I've ever known. You take chances and you're an explorer, and sometimes explorers get lost. Let me help you find your way home."

"That's way too much for me to ask."

"But I trust your instincts, and I believe in you."

"Unless I gather hard evidence for them, the US government will be after me forever and they don't stop looking, not to mention my boss and his cronies. It'll be next to impossible to get out of the office with any kind of documentation, which is what they want from me. The place is a fortress. I'd be on the run with nowhere to hide and no money. Five years in the league and nothing to show for it. Without my trust, I'm broke."

"Wall Street is full of scandals these days, Everett. If you help them shut down a corrupt company, then they'll protect you, right?"

"Doesn't work that way."

"Wouldn't they give you some kind of reward for risking your life?"

"Not hardly."

She paused. "What if we ran away, together I mean?"

"Look, you've got a career and family back here. I could never ask you to give all of that up. I don't know if I'll end up dead or in jail, or both. No."

"I know I'm not about to give up on you. You have this very special family history. It was all Virginia talked about while I was sitting with her before you arrived. Fight for it! She whispered it to you, Everett. The well? What does that mean?"

"She was delirious."

"What well is she talking about?"

"My great grandfather drilled a water well on the western outskirts of our original deed close to the river. It took him months to hit an aquifer, but that water source kick-started his soybean crop and lasted for over one hundred years. But eventually, the source was polluted by pitch."

"What's pitch?"

"A nasty, smelly, raw crude oil tar that bubbled up from the well. It had to be sealed off. My Dad rolled the dice and drilled an oil well, west of the main house right next to the water well. He had this crazy dream but went broke drilling for oil in this part of the state in the Seventies. He was close, but he never recovered much oil. It was just a small deposit that didn't last, and it broke his heart and ruined our acquifer. By the time I was born, it was not exactly a campfire story for the family."

"What if there's a connection there?"

Everett froze. "I can't believe I didn't think of it earlier."

"What?"

"Can you keep a secret?"

"I love secrets."

"When I was home for Thanksgiving, she started telling me this story about my great grandfather and Confederate gold bars."

"Gold. Like real gold?"

"Maybe."

"Then you've got to check that well, Everett."

"How about tonight?"

"What can I do?" Shelby asked.

"Find us a cheap motel on highway eighty-two with sturdy door locks. I need to sleep first. If you're up for it, we could come back late tonight and look around."

"Don't tease me."

"I like the way you think, Shelby Ford. There was always something wild about you, underneath that cheerleader outfit. I couldn't quite put my finger on it in college, but-"

"You were just too busy to notice."

"You're right. By the way, this may sound crazy but we just might be safe in Mexico."

"Mexico?"

"My client, the cocaine tycoon, happens to live there."

"Now you're the one who's delirious."

"Maybe he'll hire me to trade for him. We could make a run for the border if things break bad in San Diego. You up for that?"

"If you find buried treasure, then you won't need your trust. We could run away, and travel the world. They'll never find us and eventually they'll give up."

"No they won't."

"Frankly, I'm tired of living a safe vanilla life in the sheltered South. And now that you're back in my life, I don't want you to disappear again. And if that means helping you, then let's be bad, Everett, like desperate fugitive expatriates."

"I hate being a broker anyway. Biggest collection of divorced bipolar alcoholic drug addicts I've ever seen. Worse than the NFL."

She looked directly in to his eyes. "I believe in you, Everett Anderson. Ever since you were a teenager you were always this good-looking football player from the big house outside of town. All the girls talked about you and all the boys wanted to be your best friend. You drove fast cars and rode motorcycles to school and everybody called you dangerous. You got away with everything in high school, and you rescued me and taught me about the world."

"You're crazy. You know that, don't you?"

"Yeah. Crazy for you."

"First things first," he said as reached for his iPhone and started dialing.

After two rings the signal connected. "I told you never to call me unless it's an emergency," Vasquez scolded.

"I think this qualifies," Everett snapped. "My family's been threatened, and now Hood's occupying my house!"

"Unfortunately, I know all about it."

"You have got to be kidding. Why didn't you tell me?"

"Because I can't."

"Why not?"

"I'm in the middle of an immense federal investigation that has already cost millions of taxpayer dollars. At some point, we need a return on our investment. My hands are tied right now."

There was a long silence.

"Are you still there?" she asked.

"What if I agree to help you?"

"Look, he's making this personal for a reason. Don't you see that? He's trying to draw you offsides. If we suddenly storm in to rescue you and your grandmother, we blow ten months of surveillance, hundreds of man hours and case work, not to mention spooking every entity involved. You need to practice some restraint. You are very much outmatched right now."

"I don't exactly have the luxury of patience right now."

"Then let me do my job and whatever you do, do *not* go near your house. He *will* kill you."

There were no streetlights in the most remote rural dirt roads that crisscross the Mississippi Delta. Lights attract bugs and other curious creatures.

By midnight the lights were still on at the main house, but the loud music and drinking and shooting had stopped. Law enforcement was rarely called out to such a remote location for simple firearm discharge. Of course, all shots fired in the air would eventually land somewhere, but those rounds were of little concern to the newest members of the Buck and Wing Limited Hunting Club as they partied behind the new wooden gate.

Shelby stopped the rental car a quarter mile west past the main entry gate as Everett pointed to the north side of the road. "Pull over there, under that old pecan tree," Everett said as he hopped out of the passenger seat dressed in black jeans and a black long-sleeved t-shirt. "I used to ride my dirt bike on the trails by the old well. It's the best place to hunt on the whole acreage because quail and pheasant love to roost in the tall grass surrounding a large stand of oak trees between the house and the well. Besides, the opening was boarded up decades ago and you wouldn't know it existed if you didn't know exactly where to look."

He opened the rental's trunk, snaking the thick, black nylon rope around his shoulders and tucking it under his right arm. Next he pushed his thick arms through a large black mountain backpack, reinforced with heavy duty webbing and a lightweight metal frame strong enough to carry over a hundred pounds of gear and food. He tightened down the padded straps and laced up his parachute jump boots with heavy, jagged rubber soles.

"You look like G.I. Joe," Shelby teased.

"Count on Wal-Mart to stock everything your weekend warrior needs for a little night reconnaissance mission." He handed her one of the small hand-held walkie talkies. "Turn your dial to five and ease the volume down to one. We'll need to communicate while I'm in the hole and you're topside."

"How do I look?" she asked.

"Like the sexiest female commando I've ever seen," he said as he spread the barbwire to allow her easy access through the perimeter fencing. "Once we get to the well," Everett instructed, "stay in the woods and only whisper into your mouthpiece. Don't talk at a normal tone because sounds can carry for miles out here at night. We'll be much closer to the main house at that point.

Plus, there's no wind tonight so everything is still and quiet. We want it to stay that way."

She raised her walkie talkie. "God, you turn me on," she whispered into the mouthpiece.

"There'll be time for that later."

"Yes, sir," she said, returning a salute.

They walked for a full half hour, carefully dodging the thorny vines and pointed, dry brush that grew thick in this neglected section. Everett navigated like a hunting guide, avoiding the downed tree limbs and other overgrowth, winding his way down game trails towards the well in the dark guided by a flurry of childhood memories. Cowboys and Indians with the farm kids across the road, deer hunts and dove shoots when he was a teenager. *Six hundred acres is a lot of dirt.* California was so dense and compact, with ever square inch at a huge premium. But out here, in the sweet, cool wetness of a Mississippi autumn night, his throat tightened as he thought of Virginia and his legacy.

He stopped on the edge of a small thicket and squatted down, pointing to the small clearing overgrown with thick salt grass and vines. "There it is," he whispered, his face shiny with sweat. "Stay in the trees."

"Be careful," she whispered in his ear.

He turned and kissed her. "Remember, whisper only. And if you see some thing or some one that's so close you can't use your voice, then click three times on the talk button. Then wait a few seconds and do it again. That tells me you can't speak. You're my eyes up here, okay?"

"Okay."

He crossed the clearing quickly and quietly, then dropped to his knees. Crawling through the waist-high grass, his gloved hand felt along the ground, drawn toward the horrible smell. As the stench became stronger, he fumbled in the dark until he could feel the round concrete edge of the stone cylinder flush to the ground. Wild, thorny vines and kudzu had engulfed the wooden planks nailed over the opening. He drew a hunting knife from his belt and carefully carved an opening. There was a small gap in the rotten planking and he was able to pry open a large enough space to crawl through.

The mosquitoes were out in force and buzzed in his ears, but a brief breeze brushed them away against his face as he unwrapped the rope and began tying one end to the iron support embedded deep in the ancient mortar that once held a metal frame for a bucket and a crank.

After knotting a sturdy anchor, he pushed away the vines and grass and threw the nylon rope down the dark shaft. Eventually he heard a soft thud and glanced toward the house to make sure he wasn't seen, or heard. He carefully eased his body over the hard edge of the well and gripped the rope with both hands. The smell was overwhelming as he tried not to cough. Although the walls of the well were covered in more vines, he was able to descend fairly easily.

Once he'd cleared the opening, he stopped and removed a glow stick from his pocket and snapped it like a carrot, bringing the pencil-size fluorescent tube to life. He tossed it down the shaft until he watched it strike bottom. The shaft was overgrown with moss and vines and kudzu had forced itself through the rotted mortar cracks in the curved brick, engulfing the walls of the shaft. He would need another fifty feet to reach the base of the fast growing vine but until then, the walls were rough and rocky enough to momentarily rest his boot on. *Sealing the walls of the well, brick by brick in the hot Delta sun. Tough work.* Virginia's was a life committed to continuing the legacy. What would he find? A hole filled with dirt? Nothing but a dried up, stinking water well?

"Everett, are you all right?" she whispered.

He stopped, wrapped the rope twice around his left wrist and used the other hand to press the handheld clipped to his shirt pocket. "I'm halfway down. Everything all right up there?"

"I thought I heard something, but it's probably just a squirrel."

"Try not to talk unless you have to."

As he passed the top of the kudzu, his descent required more effort, avoiding the thick, leafy runners that clung to the walls. Contact created more noise as he tried to slide down the rope without touching the walls. He could see the soft glow of the florescent coming closer.

His eyes began to burn. Ten more feet. Then five.

Waist deep in brush and leaves, he could feel the viscous, slimy ooze beneath his boots. As he pushed the debris and stinking pitch to one side, he picked up the light to make sure he wasn't sharing the shaft with an unwelcome visitor. With the exception of a small green lizard that disappeared into the kudzu, he was sure the brush and sticks were free of snakes or scorpions or stinging spiders.

"click, click, click."

His attention quickly shifted from the chameleon.

"click, click, click."

There it was again.

Smart girl.

"click, click, click."

She held down the button so he could hear her breathing.

*

Jack recognized the caller i.d. and picked up after one ring. "Yeah."

"We have a little problem," Hood announced.

"What is it?"

"We get hack attempts all the time into our main trading database portal. During our background checks for the new rookie class, one of my best hackers discovered a little nugget of information. He used to work IT security for the US Border Patrol and he likes to use a file he compromised from their HR department as his gateway to the larger federal databases."

"Get to the point."

"Anyway, we always cross reference our existing employees whenever we run backgrounds for the new rookies and he stumbled onto a Victoria Vasquez listed on an obscure personnel file. Her social doesn't match, but her age is damn close."

"What branch?"

"We don't yet know what department, it's still being encrypted, but we do know she's paid through a government payroll service. It could be a coincidence, or someone really screwed up."

"I fucking knew it!"

"FBI, DEA, Marshal service maybe?"

"Doesn't really matter at this point now does it? We've survived hostile takeovers in the Eighties and more than one undercover attempt in the Nineties. Hell, the feds hounded my old man for years, but he always got tipped off."

"This is serious, Jack."

"I've got more important things on my mind, like a twenty million dollar S&P 500 trade working for me here in Chicago. Who did she speak to most of the time?"

"She kept to herself around the office and had no friends. A real bitch."

"There's got to be a connection with someone."

"I watched her making out with Anderson one morning in the parking garage, but didn't think anything about it."

"Man, that guy gets around."

"Our surveillance catches brokers and staff together all the time. The fire escape is a favorite rendezvous spot after a big payday."

"But Anderson's no team player," Jack said.

"I tried to warn you, Jack. He's a loner."

"Was she onboard before Harper went off the reservation?" Jack asked.

"Yeah, *and* she worked in the Chicago branch at the time."

"Go back, drill down, and re-check all the accounts she opened to earn her transfer out to San Diego. I knew I should have polygraphed her!"

"I was planning to hunt this weekend."

"That'll have to wait, Ray. Anderson's farm is all yours now. You'll have plenty of time later to hunt. Is your group watching him while he's away from the office?"

"We're all holed up at his farm, but this is supposed to be their vacation. Hell, he'll be at the hospital for days with the old hag."

"Goddamnit! You don't take vacations! He's our top liability right now. Stay on him, and call your network. We must have missed something."

"If he's at all connected to Vasquez, I could take him out when he gets back to San Diego. We've made all the money we're going to off of him. I'll make it look like he's depressed now that he's lost everything."

"Perfect."

"Then I'll bring the jet back this afternoon, but this time it'll cost you two million, cash. Anderson's confirmed on an Aero Mexico flight down to Cabo Friday afternoon out of Lindberg Field."

"I'll have good funds at the Banco de Mexico branch in Cabo."

"Roger that."

*

"click, click, click . . . "

The silence outside cracked with the sudden rattle of gunfire. Not the pop of a pistol or a shotgun blast from a drunken hunter, but the rapid report of automatic weapons fire.

Everett stepped on the glow stick, glanced at the top of the well, and saw the flashes against the round chalkboard sky. "Are you okay up there?"

"I'm fine," she sobbed. "God, it was horrible. A group of men walked right by me through the woods, then started shooting inside your house! And then they ran past me again, back toward the main road."

"You did great."

"I heard a truck start up near the main road, then drive away. Who do you think it was?"

"I have no idea. I'll be right up."

"Everett, I'll be fine," she said. "Did you find anything?"

"Not yet."

"Then stay down there and finish."

"Are you sure you're all right?"

"I'm positive."

"You're stronger than I thought," he whispered.

"I'll be waiting for you."

He clicked on a small flashlight and began digging through the soggy black leaves and dead branches that covered the bottom of the well. The pile was several feet thick. The deeper down he dug, the thicker the pitch and the worse the smell. As he slopped the heavy leaves and debris against one side of the curved stone wall, he dug down further on the other side, creating an opening, but the pitch slumped back in and covered his hole.

After several minutes, he'd dug his hands down far enough, striking a solid surface—more wooden planks under the heavy mud and brush. The planks were thick, but they felt wet and rotted under his boots. On the third stomp, one of the planks cracked and caved in. He pulled the busted wood out and shined the flashlight into the opening. Below the decking was more slop and ooze. He reached in through the hole and felt around. The dirt was soft and wet, but he felt something hard, with square corners buried in the toxic mud. He pulled one of the heavy bricks through the jagged hole and wiped off the black slime. "Shelby," he whispered.

"What is it?"

"Take a deep breath, and don't react."

"You're kidding!"

"Shhh.. No, I'm not."

"Now what?"

"I'm climbing up."

He squinted in the dark and inspected the dirty, smelly bar in the dim light. It was heavy, maybe five pounds. *One hundred ounces each!*

He reached back down into the dark mud and found another bar, then another, and then began the process of extracting and neatly packing the rest of the wet bars snuggly in the backpack.

He checked his watch. It was almost five A.M. now.

As he climbed up the thick rope, he struggled hand over hand, upward toward the top of the well. He finally reached for the bricked edge, looked around, and carefully climbed out.

The house lights were still on. "Stay in the trees," he whispered, hauling up the heavy cargo with little effort, then shouldering the backpack and heading for the rental.

26

Everett flew back to San Diego and showed up at the office later that evening. He checked his messages, returned a few phone calls, and placed several trades. He stayed for the evening trading session in bonds but the action overseas was slow and uneventful. No rumors on Reuters, no floods, oil spills, assassinations, or tsunamis, and no terrorist explosion footage. Bonds were trading sideways, and the cold-calling and prospecting was monotonous. Yet most of the brokers were still on their headsets, working the airwaves for fresh trading capital and new clients. The hum of the Grinder droned on like a diesel engine churning out commissions. It was a financial factory, trading millions by the minute. But after a year of adrenalin rushes when the markets were open, Everett had a hard time staying excited after the show was over. His days had been filled with tip-toeing through the office, careful of what he said and did, acutely aware of steel blue eyes following his every move. He shut down his screens and walked out, watching the sun disappear into the Pacific.

The artificial glow of the halogen street lights lit the sidewalks as he jogged across the intersection of Front Street and Broadway. He picked up a barbecue sandwich at the Aztec and bought a six pack of beer at the convenience store across the street. As light turned to shadow, he sat in his car, drank the beer and watched the metallic door that led to the mechanical entrance on the loading dock behind the restaurant on his building's ground floor.

The image of Ray Hood, the surfer, the SEAL, the assassin, branded itself into his mind. He could visualize the veins in the bulging neck and the striations of muscle tissue in his shoulders as he pummeled the young surfer. An anger he'd never felt before welled up inside, with no way to vent. It burned in his gut, and it tore at his soul.

Well after ten P.M., the lights on the fiftieth floor were still on. The streets were deserted, the lobby was now locked, and the downtown business district was dark and unfriendly. Clouds of heat exhaust rising from the sidewalk's mechanical grates attracted scattered homeless ghosts which seemed to levitate from corner to corner. This was an after-hours side of the urban neighborhood where he worked, and he hardly recognized it as a delivery truck pulled up to the loading dock and dumped wrapped bundles of magazines and newspapers. He could still make out the dark green Defender in the corner of the maintenance lot.

Two more hours passed, and right before twelve the sound of a hollow metal door slamming shut captured his attention. He focused his eyes at the darkness, searching toward the sound just in time to catch a brief glimpse of a silhouette leaving the building near the loading dock that serviced the mechanical systems. Everett slowly eased down in his seat and shook his head quickly in an effort to sharpen his wits. He reached for the keys but froze. The big blond surfer snapped his head to the right and left, turning and scanning the remaining parked cars in the adjacent lots on the street. Hood hesitated, then cranked the Defender and drove away.

Everett released the brake, slowly rolling into the street. The Defender disappeared around the corner as Everett followed carefully. All intersections going south were green and Everett eased behind a cab several blocks behind until the Defender entered the interstate. For a moment, he lost sight until he reached the short ramped exit to Coronado.

The green four-wheel drive Defender came into view as it entered the toll gate and continued west toward North Island.

A station wagon full of tourists from Arizona passed in front and blocked his view momentarily, but out of the corner of his eye Everett spotted the green SUV as it turned southwest onto Orange Avenue. Following discreetly, he sped through the restaurant district and followed the Defender south toward the private marinas that face the Pacific.

Several car lengths back, watching with caution as the Defender turned into the Coronado Cays Marina, he parked and closed the distance on foot. From the corner of a tiny seafood restaurant and bait shop just adjacent to the locked gangplank, he watched Ray Hood enter a private boat slip, then disappear into the cabin of a forty-five foot Alden racing yacht.

Now I know where you live, you son-of-a-bitch.

The alarm clock went off at three A.M. as Everett stepped into a pair of black Gore-Tex jogging pants and pulled on a navy hooded sweatshirt that bore three yellow initials, USN. He laced his running shoes then moved through his condominium in the inky blackness, peeking through the barely parted vertical blinds every few minutes at the four-door LTD parked across the street. He finished his coffee, slowly raised the wooden double-hung window that faced the blind side of his unit on the patio, and slipped behind the bushes outside.

The moon had already set, and he felt comfortable in the cold California blackness that hugs the human form before the dawn. The freshly-cleaned streets of Coronado were still wet and glossy from the short storm at midnight as he broke into a trot over the sidewalks of his neighborhood. Once around the corner and clear of federal surveillance, he rounded the corner and turned southwest towards Orange Avenue, scanning the area. All was still and silent, bathed in the foggy coastal dark. A Coronado police cruiser swooshed through a puddle to his left and as he turned the corner. The officer in the shotgun seat glanced around, and then continued on.

Everett picked up the pace, sprinting for two miles in front of the neat, manicured lawns and scrubbed storefronts that lined Orange, the east to west axis through the city. After jogging on the small peninsula for almost a year, he knew the sidewalks and alleys like his hometown. He bolted through several intersections of the Naval retirement haven, suddenly aware of how close his real enemy lived to him. Passing beneath the street lights, he approached the corner that led to the Coronado Cays Marina. He slowed to a walk, then traversed the sidewalk that led to the dock, watching as the boats bobbed on the black, shiny water.

He searched for the forty-five foot Alden, his heartbeat racing from the run. He looked at his watch. It was now almost four A.M. He spotted her as he sat in the corner at a dark table on the patio and removed an apple from his pocket, savoring the crisp sweetness. The run had kick-started his senses as he watched and waited in the dark corner space in front of the bait shop.

He heard a noise to his right and slowly turned his head. The wooden louvered deck door in front of the cockpit on the big sailboat at the end of the pier quickly and quietly flew open. Everett's heart pounded wildly in his chest. Ray Hood's spiked yellow crew cut emerged through the racing boat's small doorway. Once Hood stepped onto the pier and turned his back, Everett shifted carefully behind the ice machine and eased deeper into the dark shadows of the bait shop's patio corner. Hood marched quickly up the pier, swiped his keycard through the electronic lock, looked around, then walked through the gate, the metal door clanging firmly behind him.

Two sidewalks led from the ramp to the parking lot and Everett was two feet from the farthest one. Hood chose the closest route up the embankment and passed within five feet of the corner of the bait shop. With his back against the shop's wall, Everett crossed his arms quietly and covered the yellow initials across his chest, looking down at the ground. Hood opened the driver side door, slid in, cranked his four-wheel drive, and disappeared down the road.

Now certain of a clear path, Everett released a deep breath, crept onto the sidewalk, and inspected the entry gate to the pier. Metal plates had been welded onto either side of the opening to prevent encroachment. Climbing around the plates wasn't difficult and he was easily on the other side in one motion. He stopped on the back side of the entry gate and leaned against the door, his heart still jumping like a jack-hammer. The Alden yacht was moored in the last slip at the end of the dock, strategically positioned no doubt for a fast exit from the marina.

Everett walked softly as the frigid, biting, wind tested his balance on the buoyant wooden pier. There was no motion other than the gentle rocking rhythm of the floating pier and the slap of the water against the pylons. With her owner away, the powerful racing yacht suddenly looked vulnerable. He stepped over the carbon fiber body trim and onto the tongue-and-groove foredeck of the white racing yacht, carefully turning the handle.

She was magnificent. Her berthing areas were all mahogany, her trim was cherry, and she was fitted with stainless-steel and brass fixtures. Nautical maps were strewn about the cabin area. Complex charted routes were marked with red grease pencil and travel plans were obviously being constructed. Everett inspected the charts, tracing a marked route to the Hawaiian Islands, carrying Hood through the south Pacific and then on to Bora Bora, Fiji, Australia, and finally to Indonesia.

He fumbled around in the dark quarters, pulling out drawers, looking under built-in benches, and disturbing the clutter. As the yacht swayed on the water, a louvered cabinet door swung open. The storage locker was filled with survival provisions as well as several automatic weapons, handguns, knives, and a crossbow. Next to an assortment of ammunition boxes containing 9mm Black Talon rounds and Dragon's breath shotgun shells were insulin syringes and vials of Anavar, Decadurabolin and human growth hormone, steroids he'd seen in dozens of locker rooms.

Everett then cut his eyes to his wrist watch and checked the time again. The sun would soon rise. Frustrated, he checked the lower cabinets in the cabin and noticed a box with Camerone Cane S.A. written in magic marker on it. Next to it was another box labeled St. Vincent Trust. Other cabinets contained Pilgrim Capital, Baldwin Asset Partners, St. Croix Associates, Falcone Partners, and Banco de Mexico, as well as Oceanside Equity Partners, LLC. He pulled the boxes out and looked inside. *Pay dirt!* Client statements from offshore accounts, powers of attorney, insurance transaction invoices, qualified account applications and other assorted legal documents and files. *Insurance! He must have stolen them from the office to protect himself in the future.*

It took him almost an hour to climb over and around the locked entry gate and carry all twenty banker's boxes back to the bait shop. Next door was a wall of self-storage lockers for fishing equipment. Most of them were empty and all the boxes fit neatly into ten of the available lockers. He removed his wallet, swiped his credit card and tucked all ten keys from the doors into his warmup suit, zipping up the pocket. He then starting laughing softly to himself. Easing around the locked gate one last time, he scrambled down the pier and back into the yacht's cabin. He hustled to the engine room and dug through the tool box in the corner.

At the bottom of the metal box under the wrenches was a portable drill. He found a diamond bit, inserted it into the drill's teeth and checked the battery, then drilled a small, one inch hole in the carbon-fiber hull wall behind the powerful diesel engine. Brackish harbor water seeped in as the bilge pump immediately kicked on. He quickly yanked the wires from the hull that powered it.

After slowly raising his head forward and out, he checked around and behind the boat. The pier was clear as he hurried up the ramp. Passing under the Coronado street light, the Xenon bulb flickered off as darkness gave way to dawn and he jogged back to his townhouse.

Everett slipped in through the kitchen door, pitched the keys on the counter, grabbed a beer from the refrigerator and took several gulps, trying to settle his nerves, then played back a message from John Valentine about a beach party at Windansea before settling into the leather chair on the balcony with his laptop.

"You're playing a very deadly game, Everett."

Her voice made him jerk as she appeared in the kitchen doorway. "Vasquez? You scared the shit out of me."

"Good. Are you out of your mind?"

"How'd you get in?" he asked. "That's breaking and entering."

"I came here to reason with you, and try to convince you to let me do my job. I'm sorry about your grandmother."

"Thank you," he said. "I appreciate that."

"But you're too smart to play dumb with me."

"I thought I was on my own, agent Vasquez."

"Are you trying to ruin my year long investigation or are you trying to get yourself killed? I told you to be patient."

"Being patient almost got my grandmother killed!"

"I told you we would watch your back. My people tailed you for your own protection in Mississippi and again tonight to the Cays marina."

"So do you want my help or not?"

"We observed you scaling the fence of a private gated pier. That's trespassing."

"But they didn't actually see me onboard, right?"

"We can't possibly pick up every single minute detail, but we know you were there. What if he'd caught you, without us watching?"

"He didn't."

She hesitated. "So what did you see?"

"Nice trial close, Vasquez. Now *that* will cost you."

"You're just as greedy as the rest, aren't you?"

"I'm taking all the risk."

"Sorry. We don't pay a ransom for information. Either you talk or you get arrested when we take down the office."

"Bullshit. You're so desperate you broke your cover. That means you'll never be able to work under again."

"We can subpoena you, then depose you for days, and grill you in front of a grand jury. And when we ask the same question a second or a third time or a fourth time or fifth time with a different phrasing, and you contradict yourself in the slightest, that's perjury. And federal prosecutors rarely try a case without an indictment or conviction."

"You got Harper and Walker killed and now you're running out of time. Jack's suspicious enough as it is after you took a leave of absence. So let's talk terms."

"Do you have any idea what kind of individual Ray Hood is, and the men we're dealing with?"

"I've played alongside *and* against maniacs like him since I was in grade school. The NFL breeds characters just like him."

"He grew up in Hawaii. His federal file is full of details about his training in Lua. You familiar with Lua?"

"Can't say that I am."

"It's one of the most vicious martial arts in the world, and it's outlawed in every country as a legitimate fighting style. Hawaiian warriors developed it as a series of striking points that enabled them to dislocate the joints and break the bones of their enemy without the use of weapons. He's an expert, and extremely dangerous."

"You willing to wager your case on his MMA skills?"

She hesitated. "Like I said, we don't pay cash to our confidential informants. You've obviously watched too many Hollywood movies. We don't operate that way in reality."

"That cassette tape and the documents I have are my only leverage."

"So you *do* have evidence!"

"And it'll go to the highest bidder."

"A drug lord, a criminal mastermind, *and* the US Treasury all know that you've been personally involved in international fraud, racketeering, and insider trading. Not to mention Camerone's connection to Mexico's EPR."

"What's EPR?"

"The same Marxist guerrilla movement responsible for the labor strike in Brazil as well as kidnappings and attacks inside Mexico, all secretly receiving funding from Venezuela. Camerone is using the EPR and other terrorist organizations as proxies in an ideological struggle with the United States. Their goal is the destabilization of the Mexican government. EPR has members that are former Cuban agents, along with Colombians, and FARC."

"I'll take my chances."

"Perfect. You almost got your girlfriend killed. I told you not to go near your house, but no, Everett Anderson, badass weekend warrior just couldn't resist snooping around his temporarily occupied house. Do you have any idea how close your curiosity got you both to kidnapping and or death!"

"I found out what I needed to know! That's more than you could provide, and I don't exactly like having to depend on some rookie agent with promises of protection!"

"You're unbelievable. That was a death squad sent by Camerone to take out Hood and his crew, but Hood was already back in California."

Everett stared at her, motionless.

"And now you're broke and all alone in the world, Anderson! Do you think you can run from all of us?"

"I need some sleep," Everett yawned as he started up the stairs for his bedroom.

Halfway up, she rolled her eyes. "Wait," she said. "I might be able to compensate you, indirectly that is."

"Well, now we're getting somewhere."

She stared at him, trying to gauge his loyalty. "What if I told you about an upcoming market-related announcement so earth-shattering, that it could change your life if you knew about it in advance?"

"Like what?"

"Like inside information, from inside the US government."

"Now that's funny," he snickered.

"I'm serious, on a global scale."

"Then I'm listening."

"I could not only get fired, but I could go to Leavenworth for telling you this."

"You're breaking my heart."

"I can't believe I'm actually doing this."

"Sometime today would be nice."

"Alright, here goes. I happen to know about an upcoming event in the international currency markets."

"Do tell."

"But first I need to know something. How did you know to sell sugar at the top, right before the crash?"

"You really want to know?"

"Yeah. It's been driving me crazy and it might help your situation with my boss. He still thinks you're working with Jack."

"It's really simple. I found out that Jack was selling sugar in his own account the week before."

"How?"

"Jennifer told me."

"You've got to be kidding. And you trusted her?"

"I gambled on her, and now you're gambling on me. What's the difference? I believed her. Besides, if she'd been wrong, I still got all my clients out with a nice profit. Now. What's your big upcoming event?"

"After the Federal Reserve meets next week, the FOMC will actually *raise* interest rates one hundred basis points for the first time in ten years, to get the banks lending again."

"Why do I feel like I'm *really* being set up again?"

"I'm very serious. Don't you see? The stock market wants more rate cuts and easing. But if rates go up, the Dow will tank, derailing the recovery, but more importantly the dollar will rally."

"The dollar's been slipping for almost ten years."

"Exactly, and Europe is on the edge of financial collapse. Capital will flee the Euro in favor of dollars. The Fed chairman is willing to temporarily sacrifice an overvalued stock market in order to save the dollar from permanent future damage because of the billions in bailouts for the banks."

"And you know this for sure?"

"Treasury has been monitoring international option activity for months now, and there's a huge spike in November put option buying on all international exchanges. Not to mention the discreet selling of Eurodollars overseas, especially in the OPEC nations."

"So the dollar will finally start to climb, huh?"

"You would be amazed at the level of manipulation on the international financial markets. The public has no clue. Wall

Street investment bankers make a killing on the fractional moves of millions of shares driven by high frequency electronic trading while Mr. and Mrs. America buy and hold for retirement in their 401k's and IRA's."

"But you're certain about the stock market, and the dollar?"

"Look, don't turn this into something it's not. I may be young, but I've managed to associate myself with all the right people in Washington. Our personal finances are audited and monitored all the time to look for financial gain based on information we discover at work. We're all just human beings that work with other human beings and we hear things from the right people who know what they're talking about. It happens in the FBI, the IRS, and most departments and agencies in Washington. But this is not your own personal little lottery. If you trade your clients in currency futures or buy put options on the S and P five hundred, then I don't have a problem with the commissions you generate for yourself. But you damn well better not make it obvious, and if I find out you personally profited from a direct investment in either commodity, I'll come after you for the rest of my career. And no one would ever believe you if you told them you heard it from me in advance."

"I'm afraid to ask what kind of volume."

"Billions, Everett. Maybe trillions. The dollar's been dropping for years, against all major currencies. But at Treasury, we know about several connected international interests who have definitely been quietly covering their laddered short positions through multiple venues by buying dollars and selling the Euro. Wikileaks? International espionage? We also know about calculated Central Bank intervention which will finally reverse the fall of the dollar and shore it up. Now the world knows the US bailed out the EU. If you saw some of the things I've seen at the Treasury Department, it would send a chill up your spine."

"Meaning?"

"The United States is finding itself being pulled into a dark, black-box type of financial reality controlled by a shrinking number of very powerful international players. Later this month the Treasury secretary will announce sweeping regulatory changes that will alter our financial landscape for years to come."

"Like what?"

"Like merging the CFTC and the SEC. Like regulating hedge funds and private equity firms and derivatives, and taxing them like most other brokers of capital. No more carry charges. We have no choice. We're dealing with a global shadow economy of unique and poorly misunderstood financial instruments created and controlled by off-shore investment bankers and wealthy currency manipulators, including Don Carlos Eduardo Camerone. You didn't actually think Camerone lost money on his sugar trade did you?"

"Isn't that why they killed Katherine?"

"Katherine Fox was murdered because she discovered Camerone caused the crash. Continental's clearing and settlement shifted the losses into error accounts. It happens all the time. How do you think Goldman Sachs was able to short the housing markets?"

"I just thought they were pin-striped crooks."

"Over the past decade, a web of complex securities, private swaps, and wagers have made the world's financial systems so entangled and opaque that each year fewer business people understand how it all really works. And I'm not just talking about sophisticated derivatives and dark pools of unregistered capital which are beyond difficult to value, but the sheer amount of money caught up in this web is now many times larger than the world's gross domestic product. It might be anchored on Wall Street, but almost all of this capital exists outside the reach of American regulators and in the hands of sovereign wealth managers.

You don't actually think last year's market meltdown was just profit-taking, do you?"

"So basically the world is coming to an end?"

"Yeah, smartass. And options and futures prices pegged to expire this Friday, three days after the Federal Open Market Committee meeting, will be the most profitable, which also happens to be options expiration day."

"Quadruple witching?"

"Precisely. The dollar should run up several hundred basis points because of the outstanding buy imbalance, like a pig through a python."

"How do you know that?"

"The New York Federal Reserve Bank, which acts as an agent for the Treasury, will intervene in the currency markets on Friday for the first time in over a decade. The Group of Seven has secretly pledged a coordinated effort to strengthen the dollar in order to prevent the collapse of the US economy and avert a double dip recession. It may start a trend or it may just represent a short term bear rally that lasts for a few months. All you have to do is buy September in-the-money call options for your clients, and you'll clean up. If the information proves true, then we have a deal?"

"Fair enough."

"You better be careful, Everett. I warned you not to get close to your house and you ignored me. Somehow Hood escaped and now you're up to something. I just know it. And you're in way over your head."

27

Jennifer's hand shook as she dialed Everett's cell phone.

He answered after one ring. "Hello?"

"I'm outside his mansion," she said. "He just drove past me on the way to the office."

"Good. Vinnie spotted Hood leaving the marina and now he's on his way to watch Jack's house while you're inside. I'm parked right by the mechanical exit behind the building lobby and there's no sign of Hood yet."

"Jack must have surveillance at home."

"Even if he does, you'll be out of there by the time he reaches the office. You'll only need a minute to link up his system."

"I'm scared."

"You can do this, Jennifer. You've taught yourself to be an excellent hacker. You'll be able to get an I.T. job anywhere if this works. Just get his computer linked up and talking to yours, and Jack will never know you were in his system."

"Oh, he'll know."

"Then make him know it too late."

"Everett?"

"Yeah?"

"We're going to beat him, aren't we?"

"Yeah, Jen. We sure as hell are. Thanks to you."

She turned off her cell, her heart pounding against her rib cage. Even though Jack was no longer inside the huge Rancho Santa Fe estate just down the hill, she could still feel his presence and it gave her a sick feeling.

Everett had taken her to dinner the night before and told her all about the entire conspiracy, the laundering, and the lies. She already knew most of Jack's secrets and she knew that helping the Treasury was her best revenge. It'd be easy to cooperate now that she knew Jack would eventually burn for everything he'd done to her, as well as to the brokers and to their clients.

Continental's clearing firm, in co-operation with the Commodity Futures Trading Commission and the Treasury Department, finally agreed to clear Everett's currency trades for Camerone Cane S.A., with Derrick Butler handling the whole transaction. It took all week to purchase call options on the US dollar for all of Everett's clients. The clearing fee was larcenous, but the Feds paid it. There was no other choice.

Jennifer walked around the side of the estate's main house and unlocked the French doors to Jack's private terrace with a key he'd given her years ago. She never lost that key, even though she'd been held hostage there more nights than she'd care to remember. The anger and hate burned as she held her breath and inserted the key as the small light diode glowed green and she heard a click.

She took another breath, entered his private home office and sat down at his bedroom terminal. She powered up her laptop, activated the wireless modem signal and turned on the remote server that powered all of Jack's personal network. In the five years she'd worked for him, she'd developed a sixth sense when it came to using his computers. She carefully turned on the power to the elaborate network and then began typing the entry sequences, but when she hit ENTER nothing happened. She tried an alternate password. Nothing. She was even denied entry through her own pass code. *He changed all the entry codes!*

She felt helpless, but thought quickly and then dialed the office in Chicago. She checked her watch and asked for Sue Graham at the help desk, saying it was a company computer network emergency. Sue reluctantly gave Jennifer the alternate override sequences and before the coffee was brewed in the executive lounge, Jennifer was inside the company's remote access trading database, and that was all she needed.

She then dialed her cellular phone and kept the modem on her laptop computer open. She'd been up for the better part of the previous night and she'd already compromised the large Internet provider, NETCOM, and the remote secured servers that she knew Jack used for most of his trading. Continental's database was now exposed to the World Wide Web. But she'd have to wait and monitor Jack's system remotely by connecting an alarm from her laptop at home to his company computer database at the office through another wireless modem she'd established through her cellular account. The next time Jack logged on to his system, she'd be alerted. She'd then have all the necessary information recorded and decoded in order to download Jack's trading files.

She finished up and logged out as the sun came up. With trembling hands, Jennifer re-locked the door to Jack's terrace and quickly left the grounds to his estate through the thick landscaping around the side yard.

Everett finished his coffee at the Aztec and then rode the elevator to the forty-ninth floor of the California Empire Bank building later that morning. Jack greeted him enthusiastically as the polished, stainless steel elevator doors flew open. "Well, good morning, Mister Anderson! Isn't it a great day to be alive!" He'd been flirting with the receptionists in the lobby as he frequently liked to do.

"What are you so happy about?" Everett asked.

"Check the monitors, Ace," Jack beamed with a conquering smile as he stood in the middle of his luggage, waiting for the concierge. "The dollar's in record negative territory *again* this morning!"

Everett checked his messages in the large grid of pigeon hole mail slots set into the wall. He pulled the notes and glanced at the names.

"Ladies, what do you make of my top closer?" Jack jabbed. "I showed him how to trade, I gave him flawless forecasts for one full year, and now he's decided to go against my advice not once, but twice. It's treasonous I tell you!"

The girls in reception looked embarrassed.

"Our top trader here believes he knows better than the Chinese, The Russians and all of Europe, not to mention The Saudis who continue to sell dollars. How do you like that?"

Everett kept walking.

"I understand you're flying to Cabo, Mr. Anderson."

Everett froze. "Wiretapping my conversations, Jack?"

"Camerone informed me just this morning. You could use the Gulfstream, but I'm taking it to Chicago this morning. Sorry."

Everett said nothing.

"But I think it's a sensational trade, Sport! And since it's your call alone, I encourage you to close Camerone for another ten million. That's over a million dollars commission."

"Jack, you always said rebellion was the first sign of sanity."

"So let me get this straight. You want to go long the dollar in the face of the biggest currency sell-off and stock market rally in U.S. history?" Jack prodded. "You haven't spent enough time in this business to understand the meaning of the word rebellion, Sport."

"Your last example in sugar never did sit well with me," Everett said. "I think I like the other side of all your trades going forward. The Dow's due for further correction to the downside, I can feel it. I have nothing more to learn from you."

"The Dollar is in danger of violating a 15-year low against the yen! And I deliberately never taught you everything I know."

"I know my opposition was accurate in the past."

"After this morning's opening, it would appear your opposition has become an uncomfortable burden."

Everett shook his head. "At least I have a conscience."

"Ah, but conscience doth make cowards of us all."

"So you get to play king?"

"Fortunately, kings lack the caution of common men. But I'll give you some more time, and enough rope to hang yourself with. You want a showdown, you got it, Sport," Jack mocked as he disappeared with a taunting smile on his sun-burned face.

Another jab, another dig, another mental maneuver calculated to distract and disarm.

Everett entered the trading floor, crossed to his office and exchanged hellos with his senior team. There was the usual feeling of excitement in the office, and there were no secrets in the trading trenches. Everyone knew everyone else's business and everyone knew that Everett was buying the dollar, all by himself.

Going against research simply wasn't done at the Continental Trading Group. The old trading house had always perpetuated a sense of obligatory allegiance. The recommendations were always right. Always. The accuracy was unbelievable. To betray that commitment would create a small but growing undercurrent of distrust among the other brokers in the office. The gospel of Continental allowed for no dissension and no opposition to established recommendations. The brokerage's top trader was now flaunting his opposition, and it was creating doubt among the faithful. The office's brief admiration for his successful short sugar trade had long since worn off and although his reputation remained solid, Jack had since been flawless, nine-for-ten on the year. Ninety percent in commodities is staggering.

The faithful assembled on the trading floor while Bill Peterson oversaw the meeting that morning. "The dollar is expected to weaken"—came the crawling message at the bottom of Continental's casino-like sports-book scoreboard.

Everett stood in the doorway of his office with a small recorder in the palm of his left hand as a short burst of feedback came through the speaker system, signaling the morning meeting. The sound of a helicopter could be heard as Everett watched Jack's helicopter lift off for the airport.

"Good morning," Max Goldman said. "Our put options on the dollar are now in fat profits! The stock market and our December call options have been going straight up for two solid weeks now. As long as dollars are cheap, our foreign investors will buy our equities. This market is a train, folks, so get on board."

Goldman continued. "All leading economic indicators are now pointing to a test of new lows for the U.S. dollar, and the bond market is also responding well to a further interest rate reduction rumor. Dubai, Tokyo and Bejing continue to sell dollars, but in London, the dollar is violating support. We expect more buying by the World Bank, and are therefore recommending call options on the Japanese yen. If the Dow and the dollar continue in opposite directions, we will continue to profit handsomely for our clients."

Everett scanned the faces of the veteran seniors and the new rookies as the morning meeting drew to a close. He saw something markedly different in both groups. In the seniors, he saw uncertainty. But when he looked at the rookies, he saw something that scared the hell out of him. He saw Jack, staring back at him.

The elevator descended to the bank lobby of the building where Everett slipped into the bathroom and changed into shorts and a Hawaiian shirt. He put on a Padres baseball cap and sunglasses and took the emergency exit to the rear lot. He quickly cranked Vinnie's Range Rover and sped toward the interstate.

He drove east, first going fifty, then eighty, then fifty again, certain he wasn't being followed. He turned south on I-805 and headed for the Tijuana International Airport at the border crossing at San Ysidro. Although his flight on Aero Mexico was to Cabo San Lucas from Lindbergh Field in San Diego, he planned to pay cash for another ticket at Tijuana International.

His cell phone rang. "Hello?"

"Hey, Amigo. Bad news."

"What's up, Vinnie?"

"I'm at the airport now, and there's no sign of Hood."

"You're sure?"

"Positive. I've been camped in the bar all morning by your gate and I haven't seen him."

"All right. No sweat. I'm not being followed, and I'm almost across the border."

"Watch your back. Call me if you need help."

Everett hung up and slowed down the Range Rover as he approached the line of backed-up vehicles waiting for their turn to enter Mexico. The line seemed unusually long and snaked around the corner from the exit off of the highway that read: YOU ARE NOW LEAVING THE UNITED STATES OF AMERICA. The Range Rover passed the sign, rolled to a stop and waited, inching forward as each vehicle was waved across. The Friday morning traffic fell in behind him.

Everett glanced in the rear view mirror and started to look away when suddenly a flash of green startled him. He looked again and focused. Five vehicles separated him from the green Defender. He was trapped in line.

He thought quickly as he was waved up to the gate. The Mexican Federale dressed in a khaki uniform looked past him and motioned him through. Everett immediately accelerated and quickly passed the bottleneck of smoking taxis and pick-up trucks full of vegetables and cheap ceramics that collect around the border crossing.

He cut his eyes to the rear view mirror and noticed that the Defender wasn't yet through the gate. He swerved hard toward the first ramp that by-passed the main thoroughfare of Revolucion. The ramp poured him into the grid of Tijuana's crowded downtown streets. He took another road that was marked with an airplane symbol, but the street ended at a three-way stop and diverted him back to a busy, unmarked road on the edge of the city. This main road led away from the city and up a hill. He turned left and tried to lose himself in the traffic.

The road was just wide enough for two lane traffic but it was without lane markers and four lanes of vehicles in opposite directions squeezed together and filled up the bumpy, pock-marked road. He checked the mirror again and saw nothing but a crowd of vehicles frantically changing lanes and jockeying for position behind him.

The road began to climb a high hill which led westward away from Tijuana and toward the ocean. As the incline became steeper, he could see San Diego to the north in the distance.

His eyes quickly looked for an exit to the Tijuana Airport, when he suddenly felt a hard jolt from the rear. He checked the mirror and Hood's smiling face met his eyes. Everett jerked the wheel of the Range Rover to the right and barely missed a taxi, which elicited a stream of obscenities and hand gestures, and forced Hood behind the cab. With the heavy metal grill mounted on the front of the Defender, Hood rammed the cab from behind and forced it onto the shoulder where the taxi and its occupants spun to a stop in the dust. Then Hood punched the accelerator and rammed the Rover again.

Everett reached for the phone as a third jolt forced it out of his hands onto the floor board. The flow of traffic pulled back and made room once it was discovered that a personal demolition derby was taking place between two gringos. Everett sped up the hill with Hood close behind. The road had several signs written in Spanish, but none of them displayed airplane symbols and there were no guard rails on the treacherous winding state highway. Hood pulled along side Everett and jerked the wheel of his vehicle left, forcing Vinnie's new four-wheel drive into the oncoming traffic.

The Range Rover swerved further left, just barely missing a diesel Mercedes with a very loud horn as the front left wheel of the Rover rolled over the rocky shoulder on the opposite side of the road. Hood's red face in the rear-view laughed behind small silver sunglasses with oval red lenses.

As they crested the hill, the ocean came into view and the road forked. Everett crossed back to the right lane and slammed the Rover's bumper into the Defender's driver side door. Hood was braced for the blow and only wavered slightly. The two vehicles lurched against one another as they sped down the hill toward the Pacific.

The road turned sharply to the right before the fork, and Hood kept the pressure on the wheel turned sharply to the left, forcing the Rover's left tires back onto the dusty shoulder, inches away from a plummeting drop off. Everett slammed the brake pedal to the floor and both vehicles spun a full three hundred and sixty degrees, hooked together by the gouges and tears in their doors. The Rover broke free and peeled out, finding traction on the hot road surface. The Defender gave chase and banged the rear bumper again.

Everett cut the wheel sharply to the left and zoomed through the fork, which led to a circular concrete bull fighting arena by the sea. It was deserted on a Friday afternoon and Everett turned down a small, narrow road behind the arena. Hood rammed him again from behind. The smell of gasoline suddenly filled the interior of the Range Rover and Everett rolled down the window to keep from choking from the smell. The Defender pulled within inches of the left side of the Rover and Hood yanked the wheel again to the right. To the left was a cactus-filled mountainside and the Defender, and to the right was a two hundred foot drop to the rocks and waves. As Hood pushed and slammed against the Rover, Everett spotted a small dirt clearing ahead.

Hood swerved again and as the clearing approached, Everett hit the brakes, spun the wheel to the right, and wedged the passenger door open. He pitched the briefcase and dove through the door's small opening and onto the dry dirt, kicking up a dense brown cloud. The familiar and excruciating pain in his left shoulder returned as he glanced up long enough to see Vinnie's new Range Rover in flames, tumbling over the edge and disappearing on the dusty horizon. Everett rolled against a cluster of rocks on the edge of the cliff and twisted himself in to a shape that matched the small opening between the boulders. He sat still, listening to the explosion below him on the beach at the foot of the cliff's edge.

Then all was quiet as the brown cloud of dust dissipated, except for the sound of the battered Defender idling in neutral near the edge of the cliff. The crunch gravel beneath thick-soled motorcycle boots echoed in the rocks as Hood walked back and forth within inches and looked over the edge to confirm the crash.

Everett's heart pounded as he held his breath. Each beat caused the shoulder to throb painfully.

Hood took one more look around, and drove away.

"This is sloppy, Jack," Peterson shouted in a panic. "I don't like this one Goddamn bit!"

Jack stared out the window at Lake Michigan from his perch at the top of the Sears Tower. Sailboats were criss-crossing the open water through the thick glass and Lake Shore Boulevard was packed with weekend traffic. The corporate trading floor was humming with activity outside his massive office, but inside it was quiet as a church. "Relax," Jack uttered as he snorted another line of cocaine.

"You better stop using that shit, and both of us need to start worrying."

"He'll call."

"I'm beginning to think Anderson's smarter than you. He's managed to stay alive this long, and I have a bad feeling your man Hood is becoming careless lately."

"I told you to relax," Jack said calmly.

"What if we *are* being watched! All the signs are there. We have holes in our security and possibly an undercover threat posing as one of our brokers!"

"Don't go soft on me now."

"I didn't sign on for this! You were supposed to keep this nice and clean."

"We are in combat right now, and sometimes those types of decisions must be made for the good of the mission."

Everett Anderson, the gringo tourist, wasn't difficult to spot wearing a dusty Hawaiian shirt and shorts, and carrying a leather briefcase. He'd re-injured the shoulder outside of Tijuana, but he'd caught a ride to the airport with a freight trucker. After boarding a later flight and landing in Cabo, he flagged a taxi, bought a metal bucket of Coronas from a kid on the side of the road, and disappeared down the highway.

The drive to Cabo San Lucas through the desert landscape of the Baja peninsula from the airport in San Jose del Cabo was an uncomfortable ordeal. The taxi had no air conditioning but the beer was cold and the warm wind whistled through the rolled-down windows as mariachi music filled the cab. The stretch of highway that led from the airport to Cabo San Lucas was isolated, sparsely populated, and spectacular. Cactus and palms, chaparral and sagebrush all co-existed in the harsh and beautiful arid climate. He made a mental note to return under more pleasant circumstances.

When he finally reached the well-hidden Camerone complex, the armed gate guards waved him through after he was searched. He was expected. The taxi dropped him off at the main house, but the hacienda was empty. A large sunburned man with a long green cigar protruding from his thick black beard approached, dressed in tiger-stripe military fatigues. An Uzi sub-machine gun was strapped across his chest. He rambled rapidly in Spanish into a cellular phone and then gestured to Everett.

"Follow me."

Everett followed the stone steps carved into the side of the rock-hard, sun-baked hill. The crooked steps led to a boat pier and a waiting jet boat that bobbed up and down on the cobalt blue water. Everett wiped the dripping sweat from his forehead and climbed aboard.

They rocketed out to a point two miles off shore where a pristine white eighty foot Magnum was anchored. Tied to the bow of the racing yacht was a thirty-six foot Hatteras.

After pulling alongside the high-performance Magnum yacht, Everett could see Camerone on the rear deck by the transom, strapped in to a fighting chair, wrestling a black marlin. The old man rocked forward as the fish stole line and began another run for its freedom, then the drag was released and Camerone cursed and laughed loudly, admiring the fish's strength and stamina. The barrel-chested drug lord turned in his chair to greet Everett as he boarded. Against the railing on the far outside of the rear deck was Ray Hood, smoking a cigar.

"Senor Anderson!" Camerone roared. "Welcome!"

"Don Carlos," Everett said respectfully. "Thank you for allowing me this meeting, Sir."

"It was very dangerous for you to come here," Camerone said.

Hood smiled and shook his head as the old man struggled with the billfish. "I swear you've got nine lives, Anderson."

Everett nodded toward Hood. "So what's *he* doing here?"

The old man took a pull on a cold bottle of beer. "You don't think I would invest millions without a watchdog, do you?"

"So he worked for *you* all along?"

"What a smart broker you are. Knowing what you now know, you are lucky to still be alive. The sharks should be feeding on your bones."

Everett glared at Hood. "You buy a new boat, asshole?"

Hood stopped smiling. "You sunk my Alden?" he shouted, lunging for Everett. "I'll waste you for free!"

Camerone's bodyguards were larger and faster, and hooked Hood by the neck.

"Now we're even," Everett said.

"Oh you think so?" Hood bellowed.

Camerone began reeling the tired marlin against the side of the boat. "I've been told Miss Fox left you a detailed message that could be considered a liability."

"You don't think I'd be dumb enough to bring it with me, do you?"

"You have impressed me so far with how smart you are, senor Anderson. I will assume then that you have a more creative proposition for me instead?"

"I do, but we need to talk in private."

The old Mexican broke a smile. "Muy bien," he said, motioning one of his bodyguards around to the back of the boat. "Now shoot him," he ordered, looking directly at Everett.

The bodyguard withdrew the chrome-plated 50 caliber Desert Eagle from his shoulder holster as Everett's face turned ashen, bracing himself against the boat's fishing seat. Every muscle tensed. The bodyguard quickly turned and fired into the water, putting the three hundred pound fish out of its misery. The crew broke out in laughter as the bodyguard then fired another round directly into the back of Raymond Hood's head, causing blood to spout from his skull like a ruptured fire hydrant. Hood slumped forward against the boat's railing as the three-hundred pound Cuban bodyguard pressed his foot against Hood's hip and pushed the lifeless body into the dark blue water.

The whole incident happened so fast, Everett felt his chest seize up. The boat began to spin. He gagged, vomited over the rail, then turned and sat down against the inside of the boat's hull.

"You don't look very good," Camerone said as his soldier holstered the handgun.

"The son-of-a-bitch tried to kill me this morning."

"A dangerous pit bull who turns on his master must always be put down. My guess is Jack paid him to kill you. That distresses me, because family is all a man has. I understand your family is a family of planters."

"That's right," Everett said.

"My family has served the soil for five generations. Our sugar cane is our soul. To a man of honor, his blood is his soul. Hood had no honor. You, on the other hand, still work for me, and you have just bought yourself enough time to help me make more money. And that is your only salvation. So tell me your plan."

Everett eased into the empty fighting seat beside Camerone. "We're overdue for a rally. The dollar's massive short position is about to be covered overseas, right after the Federal Reserve meets next week, sending the dollar into the steepest rally in three decades."

"What is your source?"

"Let's just say I know for a fact that you've never lost a penny in your trading account with Continental."

The old man smiled. "And you are handing me this little gift for what reason?"

"I make you whole, I get to keep my life and we never meet again."

"So, you are planning your escape, no?"

"Jack's top trader in Chicago has been given immunity, and we have to act fast."

"And what about your boss?"

"All along, he's been strictly in futures contracts only, for a reason. Commodity options are considered securities, but commodity futures are not. This removes one more potential charge against him for securities fraud. I know Jack uses the futures contracts he owns to underwrite the options his brokers purchase for Continental's clients, which is very illegal."

"And if I refuse?"

"You won't."

"What if I do!" the old man shouted.

"Then I'll be forced to turn over to US authorities boxes of documents I stole from Hood's boat containing all of your original hand-written trade tickets, confirmations, time-stamped trust documents, articles of incorporation from Panamanian transfer agents and Brazilian venture capital attorneys stretching from Rio de Janeiro to Mexico City. Not to mention's your nominee shareholder trust account powers-of-attorney, very creative by the way, and every trade ticket I ever wrote for Camerone Cane, all locked away nice and neat somewhere in San Diego. If I don't make it back to the office by tonight, those records go directly to the US Treasury."

Camerone's face went calm as the sun dipped below the Pacific's deep blue horizon. "What exactly do you propose?"

"We're vulnerable if the dollar goes much lower, but we could triple your profits if we get a short term rally."

"How large a position?"

"Fifty million."

"Another ten million will be wired into my trading account on Monday morning, bringing my total balance to fifty," Camerone said.

"I'll need your signature on these powers-of-attorney. It gives me unlimited trading discretion in your corporate and insurance accounts."

The old man narrowed his eyes. "If this does not work, there will be no place on earth for you to hide from me," Camerone said as he signed the documents. "I think I have already demonstrated *my* reach."

"If this trade doesn't work, you have my permission to kill me."

28

The government Lear jet landed at Lindbergh Field well before dawn. Everett was sipping steaming coffee as the nose of the special aircraft rolled into the maintenance hangar. The cabin door folded out as two agents with ear pieces wheeled the steps into place. Victoria Vasquez stepped off the jet after the other agents and walked toward Everett. "Very impressive, Agent Vasquez," he said.

"Anderson, you remember Deputy Director Bailey."

"Mister Anderson?"

"Yes, Sir."

"I want to personally guarantee that you need not worry about being charged. I want you to appear at work this morning and go about your business as usual. We don't want Diamond spooked."

"So what should I expect?"

"You might want to leave the office early this morning," Bailey said, reaching into his coat pocket and producing a signed affidavit from the U.S. Attorney's office, and handed it to Everett. "Here's your get out of jail free card."

"And I think this is yours, Sir," Everett said, as he handed over the original micro-cassette tape of Katherine's message, all the keys to the storage units that held the bulk of accounts from Hood's boat, as well as the discs that contained hundreds of files Jennifer had copied from Jack's computer.

"You've done a good thing for your government, young man, and that is rare in the world today."

"I didn't do it for the government."

"Then if you'll excuse me, I have to coordinate today's operation. Agent Vasquez will give you the details."

Vasquez turned to Everett. "You know, I could blow the whistle on you," she half-whispered. "Conspiring with an international drug lord. Crossing the border on an illegal venture. Shame on you."

"What are you talking about?"

"I know you moved millions of dollars of Camerone's money. Don't worry. You're not going to prison," she said.

"Instead, you'll be walking in to a huge payday later this morning once you liquidate all your accounts."

"Guess it's karma."

"But you did the right thing, Anderson."

"You're quite a woman, Agent Vasquez."

"And you're one hell of a kisser."

"We were almost great together," he said, smiling. "Weren't we?"

"I wouldn't spend too much time in the office this morning if I were you."

"Don't worry. I sold my Ferrari, my townhouse is on the market at a huge discount, and I plan on being in first class on the first plane out of town this afternoon."

"Well, congratulations. Good luck and you take care of yourself, Anderson."

"You too, Vasquez."

Sunrise brought a soft orange glow to the downtown skyline as Everett stopped to retie one of his running shoes. He paused at the edge of the bay and stared across the blue water at the reddish reflection of the rising sun on the silver and black glass of the geometric office buildings. The morning run temporarily took his mind off the probable outcomes and possible scenarios he'd be facing in less than an hour. He hadn't slept all night. The aching shoulder was a constant reminder that pain has a funny habit of creating focus.

It was almost five A.M., and the currency markets on New York would be opening soon. The equity markets in London, Frankfurt, Tokyo, Hong Kong, Singapore and Sydney were in a profit-taking mode, and the overnight action set records for the decade. The debt crisis which started with Greece had infected the entire continent of Europe. Not since Black Monday had there been such short pressure on Wall Street and the U.S. dollar. Combined with a growing Chinese economy, rampant inflation on the horizon, international banking failure and an accelerating global recession, the Nikkei average was plummeting. So was the Hang Seng. So was the FTSE, the CAC-40, and the DAX. All the international network news services blamed it on the over-valued and credit-heavy American economy. The Associated Press wire called it a world-wide recession, but news reports out of Asia pointed to the United States. Even Dubai was in panic mode, suddenly and desperately buying US dollars.

As barometers for world prices, the Dow Jones industrial average carried the most weight. Regardless of the reason, the Hang Seng, which had financed a large portion of the recent gains in U.S. bond prices, suffered a twenty percent correction. Hong Kong was decimated, and now Wall Street braced itself.

After showering, Everett dressed and decided to take the ferry across the harbor to the downtown area, something he hadn't done since his first day. He checked the Bloomberg monitor in his townhouse and dressed for work. So far so good. He strolled through the quiet streets of Coronado in the early morning twilight hours, resisting the temptation to hurry to the office.

If his calculations proved to be correct, he could expect some serious selling pressure that morning in the U.S. stock market based on what had occurred overseas, but he guarded the secret that Vasquez had shared and if correct, his salvation.

The ferry crossed the bay quickly and anchored at Embarcadero Park. He picked up a cup of coffee and a copy of *Investor's Business Daily*. The headline leapt out at him. "STOCKS FALL AS US DOLLAR SURGES AGAINST ALL CURRENCIES"

He walked briskly to work.

As the elevator doors flew open on the forty-ninth floor of the California Empire Bank building, what he saw put a smile on his face. It was announced that The Federal Reserve would raise its key interest rate one percent, a full hundred basis points, unprecedented in modern portfolio theory.

The girls in reception area were frantically answering an avalanche of incoming calls and the office was full of chaos and confusion. No one noticed him as he hit the trading floor and checked the production board. The Reuters news service headline immediately exposed the awful truth. The U.S. stock market had opened down over seven hundred points as sell program breakers attempted to postpone a full collapse. Mutual funds and institutional money had tried to get out first, and the individual investor on margin was sure to make matters worse, buried in a tsunami wave of forced margin selling and securities liquidation. But the dollar was climbing like a rocket, well over 200 basis points against all major currencies. It didn't make sense, but bad news can be good and good news is often bad in the surreal world of international markets.

The panic buying had begun that morning with the Chinese. Once they tried to purchase dollars in Hong Kong, Wall Street freaked and sold securities to compensate for the loss. Then the Germans started buying dollars, then the Brits, then the French, and finally the Russians, sensing some type of edge. Before the Friday morning session was an hour old, the Dow was down one thousand points and the dollar was up three hundred. Everett's derivative put options on the plummeting S&P 500 index were now worth five times their original purchase value.

*

The vintage Rolls Royce cut across oncoming traffic in front of the California Empire Bank building and skidded to a stop against the sidewalk. Jack jumped out, pitched his keys to the building valet, and bolted through the lobby in a panic.

Once on his terrace, he pounded the keys of his computers, sliding from screen to screen in his leather chair, desperately checking his positions, calculating Continentals' full exposure to the climbing dollar and plummeting Dow Jones Industrial Average.

He stopped long enough to dial the airport.

"Good morning, Coastal Air Service," the operator said.

"This is Jack Diamond with Continental Trading," he said, composing himself. "Would you please dispatch a helicopter to my office for transport to the tarmac?"

"Certainly Mister Diamond."

"And please have my corporate jet fueled and ready for departure this morning. Have you received my flight plan?"

"Yes, sir. Your pilot has been confirmed for non-stop service to Cabo San Lucas. Everything appears to be in order."

"I'll be ready to leave in fifteen minutes."

"Your air taxi will be on-station by eight o'clock this morning, Sir. Thank you for choosing CAS."

Jack slammed the phone down. The Reuters headline continued to roll across the bottom of his Bloomberg screen, reminding him that the US dollar was now up three hundred and fifty basis points.

Everett calmly entered his office, where ten phone lines were flashing on his trading console. The interoffice email informing the company of the resignation of Bill Peterson did little to surprise him. He instead sat quietly and watched, comfortable in the knowledge that he'd finally become a disciplined player in a dangerous game.

His first temptation that morning was to remain short all morning and stay in the trade that Vasquez had given him, but the instincts that Jack had taught him to hone to an edge told him to get out. *You never really have a profit until you actually take it.*

He eased into his custom leather chair with the company crest embroidered on the back, then booted his computer and checked his positions. Five hundred points down, five hundred dollar profit for each ten points in the Dow, roughly a twenty-five thousand dollar profit per option. Camerone Cane's fifty million was worth over ninety.

"Maybe I underestimated you, Sport."

Everett looked up from his trading screen. John Valentine was leaning against the doorway.

"My advice to you is to leave the office this morning, and never look back," Everett said calmly.

"So now you're giving me advice?"

"Maybe you should have listened to me on my dollar trade."

"Maybe I did."

"No way. Jack would never have permitted it."

"My old man's in the Hamptons for the weekend. We don't talk too much. He's still pissed about how Jack seized my trust. Anyway, my salvation was your position today. I told him about your sugar trade last month and he agreed to let me use his numbered account overseas. Not bad, Sport. I cleaned up, thanks to you."

"You're welcome."

"Just called in my sell order this morning. Buy you lunch at Mister A's later this morning?"

"I meant what I said. You should take Peterson's lead."

"Fine. Just answer me one question. How the hell how did you do it? Twice?"

"If I told you, you wouldn't believe me anyway."

"Try me."

"I listened to the only two women that Jack never saw coming."

"What's that supposed to mean?"

"It means I rolled the dice, and got lucky."

As John vanished, Everett took a breath and calmly dialed Continental's trading desk direct at CME Group.

"Trading and settlement!"

"Order desk, please."

"Your name, Sir?"

"Everett Anderson."

"He's waiting for your call Mister Anderson."

"Continental!" Derrick Butler shouted from outside the S&P 500 option pit.

"Account 022759. Sell fifty thousand December S&P puts, at the market. I want you to liquidate my entire account, right now."

"Are you nuts?" Butler screamed. "Let the market fall a little further, Anderson. The dollar's just getting warmed up."

"This is a correction, not a crash. Dump it all."

Everett glanced at his monitor. The Dow was now down six hundred points and rising.

Trading timers and alarms were beeping and flashing on his computer screens and consoles, and the confusion on the San Diego trading floor was at a fever pitch.

"All right, I'll place the order," Butler said. "Congratulations, Rookie."

As he hung up the phone, Everett looked up long enough to see Jack flanked by two very large uniformed security guards marching across the trading floor straight for his office.

Everett hit eject on his computer, slid the disc into his coat pocket, and sprinted for the lobby. As he galloped through the crowded trading stations, drawing everyone's attention, the two guards gave chase.

"Do not let him out of the building!" Jack demanded.

Everett made it to the elevator lobby and pushed the button frantically. As the guards rounded the front desk, the doors opened and he disappeared inside.

"He's on elevator five," yelled one of the guards into his Bluetooth mouthpiece. "Shut it down at twenty five and have your people waiting for him! Jack's orders. We'll be right down!"

Inside, Everett watched as the digital numbers in the high speed elevator car marked his rapid descent—24-23-22-21, then a jolting halt at floor 20. He forced the doors open and crawled through the narrow opening, then ran through the law firm lobby on twenty and yanked the fire alarm, causing the sirens to trigger and alarm spotlights to flash.

The building's employees began running towards the fire escape doors and Everett melted into the crowd full of people who were unsure if this was a just a drill or the real thing. He was the first one through the door and began vaulting down the concrete steps, but the fire escape was rapidly filling up with scared people headed for the ground level exit. The higher the floor, the more uncertain the occupant. By the time he reached the tenth, the crowd was barely moving, clogging the corridor with hysteria and panic. He shoved his way through the crush of people, but was blocked by an overweight bald man. "Hey buddy, we're all trying to get out! Wait your turn!" the man shouted, shoving Everett against the wall.

"Stop that man!" shouted a security guard at the top of the stairs. "He's a thief!"

Everett punched the fat man in the gut with his elbow and spun around him just enough to leap over the handrail and land on the stairs on floor eight. As he pushed through the crowd, there was less resistance. By the time he reached the fifth floor most of the employees were laughing and discounting the event as a drill. No one smelled smoke and the mood was light as he approached the ground floor.

Everett pushed his way through the crowded fire escape stairs as people began to pour out of the building and through the metal door which opened on to the concrete sidewalk. As the bright sun forced his eyes to squint, Everett felt powerful hands on each of his arms as he was shoved into the back of a limousine idling at the curb.

*

The senior traders began gathering at the windows surrounding the perimeter of the trading floor to watch the activity in the air unfolding above the building. They sipped cappuccino and pointed.

"Check this out!"

"What the hell?"

"Jesus!"

"Did you see that?"

The thwap, thwap, thwap of helicopter blades was deafening as a Blackhawk helicopter banked in front of the windows of the forty-ninth and fiftieth floors to the north, its high-speed rotors whirling and pitching outside the tall thick glass windows. The rest of the brokers on the floor abandoned their consoles and dashboards and scurried over to the plate glass and looked up toward the roof as the helipad access doors suddenly burst wide open.

All hell broke loose as two dozen federal agents in dark blue windbreakers stormed through the roof stairs and into the office. They shut down the front desk phone system, locked the front doors and elevators, and rushed the trading floor as brokers drank their coffee and watched with amazement, marveling at their precision and coordination. With black helmets, flack jackets and fully automatic weapons drawn, the agents began corralling the brokers and lining them up against the walls, asking for social security numbers and snapping pictures with their digital cameras.

But the unfolding drama in Jack's office took center stage. As two agents kicked in the locked French doors leading to the terrace, Jack's office was empty.

"Tango zulu, this is victor charlie," the agent in charge growled into his small headset. "Suspect may still be in the building. Check every floor!"

29

Camerone torched a fresh cigar and opened the sunroof of the stretch limousine, exhaling a thick blue cloud of pungent smoke through the skylight. "Well, Senor Anderson," he said with a smile. "You have been a great disappointment to me."

"We had a bargain."

"Yes we did."

"I doubled the value of your primary trading account this morning."

"*Gracias, amigo.*"

"So what happened to the men-of-honor speech in Cabo?"

"You were flawless, except for one small detail."

"What's that?"

"You betrayed me."

"How do you figure?"

"There is no way you could have known about such an unexpected announcement on interest rates as well as the rally in the dollar without information directly from your government."

"Why do *you* care about where I got it?"

"Even my most trusted sources inside Washington were caught completely off guard."

Everett shook his head.

"You see, I never gamble with my money. I only invest in a sure thing, which is why I allowed you to move forward with our trade, once I discovered the source of your information."

"How could you possibly know?"

"I know many things. And I know many powerful people in your country and in your government. Knowledge is power but information is the most valuable commodity on earth. I know that powerful men will do anything within their means to protect that power. Men in Mexico and men in America. Why do you think your politicians will never completely stop illegal immigration? Why do you think I am able to supply America with all the cocaine it can consume? It is subject to the laws of supply and demand."

"So, that's how you import your product, disguised as sugar?"

"We have perfected the process," he boasted. "No one can tell the difference, side by side. The weight, the consistency of powdered, confectioner's sugar. It melts in your nose, not in your hand."

"I had no choice."

"I know. You were used, unfortunately. I also know that Jack is no fool. He discovered your undercover agent before he escaped, and he discovered that you agreed to cooperate with this agent."

"Jack escaped?"

"You sound surprised, Senor Anderson."

"How the hell did he do that?"

"You underestimate him. Everyone does. He is difficult to control, a loose canon as you say in your country, but he is the best at what he does."

"What's that? Lie and kill people?"

"Of course. He is my best employee."

Then it all suddenly made perfect sense. "So you own the Continental Trading Group?"

"Jack always said you were the smart one," the old man laughed as the limousine was waved through the border gate.

"Unbelievable."

"I must compliment you on your guts, as well. American football is so vulgar, but it is played by strong and stubborn men. You should have learned to play soccer. It is an intelligent game, and much easier on the body. You have visited unnecessary injury on yourself."

"We all have our own cross to bear."

"*Si.* Your cross is the location of your evidence."

"It's too late. I've already given it to authorities."

"Oh. That is too bad. It could have saved your life."

Victoria Vasquez holstered her sidearm as the action on the forty-ninth floor of the California Empire Bank Building wound to a close. "I don't believe what I just witnessed," she said as the last of the senior brokers were escorted out of the office and herded in the elevator lobby. "Diamond had a small elevator built into his office."

Deputy Director Bailey opened his cell phone and read the incoming text message. "Did you get a heading on his jet?"

"You'll have to stand by, Sir," Vasquez said. "I'm waiting for the senior air traffic controller at Lindbergh Field tower to call us back while they track it on radar. Can't we scramble some fighter jets from North Island Naval Air Station or something?"

"He must be headed for Mexico air space," the Deputy Director speculated. "That's all we need. More bad press from an already belligerent newly elected President south of the border. Relations are strained enough as it is."

"This is not good at all," she said.

The local network news crews had already found a way up the fire escapes and were setting up their cameras, asking for a comment from any agent or employee who would elaborate about the details of the daring unauthorized getaway jet takeoff that barely missed a landing 747 on runway seven-two-one at Lindbergh Field.

"At least we located the security control room," said Bailey.

"I knew it was in the building somewhere."

"It's on the twenty-fifth floor, Agent Vasquez, but all the employees scattered during the fire drill. We've got our team there right now. Why don't you go down and start the process of cataloging any evidence we can recover, then post an agent by the door. We'll be here for days anyway. And don't let the media near that floor."

"Yes, Sir."

"Surveillance cameras are positioned all over the building, everywhere. Review the footage from the different vantage points during the last several hours and cross reference Homeland Security's face recognition software."

"Right."

"Maybe we can recover any footage that'll identify the personnel who got away."

"Right away."

A cell phone continued to ring in the background.

"What is that damn ringing?" he asked. "Check it out, would you? Maybe it's an employee. Or a client that can help us."

Her eye was drawn to Everett's office as the ringing continued. The iPhone sat on Everett's desk as Vasquez entered his corner office. "Continental Trading," she said.

"Hello? Who is this, please?"

"Who is this?"

"I'm trying to reach Everett Anderson," the female caller answered. "Is this his phone?"

"It was in his office," Vasquez replied. "He's not here right now. Can I give him a message?"

"He was supposed to call me before his flight this afternoon. Would you ask him to call me when he returns?"

"Who shall I say is calling?"

"Shelby Ford. Do you know him personally?"

"I work with him."

"I'm a little worried that he hasn't called."

"I just happened to pass his office when his cell phone rang."

"Well, I haven't heard from him since last night and his scheduled flight landed here in Memphis without him."

"Probably just a missed connection."

"It was a nonstop from San Diego. Tell me your name again."

"Like I said, I'll be sure to tell him you called if I see him," she said as she turned off the iPhone, slipped it inside her fitted designer suit jacket, and entered the elevator.

"Wait. Play that back, and slow it down this time," Vasquez instructed as the Treasury's best hacker rewound the brief video footage.

"Yes ma'am."

The capture revealed, at street level, a blurred image of a man being forced into the back of a limousine waiting at the curb.

"Now frame by frame," she ordered as she studied the fleeting images. As the video footage ticked along one frame at a time, she caught a glimpse of Everett's profile as he was shoved into the limo's rear seat. "Halt it right there," she said. "Now zoom in on the tag."

After several keystrokes, the California plate was isolated and fed into a national DMV database. Within seconds, the secured search engine flashed Camerone Cane SA as the Deputy Director entered Continental's security nerve center.

"Sir, Anderson's been kidnapped. He's probably across the border already."

"Agent Vasquez, do not, I repeat, do not chase him down! I need to talk to the State Department and our embassy."

"I have to go after him, Sir."

"He's not your responsibility."

"Yes he is, Sir."

"Look. We may be able to work something out with their diplomatic authorities through sensitive channels. But this is not your own personal dogfight. Maybe we can secure a prisoner trade."

"He's not in some Mexican prison, Sir. The tags on the limo were registered to Camerone."

"What are you saying?'

"Jack Diamond escapes to Lindberg Field from the tallest building in downtown San Diego and five minutes later, Anderson is shoved into a company limo at gunpoint. With all due respect, Sir. Do the math. Diamond doesn't own the company. He never did."

"Then who does?"

"Who do you think?"

"But Camerone is a client, right?"

"He just looks like one."

"I can't authorize you for some rescue mission to Mexico. Remember the bounty hunter named Dog Chapman?"

"Yeah, and he apprehended a wanted international fugitive."

"What you're proposing would get me fired and possibly send you to Leavenworth."

"I got him into this, Sir. He did what we asked of him. Have you seen the paper trail he served up for us stored in fishing lockers in a Coronado bait shop?"

"I must admit, I haven't received the final debrief. I've been a little busy the last twenty-four hours."

"He's given us more solid indictable documentation in nine months than I could produce or provide in a year of undercover work. Now it's my responsibility to get him out of there. If I don't, they'll kill him."

"How can you be sure?"

"They must know he aided our investigation. Otherwise they wouldn't have kidnapped him."

"If you do this, you know you're on your own down there, don't you? We don't exactly have very good rapport with the current Mexican administration."

"Yes Sir. I know that."

"Good Goddamn luck, Vasquez. You'll need it."

The handset squeeked. "This is Bailey. Go."

"Sir, we've just located the storage lockers referred by Agent Vasquez," the agent said on the speaker phone. "And you're not going to like this."

"What's the problem?"

"We broke the locks on all the storage lockers and the marked boxes are all full of blank paper, Sir. We've got nothing but fifty pounds of recycled trees."

"Then standby for now," he sighed as he cut both eyes towards Vasquez.

30

Another fist was delivered to his right jaw with crushing force by the three hundred pound Cuban bodyguard, bruising then splitting open the skin covering the left cheek. Blood poured from the right ear now. "I will ask you again. Where is your evidence?"

Silence.

"Your trading courage and instincts are impressive, Senor Anderson," Camerone scoffed, puffing on a fresh cigar and watching in the dark from the damp basement corner. "You remind me of my brother, thirty years ago, before the cocaine wars."

Everett spit blood, tied to the wooden chair with electric cord and rusty wire.

The old man exhaled a thick cloud of blue smoke. "Just another spoiled American," he sighed. "Tough, but ignorant. Educated, but naive."

Everett shook his head quickly.

"I grew up in Cuba," Camerone boasted as he walked between crates of AK-47s, stored in the basement, purchased from the U.S. "When Batista was overthrown, my brother was tortured for three days, seventy-two straight hours of pure hell, with no sleep, but he never broke. Miquel arranged before his death to move us to Miami in the nineteen seventies, the golden age of the trade. And *my* cocaine fueled a billion dollar real estate boom which built the shining skyline that is on display today. Banks, car dealerships, jewelry stores, all built on our profits."

"I'm real impressed," Everett coughed.

"I was young and the world was in balance then," the old man crowed. "We made so much money in your country we were forced to bury the cash in the yards of our stash houses around Fort Lauderdale and Palm Beach. That was before the filthy Colombians tried to wage war. Everything was perfect before Ochoa and his unruly family. A golden goose sodomized by Colombia. They even sent a Godmother after me. A woman! Can you believe that?"

Everett shook his head again in disgust.

"I was a fugitive in the Everglades for months but finally escaped to Mexico on a trawler. Now I am a rancher and a respected international businessman."

"They'll find me and kill you."

"Who?" he laughed. "Your government? I donate millions to your government, and your Senators. I fly in and out of your country with impunity, and your President will never stop the flow of cocaine, or the immigration you call illegal. You and your race no longer belong in California. We have rebuilt our empire in the west as your politicians look the other way while begging for our brown votes."

Everett spit more blood on the floor, exhausted. "You're just a common drug dealer."

"I speculate in commodities. And I produce! I make *your* job possible."

"And I watched your family business ruin the lives of my team mates, and half the brokers in my office."

Another punch to the right side of the face.

"When I was twenty-one, Mister Anderson, I designed a small plane refitted with gas tanks in the fuselage and wings which could fly non-stop and unmolested back and forth from Medellin to Panama City five times a week, then turn south to Lakeland, Florida where I owned my own airstrip. Do you have any idea how visionary we were? No one was patrolling the air traffic. They were all too busy stretched thin on the east coast of Florida chasing ghosts and amateur smugglers. I was never caught, and your Customs agents were young and inexperienced, until Reagan deployed federal policemen with helicopters and automatic weapons. Now you live in a police state, a line blurred by an invading empirical fascist paramilitary that listens to your conversations in the name of terrorist protection."

"We shut you down then," Everett exhaled. "And we'll do it again."

"I enlisted the aid of the Miami police to unload tons of product from my planes and boats and they willingly transported my product in the trunks of their police cars to my safe houses, and I never involved the Colombians, which is why they came for me. All of my men were killed, but I got the message, and got out."

"Why are you telling me this?"

"Forces larger than you can imagine, greater than the mighty United States of America, now stand poised to render your country the weak and spoiled giant it has become. I have shotcallers directing sets in Los Angeles, National City, Phoenix, and Laredo who cornered the market and depressed the spot price of cocaine, forcing it to plummet after the nineteen eighties."

"So you shorted the spot price of cocaine?"

"*Si'!*" Camerone mocked. "I have never heard it put such a way, but yes, I achieved a five thousand percent return for the past twenty years, because it is a commodity, just like soybeans or corn or sugar. It was I alone who introduced cocaine as a blue collar drug, accessible and cheap, convertible to crack."

"Congratulations."

"Since the Eighties, Marijuana went up in price because coke went down. Why do you think that is?"

"I could care less."

"Your country became my best client, a client who never stops ordering. Five percent of the world population, a sad minority of walking dead, addicted to its own success," he laughed. "Even Calderon is calling for the legalization of Marijuana. Cocaine will be next!"

"You're a cancer on your own country."

"We are an insurgency! And we are coming for you and your country next!"

"Bullshit," Everett hacked.

Another humiliating jab to the face.

"Talk to me!" Camerone bellowed, throwing his cigar into Everett's face, scattering red ashes across his captive's bloody chest. "Tell me where is your evidence!"

Everett spit blood into his face.

"He will not talk, *Jefe*," said the big Cuban, circling behind Everett in the center of the basement.

"Take him from the chair, then. *Rapido!*"

The Cuban raised his boot and snap-kicked Everett in the chest, driving him backward into the stone floor. The rotted chair he was tied to splintered on impact.

"*Trae en la tabla larga!*"

The walnut banquet table was quickly dragged into the damp, dark cellar by two more soldiers. Four men in military fatigues raised one end and pinned it into the corner window at a thirty degree angle. They lifted Everett onto the table with his feet above his head and then forced a damp, mildewed cotton cloth over his face. A large bucket of water was brought in and placed next to the inverted table.

"If this does not work, then take off his head and deliver it to Washington in a box!" Camerone shouted. "I am tired of his silence!"

Everett shook his head one more time to gain his balance, but his head began to spin under the wet cloth.

Putrid water was slowly poured onto his face as he choked for oxygen and felt the grip of panic as if he was being pulled underwater, unable to breathe. Carbon dioxide accumulated in his brain, creating confusion and anxiety. He gagged, fighting for air, desperate for breath. The water was now pouring down his nostrils and into his lungs. He choked again and vomited, coughing up more blood.

"One more time!" Camerone roared. "Where is it!"

The night air blowing through the open basement window carried with it the sudden crack of automatic weapons and the boom boom of two grenade blasts, back to back. Then another explosion, louder than the first two combined.

Two more uniformed men rushed through the hallway door.

"*Jefe*! The courtyard! *Vamanos*!"

Camerone looked at Everett, motionless on the slanted table. "He's passed out. Leave him for now. Lock the door!"

The tractor chugged along through the soft black dirt, working its way between the endless rows of mature soybean plants, lined up parallel to one another like a Roman legion encampment. He'd just turned thirteen years old, having learned how to drive the harvester since he was ten. The heat was almost unbearable now, but he'd developed an immunity to it. He could labor in it for hours, days if needed. An anger welled up against it, a tolerance for it.

He wiped his brow and he bore down with that famous frown of concentration, embracing the weight of responsibility which far outnumbered his inexperience. It was all about the crop, she said, a crop that would make or break the property. The rows of mature plants blew in the stiffening and welcome August breeze, swaying like dancers on a stage, their choreography moving with the rhythm of the Earth.

He could feel his hands beginning to gather strength now, the kind of strength that would surprise those around him as he grew into adolescence. His legs ached from the pain of growth, but along with that growth came confidence. He was becoming a man.

She watched from the porch. She told him the work would help him forget. They were gone now. She said he had it in him, like the men before him, a breed apart, a tough and understanding line who rose to the challenge with a quiet grace that she'd inspired.

"Anderson," she whispered. "Can you hear me?"

He shook his head again, straining his powerful neck upward against gravity as she stood in front of him in the pitch blackness, leaning closer.

"It's me," she whispered. "Can you hear me?"

"Who?"

"You're in shock."

"Vasquez?"

"Can you walk?" she asked.

He tilted his head back and forced open one blood-caked eyelid just long enough to make her out, standing in front of him in the dark. "You can't be here, right now," he slurred.

"God. What have they done to you?" she mumbled, wiping the blood from his forehead and mouth and ears.

"How did you..?"

"I found the complex with a little GPS and satellite help from a friend in the Coast Guard. Can you stand?" she asked as she cut through the wire and rope with a diving knife and tried to lift his two hundred and twenty pound frame off of the primitive wooden table.

"Give me just a minute?" he wheezed.

"We don't have a minute," she whispered. "Camerone's men are under seige!"

"Then get under my right side. My left shoulder's dislocated."

She hooked her left arm under his right shoulder from behind, and braced against the slanted table.

"You can't support my weight."

"Try me," she said as she managed to get one of his legs under him and helped him stagger toward the small open window located high on the thick stone wall. She then knelt on all fours below the window.

As moonlight poured through the opening, he reached for the metal edges, then pulled his frame through the hole with what strength was still left in his upper body. Once clear of the window, she finished the job and crawled out behind.

"Stay close to the edge of the building, in the bushes," she whispered behind him as red tracer rounds whizzed five feet above their heads. "It's bright tonight. Full moon. Lose yourself in the vegetation. It's our best cover. Can you crawl?"

Everett started to giggle.

"What's so damn funny?" she asked.

"They left my knees alone. The only part of my body that's never been cut on."

"Then lead the way, tough guy. I cut a hole in the barbed wire perimeter fence right in front of you. Fifty feet."

"What then?" he whispered as they crawled through the landscaping.

"Then we make it to the beach."

"Our footprints will give us away."

"It'll be high tide in five hours. If we walk in the water, the waves will cover our tracks."

The shooting stopped for a moment, then restarted with a greater intensity. Then more explosions behind them.

"You got a submarine waiting offshore, Vasquez?"

"You could say that."

"No shit?"

"Actually, I have horsepower tied to the outer wall."

"Perfect."

"Can you ride a horse?"

"Since I was three."

"Good. I came in a powerboat hidden in a cave about ten miles northwest of here. But I can't call in backup until we're in international waters."

"A powerboat? Hidden in a cave ten miles north of here? And horses to get us there?"

"Well, there's only one horse, actually, but you can drive if you want."

"We're eight hundred miles from San Diego and Camerone controls the Baja Cartel as well as the peninsula."

"And your biggest client has been my personal project for the past twelve months. He owns every fishing village and desert town from here to Tijuana, on both sides of the water and in every town that Highway One touches. He owns the airports, the buses and the taxis. He pays the mayors, the Federales, the bounty hunters, the Pemex gas station owners, mercados, and all the tourist t-shirt concessions."

"But you've got your satellite phone, right?"

"I can't get a signal yet because of El Nino cloud cover, and if I use your iPhone they'll track our location."

"That's just perfect."

"Our best bet is to close the miles northwest tonight to my cave, our rally point with U.S. authorities. Either that or we scalp our way onto a ponga headed north for marlin in the Sea of Cortez."

"I don't trust the locals in this country and it's got to be close to midnight."

Vasquez checked her watch. "Wow, Anderson, it's half past. How'd you know that?"

"Internal clock. I grew up close to the soil."

"Three miles an hour puts us at my cave before four in the morning, with the cover of night. I should be able to raise naval operations before first light."

"So that's your plan?"

"Look, I took on your case because your deposition alone will change my career. I'm not about to lose you now."

"Alright Agent Vasquez. Your call."

"You don't happen to speak Spanish, do you?"

"Si! Mi español es excelente!"

"Couple days growth on your beard, dark hair, brown eyes," she whispered. "You just might pass for a local."

31

Victoria Vasquez removed Everett's iPhone from her hip pocket and hit redial as soon as he fell asleep in the dark cave.

She knew it was a gamble.

"Hello?"

"Is this the person I spoke to yesterday?" Vasquez asked.

"Yes it is, and I recognize your voice," Shelby said. "Can you tell me anything more?"

"He's safe."

"Can I speak to him?"

"I shouldn't even be speaking to *you*. That's the most I can tell you."

"How can I help?"

"I bet you know where the boxes are."

"Is he okay?"

"It's not smart for you to talk to him right now."

"But he's alive?"

"He's banged up and sleeping, but he's breathing. Yes. Now, I'll ask again. You know where the boxes are, don't you?"

"He wouldn't tell me the details because he knew it would worry me."

"I need you to trust me."

"I do trust you," Shelby said. "I guess I hear in your voice that you really know who he is. You told me you worked with him. That means you know what kind of a person he is."

"It does."

"Please bring him home," she sobbed. "If you do, I'll tell you where the boxes are."

"Just what I wanted to hear. I need you to be strong."

"I'll be happy to, if you'll tell me your name."

"You can call me Jane."

"Alright, Jane."

"I might need your help in the next twenty-four hours," Vasquez said.

"What can I do, Jane?"

"We have a mutual friend who you spoke to this morning. I need you to give our friend a message for me."

"Go ahead."

"Tell our friend, anchors away. That's all."

"Be careful, Jane."

Jack looked at Camerone as he drew a large circle with a grease pencil over a laminated map of Cabo San Lucas using a compass. "That's the only satellite signal broadcasting on land, nearest the compound. There's nothing but desert for miles outside these walls. All the other signals are GPS, or satellite, on open water."

"How do know it's him and the girl?"

"They're transmitting, and the signature is inside a thirty mile radius."

"I believe I know my own country!"

"Then I suggest we work our way north and west," Jack instructed.

"That will take all night."

"Maybe so, but it's the only way to insure they don't escape to the Pacific."

"I'll call General Lopez. He will patrol the shore."

"Let me handle those two. I'm much cheaper than the military."

Camerone stared at Jack. "Lopez would ask for ten million. I'll pay you three."

"Make it five."

"Four."

"Done. Wire the funds to my error account."

"Take everyone with you!" the old man bellowed at the crowded room of Mexican Federal Police. "Plow through every desert village and fishing port, search the beaches, and pay the local police whatever they ask!"

"Wake up, Anderson."

He slowly opened his eyes, squinting at the dark profile and shaking his head.

"On your feet," Vasquez insisted.

"Well, good morning yourself."

"I'm serious."

"Yes ma'am," he said as he pushed his bruised body to his knees.

"I tried to let you sleep."

"And don't think I don't appreciate it. Guess they picked you for several reasons."

"How's that?"

"You're young and female, and you're a rookie."

"You've got good instincts, Anderson, for a jock. Plus I grew up in Tijuana."

"So you were perfect, and the last broker Jack would suspect."

"Just wanted to do my part," she snorted, stuffing gear into her backpack and loading a full clip in her 9mm.

"Like what?"

"We need to get going."

"Try me Vasquez."

She stopped her packing and exhaled. "I lost my fiancee in Tower two. So after the funeral I applied at Annapolis."

"Wow."

"Come on Anderson," she huffed, "we better get going. I just learned Camerone was tipped off by a local fisherman who spotted us, and they're on their way here right now. We'll need to use the inflatable zodiac. Otherwise they'll hear the Scarab."

"Perfect."

She tossed him a black life vest. "I need us on the water, right away. We're to rendezvous with SEAL Team FIVE, waiting three miles offshore. They'll pick us up on radar and get us back safely to Coronado, but we still have to breach the surf zone. You ever do any surfing?" she asked.

"You could say that."

*

Shelby Ford re-played the voicemail message once again on her cell phone for the tenth time to make sure she got the directions right. She was told to come alone and arrive early, before dawn, and not to speak to anyone about the details of her visit to the off-limits section of the secret submarine base. They were very specific about the location and Shelby was given a special clearance.

She'd flown the redeye nonstop from Memphis per their instructions. After verifying the contents of bait shop storage locker 1013E in Coronado, she checked herself into a seaside hotel but couldn't sleep, glued to the TV and radio all night. Every domestic and international news outlet was broadcasting the details of the daring drug raid at the sprawling compound of Don Carlos Eduardo Camerone north of Cabo San Lucas, Baja California. CNN, Azteca, ABC, CBS, NBC, MSNBC, Skynews, Bloomberg, even Al Jazerra. It was the largest haul of cocaine in the history of the Mexican cartels. 259 million dollars in cash and 52,000 kilos of cocaine were seized, not to mention 149 vehicles, 3 aircraft, and 4 ships used by the Baja cartel, including a small Soviet submarine. U.S. officials said that morning that the Mexican

Federal Police, in cooperation with the US Drug Enforcement Administration, the Federal Bureau of Investigation, and divisions of the Department of Homeland Security had spent two years investigating and arresting people associated with the Camerone cartel—which they said had been smuggling drugs, laundering millions of dollars obtained illegally, and fueling a wave of violence along the Southern California and Texas borders for years. Agents and Marshals entered the sugar cane tycoon's vacation home pre-dawn and arrested over a hundred workers.

But all Shelby could do was stare at the black water and think about her boyfriend, pulling the windbreaker tight around her shoulders, bracing herself as another chilly Pacific gust swept past her. The Naval Station's Master-at-Arms gave it to her at the gate when she showed up in short sleeves and a skirt. As she stood on the edge of the pier adjacent to the North Island Naval shipyard, she scanned the Pacific, shaking with anticipation in the frigid morning blackness as she half-listened to the television in the guard shack, tuned to one of many network news outlets.

"International drug-trafficking organizations pose a sustained, serious threat to the safety and security of our communities," the newly appointed U.S. Attorney General announced in prepared remarks at a Washington press conference, his first as head of the Justice Department.

"We've gained access to an extremely complex international operation, destroyed make-shift labs, confiscated millions in laundered cash, and seized warehouses full of processing equipment." American politicians standing behind the AG frowned with feigned outrage, folded arms, and phony disappointment in the background of the briefing room, nodding their heads and promising more indictments.

"I might also add that simultaneously, several international banks and their at-arms-length ATS and ECN trading facilities in Antigua, Tortola, Rio de Janeiro, and Mexico City were shut down by INTERPOL while Carlos Camerone's narco-terrorist competition plundered his family's mountainside villa in Brazil," said the AG.

"Miss Ford, I'm Charles Bailey. I don't believe we've been formally introduced."

Shelby turned around, "So you're the friend who gave me directions this morning. I'm guessing you're someone important, here to see the safe return of my fiancée?"

"Fiancée? Well, congratulations."

"Thank you, Sir, for bringing him home."

"Your fiancée just pulled off a magic trick, young lady. He shouldn't be alive." He said, checking his watch. "They should be onstation any minute," he said, pointing southwest to the mouth of the harbor.

The black Mark V MAKO special operations craft was just barely visible offshore against dark clouds as it sliced through the windy surf. Her long, pointed bow and low profile made her nearly impossible to identify in the cold blackness. Once around and past Point Loma, the sleek, black patrol boat zigzagged through the busy harbor traffic, dodging sailboats and submarines. The Navy SEAL team onboard surrounded a man and a woman as the MAKO pulled alongside the dock.

Everett leapt first from the stern, wrapped in a green wool blanket.

Shelby took one long look at his bruised and bloody face, her eyes streaming tears. "Please take me home," she begged.

"Home is pretty much all I can think about right now," he uttered.

"I want us to fix up the big house with fresh paint and new furniture and huge rugs with plants everywhere," she cried. "We can do that now, can't we?"

"Oh yeah, and I want to wake up next to you for the rest of my life," he whispered.

Shelby watched over Everett's shoulders as the boat bobbed on the rough water. "And you must be Jane," she said.

"Special Agent Victoria Vasquez."

"Thank you, Agent Vasquez."

"Please, call me Vicki," Vasquez said, stepping on to the wooden dock. "Your boyfriend deserves the thanks."

"You mean her fiancée, Agent Vasquez," said Bailey. "Mister Anderson, I hope this is our last meeting."

"Me too, Sir. So what officially happened this morning?"

"A nice combination of luck and timing. The scale of Camerone's enterprise officially became a level orange threat to US national security this morning."

"Sir?"

"Satellite intel confirmed the deployment of Mexican National Militia collecting at five key transition points along the border. They stayed away from Texas, picking New Mexico and Arizona as tenderloin insertion points along half the border. Agent Vasquez and her operation were extremely sensitive and my directives came straight from the White House, once we received confirmation of Camerone's intentions. He was actually prepared to invade the United States of America."

"So Continental was Camerone's own personal ATM?"

"Much worse. Continental was the bank for the fastest growing cartel in Mexico, and Camerone was just weeks away from another 9-11. Lou Harper was the first to risk rebellion in the pits. Before he was killed, we monitored a call he made to Walker, detailing Camerone's involvement in the soybean market. Harper was on his way to give Vasquez information outside Chicago when Hood took him out."

"She's good, Sir."

"And she's smart. She found the source of Camerone's power. Most of the intel on his sugar shipments is classified, but I can tell you that he's also been helping Mexico build a multi-billion dollar Sovereign Wealth Fund for decades, with the government's help. The international debt market is a mess, and Brazil has not exactly been a helpful ally to the US. With two hundred billion alone in foreign currency reserves, Camerone thought he was protected, along with his cocaine empire. Practically every nation on the planet has an SWF, except Mexico. Why do you think that is?"

"No idea."

"Because Camerone owned the militia, bought and paid for with cartel pesos, and we just recently learned he was planning a coup in Mexico City, underwritten by his contacts in Cuba and Venezuela. Mexico is on the brink of civil war right now, and Camerone was days away from taking full advantage, starting with his border raid tonight."

"No shit."

"Thirty thousand murders south of the border in the last three years, more than Iraq and Afghanistan combined. If crude stays expensive and the cartels unite behind the military, Mexico will implode and millions of refugees will pour north over our borders into the US. And you can bet the ranch they'll bring with them Al-Qaeda cells, roadside bombs, transnational gangs, serial kidnapping, and be-headings."

"Pretty scary."

"The Mexican government maintains just enough control of the federal police to stave off a showdown, but it's coming. The army versus the police down here. And with immigration policy so polarizing right now, it's only a matter of time. The U.S. tolerated Camerone until now because there was little we could really do, but he's become extremely dangerous, requiring unilateral action direct from Washington."

"So you captured him?"

"Camerone and his son were found in an underground bunker near his compound in Cabo. Yes."

"And what about Jack?"

"He's still at large."

"No way."

"I know. It's true."

"So we got bin Laden and we got Camerone. Amazing," Everett said. "Jack Diamond seems like a bit player now."

"That's how he works. In reality he's even *more* connected than Camerone. He's made all the right international friends. I can't go into much detail, but certain interests will protect him. He did so much business last year with a small circle of offshore bankers and hedge funds that he bought an island in the Caribbean, and he had Tortola and Antigua bidding on an airstrip for him, complete with his own Customs office. But we'll find him."

"Should *we* be worried?" Shelby asked.

"Camerone will be extradited. Hood's dead. The clients are screwed. All the money at Continental was a house of cards. Receivers will sift through the rubble for years finding nothing. I don't see Diamond gaining anything from payback. He's in possession of millions offshore buried in non-extradtion countries sympathetic to his cause."

"Your keys to the boxes, Vicki," Shelby said. "Hope it gets you promoted, and decorated. The address is on the label taped to the ring."

"You two talk and catch up while I write my report, Anderson. I'll need your statement later. Then we'll locate those boxes."

"No sweat."

"Keep him out of trouble," Vasquez instructed.

Shelby hugged his thick neck. "Don't worry. We're headed home for a nice boring life in the slow lane."

"The slow lane," said Everett. "Imagine that."

Virginia Anderson walked carefully through the open screen door and onto the deep porch that wrapped around the front of the big house she was born in, along with all her sisters and brothers.

They were all gone now.

She was the last one.

Shelby helped her into her favorite wicker chair near the porch rail, then wrapped her aching legs in a blanket and handed her a steaming mug of black coffee. "You should have your own cooking show. That breakfast was perfection," she said.

"It's the least I can do now that this big old empty house is filled with voices and laughing and footsteps."

"So how do you feel this morning, Miss Virginia?"

"Well, I've been thinking all night and I've made up my mind. I'm too old for chemotherapy, dear. The cure is worse than the cancer," she said, lighting a cigarette.

"You just won't listen to anyone, will you?"

She sipped her coffee.

"So that's where he gets it," Shelby nodded.

"I prefer to spend my remaining days watching my grandson start his new life right here, with you, in his house. Besides, you and I have a lot of re-decorating to do and a wedding to plan."

"Yes, Ma'am. I'd like that," Shelby said as she eased down on to the front steps, watching Everett on horseback, working his favorite Chestnut mare along the fence line across the dark green ravine that stretched in front of the house. "You know, he'll be out there all morning," Shelby said, "until one of them gives in."

"They're just making up for lost time," Virginia smiled. "She's always been his favorite. He raised her from a weanling."

"He does have that ability to make the opposite sex crazy, doesn't he?"

Everett wheeled her back toward the house and released her in a full gallop up the pea gravel driveway toward the porch. A grey dust cloud kicked up behind them, before disappearing in the swirling crosswind.

The weather was changing now. Fall was upon them, and a chill hung in the humid air as horse and rider raced up the hill toward the house, their collective breath visible in the morning cold. He turned her sharply, and then disappeared around back.

"What's he up to now?" Shelby smiled.

"No telling. He used to ride hard like that for hours, working out whatever he was working on in his head at the time."

As the wind died down, Everett trotted slowly around the corner up to the edge of the porch, stopping in front of Shelby. "You up for a morning ride?" he asked

Shelby glanced at Virginia. "Should I?"

"He has a dangerous reputation for taking chances you know, but he's a damn good horseman."

"Then I'll take that as a yes."

"He's prone to speed, so my advice is hold on tight, dear. You're in for the ride of your life."